DECEPTION PASS

DECEPTION

PASS

EARL EMERSON

BALLANTINE BOOKS

NEW YORK

I remember the place from when I was a kid, you know, with all them cliffs running down to the water and the tide going through that narrow little channel and looking like a big boiling stew of greens because of the way it was always just churning and churning, and the bridge looming way above like it does.

When we was kids we used to fish down there for ocean perch and once in a while we'd haul in a salmon, and there was a rumor that years before, some kid fell in and was carried out into the sound by those hellacious currents and then his body was took out to sea. But you have to figure that was just a rumor. People always want you to think something terrible is just around the corner; yet it ain't always the case.

See, what I'm telling you is, basically, no matter what they tole you I done, I didn't do it. Not up there at Deception Pass. It meant too much to me. I would never wreck my childhood memories of that place by doing anything bad up there. It was just too beautiful.

From an interview with Charles Groth
two weeks before his execution

Ever since 1792 when, in his quest for a passageway to the East Coast, Captain Vancouver was deceived by this steeply chiseled, impossibly narrow chasm, the magnificent waterway of Deception Pass has more than earned its name. Visitors to the area can find peaceful little coves, secluded pebble beaches, meadows of wildflowers and sea-grasses replete with an abundance of sea-life—stately herons, basking sea-lions, soaring eagles.

But all is not idyllic here. One has only to gaze down in awe-struck wonder from the steel decking of the spectacular Deception Pass Bridge or from the perilously steep cliffs of the channel walls which plunge to roiling, unswimmable waters below to be overwhelmed by the sheer destructive power of the place. One pictures helpless boats being dashed to pieces against the merciless rocky cliffs, limp bodies being hurled from the bridge itself to be swallowed by the dark waters hundreds of feet below—lives torn and lost forever.

One might say, then, that it is only fitting that what was perhaps the most heinous and puzzling crime in the written history of Washington State occurred in a deceptively peaceful little cabin on a quiet pebble beach within sight of the treacherous walls of Deception Pass.

From The Whole Truth and Nothing But;
an unpublished manuscript by Elizabeth Faulconer

DECEPTION PASS

CHAPTER 1

Finished with my biceps, I was wrapping the tape measure around my skull when Kathy stepped into my office with a client.

When she saw what I was doing, the client let out a squawk that might have been mistaken for the first part of a giggle, a sound that stood out like a cat's screech doodling across the tranquillity of my morning.

Whatever grim business had sucked them into my office had also deterred Ms. Birchfield from editorializing, although, judging from experience, she would loose a jibe or two later that evening, probably in bed.

"What can I do for you?" I asked as I walked around the desk to shake hands with the client, whose dark brown eyes showed no hint of the amusement they'd betrayed a moment earlier.

"Lainie Smith," Kathy said, introducing us. "Thomas Black. He did most of my investigations even before he talked me into marrying him." Her eyes managed a twinkle at just the right moment. "Lainie has a question for you, Thomas."

The blue chair was a little wider and softer, so I offered it to Smith, who worked her wide hips into it while Kathy took the red one. I took a step backward and settled my rump against the edge of the desk. Lainie Smith wore a formless, ankle-length dress

3

patterned in browns and beiges, a dress you could have fit two of Kathy into.

"Fire away. I don't do very well on essay questions, but I usually hit around fifty percent on true/false." I grinned at about the same time I realized grinning was not in order.

"Mother spoke quite highly of you," Smith said, looking me square in the eye like a marine drill sergeant trying to pin me to the wall. Though I could not recall having met her before, Smith's face seemed as familiar as a box of breakfast cereal.

"Your mother is . . . ?"

"Mrs. Lola Smith."

"Ah, the canoeist," I said. When I'd encountered Smith's seventy-year-old mother, she was living her idea of the perfect retirement in a quiet, little one-bedroom cabin on a rocky beach near Gig Harbor, Washington, surrounded by a few agreeable neighbors; nothing to do but read historical romances and polish agates for her grandchildren. I was called in after a stranger routinely began paddling past her property in an aluminum canoe, and standing to shout slogans from the Korean War and various long-gone political campaigns. He was usually sans trousers when he did this.

It had taken most of one day to track him down and find out he had once processed data for the CIA and was a well-known landscape painter and a former professor of political science from Amherst. Now sinking into the early ravages of Alzheimer's, he was still clever enough to escape his wife's vigilant eye almost daily. He lived half a mile up the beach.

"If you have a question, fire away, Ms. Smith."

"Call me Lainie. Everybody does."

"Lainie."

"I came to ask you what can be done about a blackmailer."

I glanced at Kathy, who, sitting quietly in her knee-length black dress, legs crossed, was giving away nothing. "Are you being blackmailed?"

"Without saying that I am or not, I would like your take on blackmail in general." It was odd that Kathy hadn't given me a call before walking her client down the hall to spring this, but then, Kathy liked to catch me off guard. I could tell she was looking around to see where I'd ditched the tape measure.

Lainie's sockless feet were clad in sandals that laced up around her shins. Her bangs were thin and so black they had to have been dyed. They seemed to adhere to her head, perhaps from static electricity. The rest of her limp hair was cut to her shoulders and made her deep brown eyes appear even more intense. Her pale and flawless skin could have been imported from a salon in Paris and poured from a bottle. She was a pretty woman even though her nose, a little too large for her face, upturned and blunt at the tip, might have been cruelly described by sarcastic adolescent boys as a snout.

"To be honest, I've only worked one blackmail case. Not enough to be an expert, but enough to have given it some thought. There are three basic ways to deal with a blackmailer. You can pay him until you're flat broke; you can call in the police—and let your secret out to the world; or . . . you can kill him." I let my words sink in. "I assume none of these is a viable alternative?"

"No. Of course not."

"There are variations on each of these themes. You can pay him and hope he goes away. Not likely. Once a lazy person finds a source of ready cash, he's not apt to give it up voluntarily. Or, you can call in the police and pray your secret, problem— whatever it is—won't get out. If it's a videotape or some other piece of hard evidence, you might be able to keep it under wraps. Somebody might even get it back for you. If the police get it, they will see it, some of them will. Maybe somebody in the prosecutor's office will too, but probably not the whole world. If it's information—say you're a descendant of the Russian royal family—that might be a little harder to keep under wraps."

"I'm not a member of the Russian royal family," Lainie said. "And it's not a videotape. It's not hard evidence of any sort. At least, I don't believe it is."

"Of course, once you get the police into it, and *if* the secret involves anything criminal, and *if* you're involved in it, they'll have a hard time ignoring you."

She leaned back in her chair and thought about what I'd

said. Her brown eyes were targeted by huge, mascara-laden lashes, and her face registered thoughts the way very few faces do. I began to believe that, under different circumstances, she might have made an exceptional actress.

"That's all?" she said.

"I know it's not much. Blackmail is one of the few crimes where the perp and the victim have the same goal: to keep the cat *in* the bag. The perp because it would cut off the cash flow, and the victim for reasons you probably understand. Oh. There is one more way to handle it. The ostrich ploy. Stick your head in the sand and hope they go away. There's always the chance it's a bluff. This actually worked in a case a friend of mine handled a couple of years back."

"It's too late for that."

"So you've paid somebody some money?"

She hesitated. "Yes."

"To whom?"

"I don't know. It's all been anonymous phone calls. There must be something else a person could do."

"You might hire somebody to scare him off. Mess him up. But that wouldn't be me."

Smith had been hanging on my every word, her chin in her hand. Her nails were long and painted red. She wore two rings with diamonds on her right hand. The rest of her jewelry consisted of an outcropping of cherries on her earrings, more cherries on a clanking bracelet.

"And how would *you* mess somebody up?" she asked.

"Like I said, I don't do that sort of thing. Besides the ethical considerations, I'm too much of a coward."

If Lainie realized I was trying to be funny, it didn't cut through her gloom.

I glanced at Kathy and said, "Besides, if you mess him up, he's likely to let the cat out of the bag for spite. The thing to do right now is to gather as much information as you can."

Kathy studied me as she flipped a strand of her long dark hair off her shoulder and onto her back.

Lainie resumed her story: "Four weeks ago a man called and demanded two thousand dollars. He's asked for two thousand more each week. The calls usually come on Thursday; then on Friday morning we deliver the cash."

"Who's we?"

"Kent, my secretary, has done the actual deliveries. Usually to a garbage bin in a shopping mall. I shouldn't have consented the first time. I should have tried your ostrich theory, but I was so shook up I didn't think of it."

She didn't appear to be shaken now, but then, we were in an office discussing this as if it were lawn care or carpet patterns. "What is he blackmailing you over?"

"I can't tell you."

"Can you give us a general sense of it?"

Kathy replied for her. "Unless it's absolutely necessary, Lainie would prefer to keep that to herself."

"It doesn't have anything to do with preferring," said Smith. "I'm not telling. Not my lawyer. My priest. Nobody. I want you to handle it without knowing."

"So you want me to handle it?"

"Yes." She was a woman used to commanding respect. It was hard to know how I knew that, but I did, and now her life was falling into the hands of strangers, a happenstance she didn't find agreeable in the least. She glanced at Kathy again and appeared irritated for the first time since catching me with the tape around my skull. Maybe I hadn't accepted her contract quickly enough, or maybe she was simply not in the habit of asking for help.

"You realize somewhere along the line I'll most likely find out what it's about?"

"If we do find out," said Kathy, hurriedly, "whatever we learn will remain confidential."

"Even if it involves . . . ?"

"I'm your attorney," Kathy said. "Thomas is my emissary. It's the same as if he's a secretary in the room taking notes while we talk. Everything he learns will be confidential."

"Even when he finds out something outside of your presence?"

"Anything, as long as it doesn't involve an ongoing crime."

"I'll have to hire operatives," I said. "It's going to run into some money."

"Mr. Black. If it was only going to be two thousand dollars a week, and I knew my life would remain undisturbed, I would pay for the rest of my life and not think twice about it. Money is not the problem. It's the idea of somebody knowing what he cannot possibly know. And what else he might do with that knowledge. It's driving me crazy."

"And, of course, you're not going to explain what that means?"

"No."

"To date, you've given this person how much?"

"If we pay this week, it'll be eight."

"And you think he'll call tomorrow and ask for two thousand dollars? What if he ups it?" She was quiet. "Yes, well. It doesn't much matter. We'll just have to put the kibosh on the whole business. Tell me everything that's happened. Step by step."

She looked at Kathy again, probably for succor, but Kathy was watching me. I could tell she was still trying to figure out why I'd been measuring my skull.

Along with two other lawyers, a couple of paralegals, and an affable receptionist/secretary named Beulah, Kathy and I shared offices on an upper floor in the Mutual Life Building at First and Yesler. Though there had once been a fortune-teller across the street, I was the only private investigator on our floor, which meant I was saddled with ousting salesmen and spiders. I had once even been elected to carry out a dead rat. They saved all the rough stuff for me.

CHAPTER 2

"Four weeks ago I got this call. A man. He sounded . . . I don't know . . . scary and large, if you can sound large on the phone. I didn't recognize the voice. He said he needed 'two thousand bucks' by Friday and that I was to put it in a paper sack and have somebody drop it in a trash bin outside the knife store at the Southcenter Mall. I had Kent deliver it. He's a weight lifter, so I thought . . . well, that he would be able to handle whatever came up. The next week it was a waste bin outside of JC Penney. And last week it was the Orange Julius place. Another garbage can."

"All of these were at Southcenter Mall?"

"Yes."

"Did Kent see anything?"

"The man on the phone said not to hang around. He said we were to put the sack in the garbage and keep on walking right out of the mall. That's what Kent did."

"And Kent's always done it exactly the way the man on the phone asked?"

"Yes."

"You didn't have somebody follow Kent?"

"No. Listen. I don't want you guessing about this. I'll only say that somebody knows something I don't want out. I want you to find who it is and stop it."

She didn't want me guessing. She might as well have sat Kathy on my lap and told me not to think about sex. I could see the same reaction in Kathy's eyes. Not the sex, but the guessing. Between the two of us, we would figure this out. No guessing? Who did she think we were? She was talking to the best guessers in town.

"The calls come to your home?"

"Both numbers. I have a condo with an office on the same floor as my residence, and they've come to both numbers."

"You're in the book?"

"No. But a million people know those numbers. They haven't been changed in four years."

"Okay. Will you be in this afternoon? I need to install a recorder and put a trap on your phone line."

"What's a trap?"

"A machine that tells what number somebody is calling from."

"I have one of those already. I have a friend who works for the phone company, and she checked all three phone numbers. They were pay phones on Capitol Hill."

"You've been busy." Nothing else in the morning's conversation had embarrassed her, but my discovery that she'd been sleuthing on her own had. "One other item, Lainie. I want to do an electronic sweep of your premises. For bugs. Tapped phone lines. Listening devices. It should take less than an hour."

"I'll be there the rest of the day. But there is no way anybody could have found this out by bugging my place. I've never spoken of it."

"Humor me."

"Sure."

"Let me just walk Lainie out," said Kathy, standing as Lainie worked to lever herself out of the blue chair. Her movements lifted the legs of the chair an inch off the carpet, an event we all pretended didn't happen.

I said, "Of course, there's one way to stop the whole deal, and it won't cost a red cent."

"What's that?" Lainie asked.

"Spill the beans."

Unimpressed by my smile, the dimensions of my biceps, my hat size, or my suggestion, she shook her head. "Believe me, I've thought about it, but no."

CHAPTER 3

I was staring out the window at the slanting October sunshine, waiting for our client to emerge on the sidewalk three stories below, when Kathy came bustling back into the office, carefully examined the floor, rifled a drawer or two, then sat on the corner of the desk as if it were an English sidesaddle. "That was cute. Did you do that on purpose?"

"What?" I turned and kissed the spot where her hairline met her brow, tasting just a hint of perspiration.

"Where'd you hide the tape?"

"What tape?"

"Let me see now. What do boys measure besides their heads? Their muscles? Their waist? You weren't measuring your tinkle, were you?"

"Hey. I wasn't measuring it, and it's called a wang. I know Smith from somewhere. Where do I know her from?" In the street a man with a ponytail and a long gray wool overcoat escorted our client toward a loading zone where a brand-new black Volvo station wagon waited. They climbed in, and a moment later the car merged smoothly into traffic.

"Of course you know her. That was *Lainie Smith*. The woman who founded Children's House. The Red Teddy Bear Foundation. The Seattle Grand Children's Choir?"

"A couple of years back she and three others put an unsuccessful bid together to buy the Seahawks?"

"That's the one."

"But she's only, what . . . in her thirties?"

"Thirty-four. And she thinks you're cute. If you weren't stuck with me, you could have snagged yourself a rich wife."

"Drat. And I got stuck with a beautiful one."

"Aren't you nice. Her mother's been a client for just over a year. This is the first time Lainie's come to me. I guess she didn't want her regular attorneys involved."

"What did you tell her outside?"

"I told her not to mind that you looked a little squirrelly. I told her the medication kicked in when I could get you to take it on a regular basis. I told her you were one of the top fifty or one hundred investigators in this part of town."

"You really put me on a pedestal, didn't you? What's she worth, anyway?"

"Who can keep track after the first hundred mil?"

Kathy thrust a newspaper article at me, a full page folded several times from a Sunday section that had run a year or so earlier. It was anybody's guess where she'd been carrying it, because her dress didn't have any pockets and I hadn't seen it in her hands.

While I read, Kathy, looking for the tape measure, rummaged through my desk drawers and then my pockets, a process made more difficult when I tilted my chair back on two legs to better peruse the article. Lainie Smith was, according to the *Seattle Post-Intelligencer*, a natural resource if not a national treasure, a fountain of largesse who blessed Seattle at every turn.

After an unremarkable college career at the University of Washington, where she majored in math and computer science, Lainie embarked on a career writing computer game programs for a then-small software company called Globe Xenotronics. Teetering on the brink of bankruptcy for most of their first year, Xenotronics was comprised of a small team of computer geeks, entrepreneurial eager beavers, programmers, and avid gamesters—a strange and, they all thought, winning brew. However, their reserves went from meager to zilch after their founder staked everything and lost it on a video arcade game called Gonzago.

The CEO begged for faith and commitment, encouraging those who could to keep working—not for salaries, but for shares in the company, shares that might ultimately be worth nothing. Four of the original eight founders were forced by family obligations to abandon. Four others stayed—two at reduced salaries, one for medical and dental only. Lainie, still residing at home with her parents in Auburn, agreed to work for stock shares alone, paying for clothes, gas, car insurance, and Christmas presents with a second job waiting tables in a Pioneer Square pub, Doc Maynard's, which was just across the street from our building.

For almost three years she worked fifty to seventy hours a week collecting speculative stock shares instead of a salary. Then, in the space of two months, the company located willing investors with deep pockets and began producing an original series of home computer games. Globe Xenotronics branched out, writing specialty programs for professionals and piloting experimental projects for the Internet.

By the time Xenotronics resumed paying her salary, Smith had accrued nearly fifty thousand shares, more than any other single individual except the CEO, who was killed the day after Thanksgiving when his Carrera, traveling a hundred and ten miles an hour, hit a patch of black ice on a freeway overpass. His stock was divvied up among four relatives. Smith had gained a position in the company that was to set her up for life.

By the time Lainie quit, Xenotronics was employing over three thousand people, and its stock, valued optimistically at a dollar a share during the three years Smith had been stashing it away, had split six times. Nobody knew exactly what Smith was worth, but it was a lot.

Four years earlier, on her thirtieth birthday, Smith quit Globe Xenotronics to become an immediate presence in Seattle, sponsoring halfway houses for street kids, homeless shelters in downtown Seattle, and opening two small manufacturing plants devoted exclusively to giving jobs to the homeless, as well as free day care to parents while they worked.

"Mother Teresa with a bankroll," I said, looking up at Kathy.

"She supports the symphony, the ballet, the art museum, the zoo, every children's theatre in the area. There are artists around Seattle who are eating only because of her. She's an advocate for children and for the homeless. And believe it or not, her mother once told me the bulk of her work is done in secret."

"You'd think Smith would have used a big firm to get rid of a scuzzball blackmailer," I said.

"If you think about it, what she did was go to somebody her mother told her she could trust. Somebody small and reliable and unknown. Us. Clearly, she doesn't want it kicked around at board meetings."

After picking up the requisite tools and machines, I drove to Lainie Smith's condo on First Hill. She owned the entire tenth floor of a security condominium building; offices on the south side, living quarters and guest suite on the north.

Though I could hear her talking in an adjoining room, I didn't see her during my visit. I was shown around by her secretary, Kent Wadsworth, the man in the ponytail who'd been waiting downstairs earlier that day, the man who had been making the payoffs. While I worked, he spoke at length about his wine collection. After about an hour of this, I felt as if I were on the wrong end of a blind date gone bad.

The remainder of the day was spent driving to the pay phones Smith had already identified and making calls on my cell phone to assemble a team of operatives for Friday.

Late that evening in bed, Kathy said, "I've been mulling it over all day. And all I can think is that Lainie has been working twelve- and fourteen-hour days since she got out of school. Before that, she took a full load at the U and worked to pay for it. Her father died when she was a freshman, and her mother never really had any money until Lainie gave it to her. So, where did she have time to mess up so that somebody could blackmail her?"

"Maybe she stumbled onto something she shouldn't have stumbled onto and it just took a minute to see it and be in trouble. It might have been one of those rare times in life when you're presented with a dilemma and have about three seconds to make a decision. And you make the wrong one."

"Like witnessing a mob hit or something?" Kathy asked.

"Something."

"Or a drug deal? An undercover cop was getting shot in a drug deal, and she just happened to be driving by? And she never came forward? Or a hit and run. You had a case a while back that revolved around a twenty-year-old hit and run."

"A hit and run. I think you've got it. Yes, you've definitely figured it out. Let's make love."

"Don't kid around."

"Who's kidding?"

"No, she's been too busy to get into trouble as an adult. It was something she did when she was younger. Maybe she was a rock groupie. Did a bunch of disgusting drugs and sex."

"A lot of people were groupies. Nobody remembers them."

"Maybe she was a teenage streetwalker."

"You're going to keep guessing, aren't you?"

"Only until we figure it out. It would go faster if you helped."

"You don't want to make love?"

"Of course I do. But later."

"You're going to work this like an old dog with a bone until you think you know why she's being blackmailed."

"Well, sure. That's the whole fun of it, right?"

"Okay. Let's see. She was a porno actress. Some of the old stuff has resurfaced, and she's embarrassed to death."

"That's just like a guy. A porno actress. Lainie would never do that."

"You just said yourself she could have been a teen hooker. It makes more sense than being a hooker. If she'd been a prostitute, there probably wouldn't be any proof. If she'd been in films, there would be the films."

"My other question is, why is the price so low? Two grand? Lainie could pay a hundred times that."

"Maybe they don't know what she's worth. Now let's you and me horse around for a while and then go to sleep, okay?" When I kissed her, Kathy, wrapped up in her own thoughts, was about as responsive as an old woman goosed by a stranger in an elevator. "I might have to chase a blackmailer all over the mall tomorrow."

"Tomorrow she gets the call. Friday you chase the black-mailer all over the mall. Say, while you're there, I've got a scarf waiting at Nordstrom. Could you pick it up?"

"Sure. I'll put it in my machine-gun case."

"Maybe she lived with somebody she no longer wants to be linked to? Some sleazeball. A drug kingpin. What do you think?"

"I think we should make love and go to sleep."

"No, really. What do you think?"

"I think she seems pretty righteous, although you can't tell from a ten-minute interview. Not for sure. But she seems that way, and her public persona bears it out."

"Maybe her father did something before he died that she doesn't want leaked out. I *know*. She's a heroin addict."

"Being a junkie shouldn't be that much of a problem. She could *buy* a doctor. Hell, she could buy a *hospital*."

"Thomas!"

"What? You want to make love?"

"She's a guy! Lainie. Lane. She was born Lane Smith. Doesn't she look like she could have been a guy?"

"No."

"How do you know?"

I yawned. "I'm going to sleep."

"Don't you think she might be a man who's gone through all the hormones and whatnot? I mean . . . they do excellent work these days. . . . Thomas? Don't go to sleep on me. I thought you wanted to make love."

"I'm too tired, Sister."

"Okay. Be a spoilsport. But could you answer one question without a lot of funny business?"

"Ummm?" I mumbled into my pillow.

"What were you doing with that tape measure wrapped around your head?"

"What tape measure?"

CHAPTER 4

Thursday morning was as bright and sunny as Wednesday had been, the sunlight exploding into a blaze in the yellowing leaves of the maples across the street from my office. Kathy called at eleven-thirty. "Thomas? I've got Lainie Smith on the conference line. Lainie?"

"I'm here."

"Good to talk to you," I said. "What's going on?"

"He telephoned about five minutes ago. It's exactly like before. He wants us to put two thousand dollars in the trash bin closest to B. Dalton in Southcenter."

"Do you have the tape there?"

"Yes."

"Can you play it for us?"

"I think so."

When the voices came on, they were so clear I thought they were live:

"Lainie Smith."

"Listen, lady. You know the routine by now. Two grand. Small bills. The trash can in front of that bookstore at Southcenter. You know the one?"

"I believe there are a couple of bookstores."

"Ah, it's the one on the main drag. Faces north."

"That would be B. Dalton."

"Yeah, that's the one. B. Dalton. Have your guy put it in the garbage and walk away. I figure by now you're ready to try something funny. Don't. I wouldn't like to see you on the front page of the *Times*, sweetheart. Wouldn't want people to know how cold-blooded you really are."

Lainie had paused as if thinking, or as if she had to work off some fear. "What time do we bring the package?"

"Oh, the time. I almost forgot. That would have been bad. Coulda got you in a lot of hot water, deary." He laughed. His voice was a little rough around the edges, making it hard to guess how old he was. "Today," he said. "Two o'clock. We're going to vary it a little just in case you're getting ideas."

"I'm not getting any ideas."

"Two o'clock. Don't fuck up."

Lainie's voice was almost inaudible when she said, "I won't."

The tape ended, and then Lainie was back on the line. "He changed the day," she said.

"Was that the same person?" Kathy asked.

"Yes."

"Is the money ready?" I asked.

"We have it right here."

"Send Kent just like always, and we'll take it from there. Hang on to that tape. I'll pick it up in a little while." I made five quick telephone calls and then met Kathy in the foyer in front of Beulah's tall, circular reception counter. Beulah had her back to us and was typing on her computer keyboard.

"You know, I've been thinking about this," Kathy said.

"I know you have." I leaned down and kissed her cheek. "What's your theory now?"

"Just this. If our blackmailer was smart, he'd be asking Lainie to mail this to a post office box. Then he'd have some panhandler pick up the merchandise so he could follow him around the Public Market until he was sure he wasn't being followed."

"Yeah, well, he calls her up and forgets to give her half the instructions. Doesn't know the name of the bookstore he wants to use. It sounded almost as if he was on drugs."

"Dumb."

"Still, I'm not going to automatically assume we're smarter than he is. That phone call could have been a ruse. When we get there, the pickup person might well spot us all in fifteen seconds and pepper our butts with poison darts."

"Don't get careless, big guy. I like your butt the way it is."

"You might like it better with feathered darts."

"Be careful. It's a pretty big target."

"My butt?"

"What are you two talking about?" Beulah asked, looking up from her work.

"Nothing," I said.

"Thomas's butt," Kathy said. "Don't you think it's the best butt you've seen on a white guy?"

"It's cute," Beulah said. "Everybody in the building thinks so."

Thoroughly embarrassed, I rode the elevator to the street and handed fifty cents to a man with bloodshot eyes on the corner. I retrieved my Ford Taurus SHO from its stall in the Allright Parking garage a block away and drove to Lainie's condo on First Hill, where I double-parked and picked up the tape, which was waiting for me in a brown sack at the guard counter in the foyer. Then I took Interstate 5 out of downtown Seattle to the Southcenter shopping mall. It was a fifteen-minute drive.

I pulled into the lot of a movie house at the northwest corner of the mall and waited for the others. *Jerry Maguire* was the current attraction.

It took fifteen minutes for our little covey to assemble. Bruno Collins, a black private eye I'd worked with in the past, was the last to arrive, driving a pale green vintage Chevrolet with plates that said DETECT1. I'd forgotten about his telltale plates. He could ride with me, and that way, should the need arise, we could put somebody on foot quickly. All told, I had five portable radios to pass out, each with a range of up to seven miles when hills or buildings didn't interfere.

In addition to Bruno Collins there was Bridget Simes, another licensed private investigator I'd worked with before, a jogger about my age who could change her look with a hat or a pair of glasses; and two senior citizens, Hazel and Thelma, both of whom drove like demons. Thelma, who wheeled around in a Jaguar coupé, had recently gone straight from red hair to solid blue, thus sidestepping all the salt-and-pepper years in between. Hazel took her Buick out each year at the first snow and practiced spinning around in empty parking lots. Registered private investigators, the two would have worked for peanuts if I'd let them. They practiced thumb holds on each other until I got sick of watching.

Our spotter, the person I'd chosen to sit outside the bookstore and snap pictures with a concealed camera, was a black woman who'd been fired from the Seattle Police Department for reasons I wasn't privy to. I'd never used her before, but Bruno swore she could be trusted. Her name was Latasha, and I'd asked her to come dressed as uncoplike as possible. She said she could do better than that and surprised us by bringing along her sister's thirteen-month-old son. I wasn't thrilled about that, though Thelma and Hazel were soon cooing up a storm.

Motors running, Thelma and Hazel would be on opposite sides of the mall listening to their portable radios and ready to angle in from either direction.

Bridget was to follow our target inside the mall and tell us what exit he was headed for. She had ridden in on a BMW motorcycle, so if she could reach it in time, at least one of us would be able to follow him just about anywhere.

Thursday afternoon traffic probably wouldn't be bad, but the Seattle area was so congested and there were so few alternate routes, it took the freeways only a heartbeat to choke up like a fat boy in an all-you-can-eat restaurant.

At 1:59 Kent Wadsworth came breezing down the main hall from the west, as punctual as a clockmaker arriving for a job interview. Without stopping, he dunked a small package wrapped in a brown paper sack into the low, cylindrical garbage bin outside the bookstore, continuing on to overtake a trio of elderly women using the mall for their daily walk.

Kent wore Dockers, earrings, a white polo shirt, and moccasins. His hair was in a ponytail. His biceps were bulging, but not enough for him to wing his arms out to the side the way he did. Even from where I was standing at the end of the mall, he looked like an arrogant twit who was a likely candidate to have his soup served with a waiter's spit in it.

My time with him yesterday afternoon had been barely tolerable. More than impressed with his connections to Lainie Smith and the power elite of Seattle, when he wasn't talking about his wine collection, he'd chatted away with annoying familiarity about the mayor and the governor and had ordered me about as if I were a servant. He was a good-looking man in his late twenties or early thirties, maybe five years younger than me, with widely spaced blue eyes, a good nose, and a square jaw.

He walked within thirty feet of me, and perhaps because he was so busy looking at his reflection in the shop windows, he failed to see me.

Showing up thirty-five minutes later, our target was quick and smooth. He wore a navy-blue watch cap, wraparound sunglasses, a mustache, a long raincoat, jeans, Adidas running shoes, and wool glove liners. He came out of B. Dalton, walked directly to the garbage bin, took the lid off, scooped out the package, and walked away.

He appeared to be heading directly at me, so I turned my back to him and walked toward the exit north of where I'd been standing so that if he kept up his pace, he would pass me just before I reached the door.

"Latasha," I said. "Anybody watching besides us?"

"Not that I can see. He's wearing a long brown raincoat buttoned to the neck. He's just under six feet. Skinny. One fifty. Maybe one forty. Caucasian. He's walking fast. I'd say he's in his late teens or early twenties."

By the time he passed me at the exit, I was on one knee tying a shoelace. Thelma rounded the corner in her Jaguar coupé. I could see Bruno idling my Ford, pretending to wait for a space. Our target went outside and bisected the parking lot on a dead run.

He climbed into a dark green Jeep with a soft top, canvas zippered windows, a roll bar, and mud spattered all over the back so that the license plate was close to unreadable.

There was a passenger, a black man, maybe thirty-five years old.

The Jeep zigzagged in and out of traffic. After we latched on, we followed from about eight car lengths back on Interstate 405, Bruno all the while telling me about the greasy spoon he wanted to open when he'd saved enough money. "The secret to a good greasy spoon," Bruno assured me, "is a quality product that people don't mind paying a few extra pennies for."

Bruno was recently divorced, and the celebrities and dignitaries who'd been hiring him as a bodyguard had, for one reason or another, wearied of his services. When he wasn't working, he played backgammon in the back of a shoe repair shop a few blocks from our office.

With four trailing vehicles and good radio communication between us, we didn't have much trouble. We followed the Jeep to Bellevue, where it exited at Northeast Eighth, turned south as far as the Red Lion, circled the parking lot, then got back onto 405 and crossed Lake Washington on the 520 floating bridge. Once in Seattle, the Jeep took the Montlake exit and went south on Twenty-third, up the hill to Madison, where it began a series of long, looping circles on Capitol Hill.

When the Jeep parked on East John Street, Thelma radioed that two men had gotten out and were walking east past some apartment houses. Bridget said she could tail them from her bike, but then, a minute later, Thelma let out a howl over the airwaves.

"Get in here. Somebody get in here. He's going to clobber Bridget."

We'd been double-parked around the corner, Bruno expounding on what made one batch of french fries crisper than another, and as we raced around the corner onto East John, we spotted Bridget facing off with a black man in a raggedy coat. He looked mean enough to make a train take a dirt road.

CHAPTER 5

Eyes locked on her foe, Bridget was in the street in front of her parked bike, primed for a getaway but clearly afraid to initiate it.

The black man on the parking strip was the passenger from the Jeep. He moved toward her in small increments like a cat creeping up on something he wanted to kill. The driver, who had picked up the package, was nowhere in sight.

Bridget was eight feet from her nemesis, her helmet still on and her dark shield down, so that with her bulky leather jacket, the man on the parking strip might not have realized he was facing a woman. I hoped she had the good sense not to provoke him.

The situation annoyed me because I was painfully aware we hadn't formulated any sort of battle plan, and ultimately, whatever happened would be my fault. I was tweaked at Bridget for getting us into this pickle. We'd tailed these two twenty-five miles on freeways, through Bellevue and then across the lake without arousing any suspicions, and now Bridget had launched into a staring contest with a man who looked like he could piss farther than anybody else in cell block G.

"Problem here?" I said, as if I'd stumbled upon the scene by accident.

"Stay the fuck out of it," said the man, without turning his head from Bridget, who had her right hand in her jacket pocket, grasping, I felt sure, either a canister of Mace or pepper spray, her weapons of choice. He could probably take her head off before her hand cleared her pocket.

"I wasn't doing anything," Bridget said, her voice so unnaturally calm and lacking modulation that you could tell she knew she was in trouble.

"You followin' me, bitch."

"I was just looking for a place to park my bike."

"Now you callin' me a liar."

"Why would I be following you?"

"You tell me."

A gentleman would have run a prompt interference, but leaving them alone for the moment gave me time to evaluate our opponent and size up our resources.

He was a few inches shorter than me, maybe five-ten or five-eleven, but he looked solid, weighed around 210 or 220, and although he was not in a traditional fighting stance, there was something about the manner in which he held himself that made me think he knew martial arts.

He had a wide nose and a bulldog jaw spiked with dark stubble. His face was throbbing with anger. His hair was short enough to be beard stubble, chevrons chiseled on both sides and in back. He had a tuft of hair just under his heavy lower lip and was dressed like a man who made his living cleaning crawl spaces and cesspools. He wore work boots so battered they might have been passed down from an earlier generation, baggy gray trousers spattered with various colors of paint, and a filthy jacket zipped to the neck and torn where it wasn't already patched with silver duct tape. It was the kind of coat you put out in the dog-house when your dog is sick.

There were four of us: Bridget, Bruno, me, and Thelma, who was behind us in her car and wouldn't be handy for anything but calling the ambulance crew for us when the dust cleared.

"He just got out of the joint," Bruno whispered to me.

"What'd you say?" The man in the coat turned and squared himself up with me. We'd had enough sense to spread out a bit and angle around past the sidewalk into somebody's yard where our landings would be softer. I was glad to have Bruno beside me, because, besides outweighing me by fifty pounds, Bruno was a professional bodyguard and might know some tricks. Our opponent looked directly at me. "What the fuck you say, grinnin' boy?"

"Not a word. Not a blessed word."

"No, grinnin' boy. You said something about the joint."

"Not me." The body language, the tenseness, the hard eyes and uncompromising demeanor in the man, made me think Bruno had pinpointed it. If he hadn't been let out of a very tough prison recently, then he'd certainly gone over the wall of a mental institution. For a moment I thought about what might happen if he tackled me. From the look of coiled tension in his limbs, this guy would kick your head around the block just to show the neighbors what he had.

"No, you said something. One of you two fuckers said something." As he said the word *two*, he split the index and middle finger of his left hand and pointed at each of us. His fingernails were long and dirty, his fingers like water pipes. He glanced at Bruno and then at me.

Of the three of us, Bruno was the largest, about the same height as our customer but heavier; yet with his walnut cheeks, his baby face, and tiny, rosebud mouth, Bruno had the handicap of looking like a teddy bear. Even when he was mad he looked like a teddy bear. It didn't help that his navy-blue, double-breasted suit was what a little boy would wear to Sunday school.

"What the fuck you say?"

"What do you want with this lady?" I said.

"I asked *you* a question, motherfucker." He was pointing at me. "You gonna answer me or you gonna dance with Papa?"

"Whatever happened between you and this lady, it's not worth doing time over."

"Time? What you talkin' about, time?" He glowered at me for ten seconds. It was hard to hold his eyes without either pouncing on him or running away, and my inclination fell strongly toward the latter. I was pretty sure he could take Bruno and me at the same time, and I could feel Bruno beside me coming to the same conclusion, for Bruno was trying to be as quiet as possible; Bridget was too. Even Thelma back there in her car was sinking down in her seat.

"I asked you a question, motherfuck," he said, his voice lower and softer. I took that as a sign he was about to make a move. Bridget stepped farther out into the street toward her bike. Without looking at her, he said, "Don't budge, bitch!"

She froze.

"Go ahead. Get on your bike," I said to Bridget. "And *you*. Leave her alone."

"You gonna make me? Is that it? You think you can make me?"

"Leave her alone."

"One more move, bitch, I'll break your neck." Bridget remained frozen. He'd kept his eyes fixed on me while making the threat, and I kept thinking about all the crippling stratagems a man with martial arts experience could use.

Bruno whispered, "What are you gonna do?"

"You know this bitch? You know this bitch? You motherfuckers been following me? All of you? You know this bitch!"

He took a step forward, and without much movement his boot was six feet in the air and brushing the tip of my nose. As he made the move, I pulled back, but he managed to jump almost as high as I was tall, flinging his foot at my head. The whole maneuver took a little less time than it took to snap your fingers, and as he landed on both feet, I rushed him like a psyched-up walk-on tackle trying out for the Huskies. Clearly, it was the last tactic he expected.

He stumbled backward a few paces and then went down with me on top, and I heard the air go out of his lungs and heard his elbows and back and head clunk on the sidewalk.

Banging hips, knees, shoulders, and skulls, we rolled across the sidewalk and into some shrubbery in front of a brick apartment house. Bruno tried to help, but we were moving so quickly, I never really got a handle on where Bruno was in relation to us. At one point my opponent's beard stubble burned my smooth-shaven cheek. As we clutched each other, he smelled of grass clippings and motor oil and malt liquor.

Twice he went for my eyes with his long fingernails. He tried to bite. He tried to knee my groin. I'd taken him out of his game, and he was frustrated. I could hear it in his breathing.

Then Bruno screamed. It wasn't until my eyes began watering that I realized Bridget had hit us with her pepper spray—all of us.

Suddenly it became difficult to inhale and even more difficult to keep my eyes open. Bruno got to his hands and knees and was retching, but nothing came up. The man we'd been fighting climbed to his feet now, and so did I, at least partially. I was trying to hold him, and he was punching me repeatedly in the stomach. If I hadn't already been all crunched up from the pepper spray, he probably would have knocked all the wind out of me, but my stomach was hard and cramped and pulled tight, and his blows were weakened considerably by the sting in the air.

Then Bruno, issuing a woof sound, tackled us both. I remember hitting the sidewalk on my side, cracking my head on the concrete one more time, and then climbing to my knees, unwilling to remain prone near this lunatic for fear he would jump on my neck and turn me into a quadriplegic. I couldn't see much, but I knew Bruno was on the sidewalk on his back moaning. He'd hurt himself more than he'd hurt either of us. The man was backing away. As he drew even with a phone pole, he gave it a couple of whacks with the edge of his hand, and you could hear the contact against the pole like a hammer striking a two-by-four.

After another brief moment of staring, he sauntered around the corner and out of sight.

"Are you all right?" I asked, leaning over Bruno. "Can you get up?"

"I'm resting."

"Don't worry. He's gone."

"I'm not worried. I'm resting."

"Why didn't you guys get him?" Bridget said, standing over Bruno with a small can in her fist.

I knuckled my eyes again. "We were trying to when somebody filled the afternoon with Grizzly Attack."

"He was going to kill you both."

"Yeah, I think you're right. You probably saved us a pretty good beating."

"I had to. I'm sorry, but I had to. You were like a couple of dogs who'd gotten stuck together."

"Nice simile."

"He was about to kill you. Didn't you see the knife?"

"No, but thanks, Bridget," I said.

"Next time you use that spray," Bruno said, "could you wait until me and Thomas are in the next county?"

"It didn't seem to have much of an effect on *him*," I said.

"It didn't have *any* effect on him," Bridget said. "They say some bears are immune to it too."

"He felt like a bear," Bruno said, heeling his eyes with his palms. The sidewalk on both sides of his head was starred with tears. "You know what else, Thomas? He looked like a Shaolin priest. You know? From that old *Kung Fu* TV show? Ah, Grasshopper. Man in rags fight like warrior. Move like wind in poplars. Man in rags—"

"I don't understand why you guys couldn't take him," Bridget said. "There were *two* of you."

"We were going to take him, but we wanted to play with him first."

"He had *joint* written all over him," Bruno said, climbing to one knee. "That man's done *hard* time."

"I got the cuffs," Bridget said, dangling a pair of regulation handcuffs. "If you could have held him for a minute, we could have handed him over to the police."

"Or he would have handed us over to the coroner," Bruno said. A small crowd of concerned neighbors had gathered. A woman in her late sixties with dyed black hair wouldn't leave until I assured her my bruises and scrapes did not hurt, though they hurt like hell, for pepper spray had gotten into them. People always came out of crowds to mother me. It was hard to know why.

"They parked the Jeep," Bridget said, "and the white guy went east, and the black guy just stood there. He was staring at Thelma. He'd spotted her and was going to do something, so I got in front of him. I guess it was a bad move."

"Not necessarily," Bruno said. "He was probably going to go over and thumb Thelma's eyeballs out so he could make a sandwich out of them."

"I still can't believe the two of you couldn't take him."

"We coulda took him if we wanted to get rough," Bruno said. "But we didn't want to get rough."

"No," I said, touching my hip through my trousers. It was wet with blood from abrasions. "We didn't want to hurt the poor guy. He's probably got a family. He's probably got a cat."

"And a hamster," Bruno said.

Thelma stayed in her car—a thoughtful move in case we were being watched. Bridget mounted her bike and headed for my office. I got into the double-parked Taurus and used the walkie-talkie to tell everybody it was over for the afternoon.

Bruno climbed into the Taurus and said, "There's some nice apartment buildings around here. I wish I could afford one. Rental property is definitely the way to go."

I called a friend who worked for the SPD, and he ran the Jeep's plate while I waited. It was owned free and clear by a John Jacob Bowers.

The driver's door didn't lock properly. I popped it and hopped in.

Empty Talking Rain water bottles carpeted the floor in back. A regional newspaper from Auburn, Washington, lay open on the backseat. In the glove box I found a registration made out to John Jacob Bowers, with an address in Kent, a student admission ticket to an Olympic High School event featuring a team called the Trojans, a worn map of Montana, a newer map of Oregon, and a receipt for Les Schwab tires, documentation that would get him free rotation and flat-tire repair. On the dash were a couple of realtors' business cards, both based in Kent. I found an appointment reminder from a dentist in Renton. A Farmers insurance card made out to John Jacob Bowers in accordance with a state law obligating drivers to carry proof of insurance. And a brochure for a lodge on Lake Okanogan in Canada. Prices had been inked in with a ballpoint pen and a shaky hand. There was a receipt for $29.61 for a motel room in Astoria, Oregon.

Bowers had made the mistake of leaving receipts with his credit card numbers on them. I wrote the numbers down, then called an information broker in Oregon who took notes as I spoke and told me she'd get back to me.

On the drive to Southcenter to pick up Bruno's Chevy, he went off on a riff about rental property as an investment, a riff I decided was his way of distancing himself emotionally from what had happened.

In the Southcenter parking lot an impatient man in an Isuzu Trooper fumed behind me and tapped his horn in little burps as Bruno stood alongside his parked Chevy and said, "I guess you woulda took him if I hadn't butted in, huh?"

"The only reason he didn't unscrew my head and talk directly to my brain was because I startled him."

"Whooee. He was something, wasn't he?"

"I sure hope we don't run into him again."

"I think we better get plastic surgery," said Bruno. "So he won't recognize us."

We looked at each other and laughed. We laughed until the man in the Isuzu backed out of the row in disgust.

On the drive back to my office in Pioneer Square, I decided the worst part was the feeling all along that the Shaolin had nothing whatsoever to lose. A fight is always a gamble, but only a fool gambles with somebody who can afford to lose everything.

CHAPTER 6

We crowded into my small office: me, Thelma, Hazel, Bruno, Bridget, Latasha, and her charge, Reginald—the rest of the office grinding to a halt to fuss over Reginald. We seldom had babies in our aerie, but when we did, they almost always ended up on my lap, and Reginald was no exception.

I thought Reginald had the largest head I'd ever seen on a child, but nobody seemed to agree, because when I said something along the lines of, "Check out the melon on this baby," it provoked a chorus of chastisement. "I just meant with this much weight to balance up here, he'll never learn to walk." Reginald looked up at me with wonder and love in his huge brown eyes, then, much to her chagrin, he howled and balked and clung to me when Thelma tried to pick him up.

Before we settled down, my information broker, Hilda, called from Oregon with some preliminaries, one of which was the fact that John Bowers, the owner of the Jeep, was fifty-eight years old, which meant he couldn't have been either of the men we'd seen. I wondered if the Jeep had been stolen and told Hilda I would get back to her.

Latasha had taken four photographs of our perp, though the fish-eye camera lens, his disguise, and the blur of movement compounded to produce fuzzy, almost unrecognizable images similar to the blurred photos of bank robbery suspects you see in the newspapers.

After I'd cut the checks, Bruno, the women, and the baby left me with my skinned elbows, bruised knees, and a dab of prune custard on my slacks.

I phoned John Bowers, the owner of the Jeep. Sounding as if he'd just run in the door, Bowers answered the phone on the twelfth ring. "I wasn't there myself," I said, "but my car was parked on East John this afternoon, and witnesses tell me your Jeep put a scratch down the side of my BMW."

The line was silent for a few beats. "Now don't try to blame this on me. My nephew's been driving the car for two weeks—thinkin' of buying it. He'll make good. I'll see to that." Bowers supplied a phone number but couldn't recall his nephew's street address. "Hey, listen. Go easy on him? I'm sure he didn't realize he damaged your rig or he would have wrote you a note. He's a little twitterpated, but basically he's a good kid."

"What's his name?"

"Nat Bowers. Nathaniel. And, listen. If you could keep this off my insurance, I'd appreciate it."

"All I want is my car fixed."

My CD-ROM telephone directory had five N. Bowers listings up and down the West Coast, a John N. in Seattle, but the only Nathaniel Bowers was in the Fremont District on Northwest Bowdoin. The phone number didn't match the one the uncle had supplied, so I called a contact at the phone company and gave her the number Bowers's uncle had given me. She quickly pegged it to an address on East Republican, four blocks from where we'd met the Shaolin.

I sicced Hilda on Nathaniel, and half an hour later she called back. Nat Bowers had been born at Swedish Hospital in Seattle. He was twenty-five and had no criminal history. He had made several applications for credit cards and vehicle loans, all without success. His listed profession was *student*, and his last known place of employment was a pizza house on Madison. We'd driven past it when we followed him into Seattle. His uncle was probably selling him the Jeep on a personal contract, cheap, doing him a favor.

When I called Lainie Smith's office, Kent Wadsworth bombarded me with questions about Lainie's blackmailer—none of which I answered. I had the feeling Kent thought part of his job description was harassing the hired help. He finally told me Smith was spending the evening in a gallery in Pioneer Square, coincidentally only a few blocks from our office, and that I was to contact her there if I called.

Armed with what I knew about Bowers, the four photographs Latasha had taken, and a mental description of the Shaolin priest, Kathy and I rode the elevator to the lobby, traipsed down the worn marble steps into the crisp evening air, and inhaled the smells of autumn leaves, catalytic converters, barbecued ribs, and chocolate chip cookies from the shop across the street.

We crossed the intersection at First and Yesler, where a cabdriver in a turban gave Kathy a lingering look. It was after hours, and Kathy was wearing a hat and coat from her 1930s collection, the coat with a real fox collar. For me it was embarrassing to watch the stares she garnered, mostly from women on their way home from work. Dead foxes were not a hot fashion item in Seattle.

We walked south through the bustling crowds along First Avenue to Jackson and then east to Occidental, a quiet, brick street open only to foot traffic and lined with quaint shops, antiques stores, and art galleries.

The Beekman Gallery faced east and was situated between Jackson and King streets. A carpet store on one side, an antiques dealer on the other, it was a small gallery at street level and presented Occidental Avenue with nothing but windows and culture. It was long and narrow and tall, with a small mezzanine in the back. Tonight it was bristling with glass objets d'art and the rudiments of a good-sized crowd.

"You said there were going to be cowboy pictures."

Kathy turned to me. "I said there was going to be some good art. The people who work for Lainie have excellent taste. This is all very Northwest."

"It's nothing but colored glass. A ten-year-old with a pellet gun could take care of this in about four minutes."

"These glass pieces are wonderful. They're evocative and timeless, and they just about take your breath away."

"Maybe they have some WW Two pictures hidden in the back room. A Messerschmitt going down in flames, the German pilot screaming in agony, a P-38 tipping its wings in victory. Where's the back room?"

"There's Lainie now. Do me a favor and don't ask her where the Messerschmitt pictures are."

Emerging from a group of women, all of whom wore fall coats that weren't from the 1930s, Lainie swept over and hugged us each in turn, cheek smooches for me. She wore a voluminous dress that concealed everything but her forearms, a brace of clanking gold bracelets on one wrist.

"Some nice pieces here," I said. "It's all very Northwest. They're evocative and timeless. They just about take your breath away." Kathy gave me a sour look.

"Thank you. *We* like them. What did you find out? Kent didn't see you. He said he thought you might have gotten the wrong mall."

"Is there someplace we can talk?"

She led us through the gallery and into a small, untidy office constructed of two-by-fours and plywood and butted up against a bare brick wall. The office had no ceiling, and we could hear the din of voices in the gallery, though nobody was close enough to eavesdrop on us.

"What is it?" Lainie said, trying to catch her breath as she closed the hollow-core door behind her. Kathy stood between piles of books on the floor, and I squeezed into the open space behind the cluttered desk, trying not to bump into a rack of paintings standing on edge against the wall. Lainie kept her hand on the doorknob as if she might need to flee at short notice.

"There were two of them," I said. "A salt and pepper team."

"You saw them?"

"I don't know much about the black guy except what he looks like. The white guy? We've got a name, an address, and pictures of him picking up the package. What we have to talk about now is the approach."

Lainie started to say something and then sagged against the door without speaking.

I continued. "I can think of a lot of things that could go wrong at this point. I might have a chat with him and he might go underground, in which event we'd have to find him all over again. Or I might talk to him and he might afterward go out and destroy something you don't want destroyed. Right now we have at least a partial element of surprise. I'd like to use it to our advantage."

"Tell me . . ." Lainie said, her breathing rapid. "Who is he?"

"I think I know his name, but I'll need to verify it before I can give you any information on him." Leaving out the scuffle, I detailed the afternoon's events and gave her a description of the men.

"You say the driver is twenty-five? That's not possible. He couldn't be twenty-five and know what he knows."

"He's the one who picked up your package."

"Then he's working for somebody."

"Maybe so, but this is a relatively unsophisticated setup. Add to that the fact that the amount of money they've asked for doesn't show a whole lot of ambition or confidence. My feeling is, if they're hiding something, they're not hiding it very well. I might be able to retrieve it."

"I told you yesterday. There isn't anything to retrieve." She pulled a chair out from under a small table next to the door and sat, tipping it forward precariously on two legs.

"You realize that by not explaining what all this is about, you're making things very difficult."

"Tell me what he looks like again."

Kathy's Elizabeth Taylor eyes were signaling me not to show her the photos, but I already had them out, was moving across the small room. Lainie studied them eagerly, rotating them in her hands as if they were poker cards and she'd just wagered her houseboat.

"It's hard to tell, but I don't believe I've ever seen him before." She stacked the cards together in the precise order she'd received them, tidied the edges until they looked like one, and handed them back. "And there is absolutely no way a twenty-five-year-old could know about this."

"Is there any way a man in his thirties, maybe early forties, just released from the pokey, might know about it?"

"What are you talking about? Prison?"

"We thought maybe the black man had been in prison recently. He had the look."

"What prison?"

"I have no idea. It was just a hunch. I have a couple of people working on it, but right now we don't even know his name."

"Pri . . . prison? Why would . . . ? Yes. It's possible somebody from a prison might be doing this."

We thought about that for a few moments. I walked around the desk. Kathy moved toward the door.

Lainie said, "I . . . I'll trust you to handle this the way you see fit."

"Fine. I'll call daily with a progress report."

It was refreshingly cool outside, Occidental Avenue having cleared itself of foot traffic while we were in the Beekman. Outside the gallery we sidestepped a trio of young women teetering carefully so as not to catch their heels in the cracks between the bricks. Up the street at Jackson, a horse and buggy carried a couple—tourists from Denver with gout, I speculated, to be countered by Kathy's hypothesis that they were star-crossed lovers from Iran running away from her angry father. The buggy was too far away to confirm either love or gout.

"Cowboys would have been good," I said as we passed under one of the grape-cluster street lamps, replicas copied from turn-of-the-century photos. "Or a picture of a Cree Indian on horseback hunting buffalo."

"Poor Thomas. I'm sorry the gallery didn't meet your aesthetic expectations. Is this thing you're doing for Lainie turning dangerous, do you think?"

"I doubt it."

"Bridget told me about the fight. She was worried about you."

"The fight? Oh, that. We had a little shoving match. School-yard stuff. Nothing much."

"Bridget said it was a monster fight. She said if she hadn't sprayed you, somebody would have been badly hurt."

"Yeah, we were just about to trounce him when she stopped it."

CHAPTER 7

Still in his double-breasted suit, Bruno was standing next to his parked car when I pulled up behind him at ten o'clock that night at Eighteenth and Republican, two blocks from Nat Bowers's rooming house.

Bruno said, "Is Bridget a little bit stuck up?"

"Not that I've noticed."

"Today was the second time I asked her out, and she doesn't say 'I'm busy' or 'Not tonight.' She says 'Nooooo.' "

"Maybe she doesn't want to go out."

"I'm not such a bad guy, am I?"

"Not since you got rid of all those lip tattoos."

"What lip . . . ? You didn't tell her I was in prison, did you?"

"Were you?"

"It was one weekend in jail, and I didn't even—"

"I didn't tell her anything."

"She doesn't want to go out with a black guy, is that it?"

"I think it's more like she doesn't want to go out with a *guy*. She's a lesbian. You see anybody up the street when you got here?"

"Naw. I only been here ten minutes. Did she tell you she was a lesbian?"

"No, but she is."

"How do you know?"

"Trust me."

"Oh, boy. She must think I'm a dope."

"That's a possibility. You get the flowers?"

"In the back of my car. Are you sure about this lesbian stuff?"

"Pretty sure."

Opening my trunk, I removed a white service jacket with a small red emblem on the chest that Kathy had sewn on for me. At a distance the emblem looked like a chameleon, but if you examined it long enough, you saw it was a smoking machine gun. I buttoned the jacket, slipped a cell phone in one pocket, an array of common tools in another. I put a porkpie hat on, along with a pair of horn-rimmed glasses.

Slinging a camera around my neck under my jacket, I walked to Bruno's Chevy and picked up a heavy flower arrangement from the backseat. "This is a window planter, for God's sake," I said. "How much did this cost?"

"I forget, but I got the receipt in the car. My aunt gave me a deal on it."

"Your aunt, huh? You keep your motor running and watch the front. Call me if you see anything. I don't want to get caught."

"Thomas, is this ethical?"

"Breaking into a blackmailer's room? I don't know."

With the hat and glasses, a round-shouldered posture, and a stiff-legged limp, I felt sure nobody would recognize me. It wasn't until I was actually in the neighborhood that I realized how nervous I'd been facing down the Shaolin that afternoon. He'd been on foot when he confronted Bridget, so it was possible I was standing in front of his place now. He might even be a housemate to the man driving the Jeep.

It was a quiet neighborhood, full of student housing, shared rooms, three-story brick apartment buildings, most of the residences situated close to the sidewalk, lights from various windows softly meshing with the harsher light from the street lamps. Bruno had done well to find two parking spots, because I didn't see another one anywhere.

It was an old house, three stories, badly in need of paint, yellow at one time, lime-green another. There were five little black mailboxes screwed to the wall next to the front door, each shabbier than the last, all with kerchiefs of mail sticking out.

Faint strains of a string quartet seeped from a brick apartment building next door. The crooked wooden stairs had been wiped clean of paint by a decade of shoe leather and hasty people. They squeaked when I put my weight on them. The lowest mailbox was labeled N. BOWERS, the name penciled onto a strip of masking tape. He had three pieces of mail: a phone bill, a record club solicitation, and a campaign flyer from a man running for lieutenant governor.

Though locked, the front door was glass, and through it, under the dim bulb in the hallway, I could see a frayed rug, a table spotty with junk mail, and a set of switchbacking stairs leading to the second floor. The wallpaper was about my mother's age.

I was preparing to spring the simple door lock with a knife when a young woman with dyed black hair, a nose ring, black lipstick, a black shirt over black jeans, and a face made white with powder, came bouncing down the stairs towing by the hand a long-haired young man in baggy shorts and a Pearl Jam T-shirt. They both wore unlaced black combat boots. As they exited the house, the young woman politely held the door open for me.

"Those flowers aren't for Rosenblatt, are they?" the woman asked, getting ready to smile.

"Bowers."

Visibly disappointed, she got over it quickly and said, "Top of the stairs. First door on the right."

"Thank you."

As they headed down the sidewalk, I could see the blush of headlights in the street from Bruno's idling Chevy. I'd frightened myself thinking about it, but it was possible, maybe even probable, that the Shaolin and Nat Bowers were one and the same. Maybe I was about to break into the Shaolin's room. If he was inside and he shot me, I doubted the authorities would lose any sleep over it.

I went up the stairs quietly, the woodsy smell of the flowers

mingling with the odor of the house, which was like newspapers
too long in the sun. At the top of the stairs four closed doors and
an open bathroom surrounded a small hallway. A padlock se-
cured the door on the right. He wasn't inside if he had a padlock
on the outside.

Grabbing the lock around the body, I tugged, and as happened more often than one would think, it pulled apart. He'd
forgotten to set it. I put the flowers down in the corridor and
stepped into the room.

Despite the fact that one of the two windows overlooked the
street, I flicked on the overhead light, which turned out to be
two low-wattage bulbs inside a small, floral catch basin filled
with dead flies. It was a small room, tidier than I would have
imagined. A bed to the right of the door was barely rumpled. In
the corner beyond the bed sat a battered leather easy chair. A
mountain bike leaned against the wall between the chair and the
bed. The opposite corner was occupied by a large desk, a window on either side.

I pushed the timer on my stopwatch and opened a closet to
my left. On top of a trunk on the floor were a navy-blue watch
cap, wraparound sunglasses, a false mustache, and wool glove
liners: the white guy's disguise from that afternoon. The Adidas
running shoes were missing, but the raincoat was dangling from
a hanger like a jailhouse suicide. Next to it several shirts hung
like onlookers.

When I opened the trunk, it was full of used school text-
books and student paraphernalia. A backpack hung on a hook
on the wall. A clot of dirty T-shirts and shorts were wadded into
a ball on the floor next to two pairs of hiking boots, one style for
summer, a stouter pair for winter. Against the back wall were a
pair of old-fashioned wooden snowshoes along with a couple of
bent ski poles.

The only newspapers in the room were in the closet under a
pair of muddy mountain biking shoes. He read car, music, and
mountain biking magazines. Tipped over on a stand next to his
bed was a bottle of prescription medication for high blood pressure, and beside that, vitamin supplements and a vial of vitamin E
capsules. On the end of the bed sat an unopened carton contain-

ing a car stereo system. When he finally bought the Jeep from Uncle John, he would install the speakers and amp. He didn't need much. He had the richest woman in town at his beck and call, but all he wanted was a used Jeep and some loud music. The kid didn't have enough brains to be greedy.

The walls were covered with pictures. James Dean. Judy Garland. Fred Astaire. Male models with rippling stomach muscles. More male models, and almost hidden, next to the bed where it would be the last thing he saw before switching off the small lamp on his bedside table, a small photograph of four naked young men standing next to a car.

On the desk was a well-thumbed copy of *Seattle* magazine, an issue from about a year ago featuring an article about Lainie Smith.

The desk had drawers that pulled out only with difficulty and were empty except for pencils, pens, colored markers, stamps, and some small change rolling around in the bottom of the middle one. On top of the desk, in addition to the magazines, were notes and a penciled draft of an essay on capital punishment. There was a closed game board—maybe chess or checkers—no pieces in sight. Above the homework were several manila envelopes, the first filled with cash, stacked and girdled tight with rubber bands in bundles of fives, tens, and twenties, a hundred bills in each stack. Four thousand dollars. A second manila envelope contained pocket change and unbanded singles. The third envelope was pregnant with newspaper clippings.

I pulled them out in a single loaf like a baker sliding bread out of the oven, and, after checking the window and being reassured by Bruno's Chevy in the street, I sat down at the desk with them.

The clippings were mostly from local papers, although several were from the *Baltimore Sun*. All of them were about a man named Charles Groth.

Everybody in Washington knew about Groth. Four months earlier he'd been executed at the state penitentiary in Walla Walla.

CHAPTER 8

Twelve years ago Charles Groth had been tried and convicted of murdering four people in Skagit County. The crime was sensational, the five-year search for the killer protracted, and the details dizzying enough that before the execution the newspapers exhumed every gruesome feature of the killings, the investigation, and the trial, as well as ransacking every detail of Groth's life and the lives of his victims. What made the issue particularly compelling was that Groth proclaimed his innocence right up to the last; and a good number of people, especially the anti-death-penalty contingent, wanted to believe him.

The phone in my pocket rang before I could do much more than spread the articles out. "Yeah?"

"I think it's him. You better git."

When he came through the front entrance and headed up the stairs, he was reading his mail. I was already outside his door. I used a cough to camouflage the sound of the padlock snicking shut, quickly got out a pen and a three-by-five note card, and was scribbling a message on his door when he arrived.

"You mind?" he said, poking two skinny hands past my nose to fumble with the padlock. I moved aside.

"Nat Bowers?"

He stood back from the lock and gave me a long look while I
did a jitterbug performance with my eyes behind the horn-rimmed
glasses, inhaled wetly and ducked my head. "Who wants to
know?"

Fumbling in my pocket, I fished out a business card: ROY
WHITAKER. FRESH SEAFOOD BY THE CARLOAD. He took the card, read it,
and dropped it on the floor, causing me to stoop at his feet to recover it. I meticulously replaced it in my wallet. I was bigger than
he was, but I was acting smaller, and he seemed a natural bully.

"So?"

"You drive a Jeep?" I gave him the license number.

"What's it to ya?"

"I don't really know how to say this. Some people . . . I
don't know . . . they could be wrong . . . but they said your Jeep
scratched my car up the street here. That's what they said."

He looked younger than twenty-five, with short cropped hair
so dark brown as to be almost black and sideburns that ex-
tended to the bottom of ears that stuck out like kites. His eyebrows were heavy, his eyelashes long and feminine. His pointed
nose was fine and long and drifted off to one side ever so slightly.
It had never been broken by anybody like me. He had a weak
chin, but his teeth had had a long relationship with a good
orthodontist. He wore baggy jeans and a coat that stopped at
mid-thigh. He was almost my height but weighed maybe thirty
pounds less than my 180. He clearly wanted to be sarcastic and
bad, and even though I could have pinned him to the wall with
one arm, I sniveled and crouched and avoided his eyes.

"I didn't do shit," he said. "How'd you get in this house?
The front door's locked."

"You mean in here? That lady let me in."

"Across the hall? She'd go apeshit if I let somebody in."

"I didn't mean to get anyone in trouble. I was going to
write you a note. I was going to put it in your mailbox, but I
was afraid somebody would snitch it. See, my name is Roy
Whit—"

"You told me your name. Listen. I didn't do it, okay? I would
have known if I had, and I didn't."

"I don't mean to disagree, but these people were right down there on the street, and they—"

"I'm going to have to ask you to leave." He was one of those young men whose sneering, arrogant look made you want to slap him just for the hell of it, and it wasn't only because I knew he was a blackmailer. It was ironic, Bowers with a face begging to be slapped, riding around in a Jeep beside the Shaolin, who was so anxious to slap somebody that he practiced on telephone poles.

"I'm just sure these people were right. I mean . . . I mean . . ." I pushed my glasses up my nose until they were so snug on my face they hurt and then tipped the brim of the porkpie hat down.

"Of all the pricks in the world that could have done this, you decide I was the prick? How did you even find my address?"

"Your address?"

As we spoke, a large gentleman in a bathrobe and slippers, a towel draped loosely around his neck, emerged from down the hall. His hair was combed straight back and his legs were as hairy as two cats. Bowers said, "Brad, this guy won't leave," as if it were one word: *Bradthisguywontleave.*

"What's the problem?"

"No problem. I don't have any problem." I stooped and picked up the plant, then moved toward the stairs.

"What's with the flowers?"

"It's for my grandma. But you did scratch my car. There are eyewitnesses."

"You just take those eyewitnesses and stick 'em in your ear," Bowers said, shored up by the presence of his burly housemate. As I descended the stairs, he added, "Where do pricks like that come from?"

The housemate said, "Hey, man, in Seattle they grow on trees. I never knew nobody like that back in Milwaukee."

"Then go back to Milwaukee," I yelled from the foyer.

"Up yours!"

As I crossed the street past his Chevy, I told Bruno, "That's all for tonight. Thanks."

"Find anything?"

"Hard to tell. You want the flowers?"

"What am I going to do with them?"

I carried the pot two blocks to my Ford, placed it on the floor on the passenger side, then, still in costume, drove home. Nobody followed me. I'd briefly considered bracing Bowers about the blackmail, but I was glad I hadn't. It was still possible the Shaolin lived there. And then there was the vague feeling I'd had that, besides being immature, smug, nervous, and defensive, Bowers was carrying a gun.

Kathy was reading in bed when I got home. "How'd it go, Cisco?"

"I'll tell you about it in the morning after I do a little research."

"Flowers? For me?"

"Sure. You can have 'em. I was going to give them to Horace next door, but I guess you can have 'em."

"You're so romantic."

"I just hope Horace isn't hurt."

The shower stung both elbows, both knees, and a hip—all abrasions sustained in the scuffle with the Shaolin that afternoon. The wounds on my knees were weeping, but I figured if I cranked the heat up in the house and slept with only a sheet for covering, they wouldn't need a dressing. I'd been in a couple of good bike wrecks, so I knew the last thing I wanted to do was slap a gauze dressing on a weeping wound. It was torture peeling them off, and despite what the experts claimed, I was convinced they healed better without a dressing.

The light was off when I came out of the bathroom, so I tiptoed into the hall, fiddled with the thermostat, then quietly stepped around to my side of the bed. I hadn't even pulled the sheet over myself when Kathy rolled up against me, her hands moving along my spine, her skin hot. She was wide-awake and wearing about what I was. Nothing.

"Ohhh," I moaned.

"You like, big boy?"

"Ohhhh."

"What's the matter?" Kathy tried to release me, but I wouldn't let her.

"Not a thing. I just thought you'd want to go to sleep."

"Oh, come on. I talked you to death last night. Let me make it up to you tonight."

Afterward we lay in a sweat—the furnace had come on—listening to the sounds of the University District. In the downstairs apartment we rented to a Swedish student, a door closed, then the low, almost inaudible sound of weeping began. It went on for a while, and then the rumble of a television washed it away. Perhaps uncharitably, we called our renter The Mole, since we rarely saw her emerge from her underground abode.

Neither of us mentioned the crying, and I was almost asleep when Kathy opted for conversation. "That's the first time you've ever moaned more than me."

"*You're* the one who does that? I always thought that was some woman hiding in the closet."

"And you brought flowers because of what? Feeling guilty about something?"

"The flowers were for Horace."

"Oh, that's right. I forgot. You know, she's been down there all evening singing to ABBA records, and now she sounds so blue. I wonder what's wrong."

"Why don't you go down tomorrow and ask?"

"I couldn't possibly invade her privacy like that. But I have been thinking—not about The Mole, though. I've figured out what Lainie's being blackmailed for."

"You have, have you?"

"Think about this. All that computer stuff she was supposed to be so good at. It was plagiarized. She stole the work from somebody else."

"I think you've got it."

"Now you're patronizing me."

"No, I think you've got it."

"Really?"

"It's gotta be. That or she's from another planet."

Kathy pushed me playfully.

Later, in the middle of the night, half awake, I rolled over to get more comfortable, and perhaps it was my imagination, but I thought I heard more crying downstairs.

CHAPTER 9

When the security custodian rattled his keys in the glass door, there were eight of us waiting at the Fourth Avenue entrance to the main branch of the Seattle Public Library: a muttering woman with coarse hairs growing out of her face, a homeless man carrying a laptop computer wrapped in his sleeping bag, five homeless men without computers, and me, also without a computer.

The hazy October morning air had washed all the downtown buildings a grayish brown, the same shade as the sky, all of which portended a fine fall day if the smog burned off and the chill lifted.

As we filtered into the warm building and raced, each for his or her own niche in the stacks, my rivals, these habitués of public offices and private gardens—most of whom had slept atop pieces of cardboard in the shrubbery outside the building—looked neither right nor left, but kept their noses in front of their pumping knees.

A perky young librarian with sensible flat shoes, a long gray dress, and lively gray-brown eyes almost the color of the sky outside, helped me find microfiche from the Everett *Herald*, *The Seattle Times*, the *Seattle Post-Intelligencer*, and the *Journal American* for the dates I was interested in.

Even now, twelve years after the trial and seventeen years after the murders, it was easy to remember and jarring to recall the impression the trial had made on the local consciousness, as each night local newscasts replayed footage of the death cabin and the beach in front of it, along with film clips of Charles Groth being led, handcuffed, belted, and chained, into and out of the courtroom. Each night in front of the camera, the prosecutor proclaimed Groth's guilt and his own confidence in a guilty verdict.

Thinking back on it, you could see how the media and the letters columns in the papers had lynched Groth long before the state managed to slip its rope around his neck.

Last spring's stories at the time of the execution were abridged versions of the earlier articles, rehashing the crime, detailing the aftermath, interviewing relatives of the victims and people who'd worked the investigation. The original judge now had senile dementia. The prosecuting attorney had died in a car accident in New York State, but the defense attorney, though she had been almost invisible at the time of the trial, was featured prominently in many of last spring's articles as she railed against capital punishment.

Ninety-two and living in a Santa Cruz nursing home, Groth's mother, who had always professed her son's innocence, expressed remorse only over her unfortunate choice of wording twelve years earlier when a radio reporter overheard her say, "If he was going to make up a story, why didn't he make up a story I could believe in?"

The murders were committed in a cabin on a beach across the bridge from Deception Pass State Park, located an hour and a half north of Seattle on the northernmost tip of Whidbey Island. On a Monday morning in late August seventeen years ago, a gas meter reader walked past the cabin and through the kitchen window noticed a clock hanging awry. Stepping closer, he spotted what appeared to him to be random smears of brown paint on the walls. The crime, at that point, was already three days old, and the smell of death drifting through a partially open window choked him.

Summoned by the meter reader, the police discovered four bodies inside the five-room cabin: two women and two men. Both of the women and one of the men had been tied to chairs with strips of bedsheets and nylon stockings, gagged, stabbed, and bludgeoned as they sat bound and helpless; though inexplicably, the second woman's hands had either been freed or she had freed them herself before death.

The second man, the loser in what apparently had been a long and nasty scrimmage, was found crumpled in a corner of the kitchen, a butcher knife planted in the center of his chest like a surveyor's stake in a vacant lot. None of the victims had been sexually assaulted, and none had been involved with drugs.

Three of the deceased had been attending the University of Washington, and the fourth had recently graduated. The oldest was twenty-two, the youngest nineteen. All had been in good health. The two women had been pretty, the men square-jawed and stalwart-looking.

Though the cabin had been ransacked, it was unclear what, other than some petty cash, had been taken. When the police arrived, the victims' automobiles were still parked outside, although the keys to one of them were never found.

The victims were Raymond and Amy Brittan, married for less than a year; Tess Hadlock, single; and Jack Schupp, who was going steady with a young woman who had remained in Seattle to study for summer-quarter finals. Tess, Jack, and Amy had been tied to chairs in the living room. Raymond was found in the kitchen.

The police collected more than ample physical evidence: fingerprints, blood spatters, bloody footprints in the house as well as outside in the yard. Fingerprints on the Brittans' car. There were three other houses within hailing distance on the beach, but none of the occupants had seen or heard anything unusual.

The quartet had borrowed the cabin from Schupp's father, whose family had owned it since the late Thirties.

Half a mile away, not far from a beach cottage where a shirt had been stolen off a clothesline the night of the murders, police dogs from Everett sniffed out a man's bloody shirt stashed under a log alongside a local road. Lab tests matched blood on the shirt to two of the victims.

Even with the surfeit of hard evidence, years passed without a suspect surfacing, and Skagit County, which had not had a similar murder in anybody's memory, circulated rumors faster than bad money at a counterfeiters' convention. One favorite was that the murders were the work of a devil-worshiping cult, and the reason Tess Hadlock's hands had been untied and her jeans unzipped was so they could ascertain whether she was a virgin before giving her to the devil—that when they found she was not a virgin, they slaughtered her with the others. Police said her jeans had most likely become unzipped after the murderer left, as she crawled across the floor on her belly. And the medical examiner, probably to combat the devil-worshiper rumors, announced one day out of the blue that Hadlock *had* been a virgin.

Another rumor suggested Raymond Brittan had gone berserk, murdering all except his wife, whom he freed before changing his mind. The conjecture was that in a fit of further madness and remorse, he then slashed himself with the butcher knife, tore the place apart, and eventually fell on the blade in the kitchen. The hitch in that particular rumor was that the woman who'd been untied was not his wife. Also, there were unidentified fingerprints on the knife that killed him.

So many people had used the cabin in the two years prior to the killings that the police didn't know who to match fingerprints to. In only the six months preceding the crime, seventy-eight different individuals had been inside the house.

Two of Brittan's fingertips had been cut off, but nobody seemed to know how that had happened, unless it had been the result of a defensive wound.

A local radio station initiated a ghoulish contest in which listeners were invited to call in theories of what might have happened, the best theorist to win a paid overnight stay on Halloween at Rosario Resort on Orcas Island. Eventually the station canceled the contest and apologized to the relatives of the deceased, two of whom had complained bitterly about the station turning their tragedy into a parlor game.

It wasn't until five years later that a man named Charles Groth, awaiting arraignment in the Pierce County Jail in Tacoma on a burglary charge, was fingered by one of his cell mates, who said Groth told him he had knowledge of who had killed "those four college kids up at Deception Pass five years ago."

When questioned by the police, Groth clammed up until the State Patrol lab matched his fingerprints to prints in the cabin and to prints on the knife that had killed Brittan.

Groth's explanation was that, yes, he'd been at the cabin, that he and a young woman named Cherokee or Chance— he wasn't sure—were drinking and doing sex and drugs on the beach. He claimed that she decided they should rob one of the local homeowners, that they then broke into the cabin and tied the victims to chairs at knife point. When they found only twenty-seven dollars in cash, his woman companion went on a killing spree so brutal that Groth blacked out for two days, regaining his senses several miles up the beach, where he found himself covered in sand and knife cuts.

The jury didn't believe Groth, neither the police nor the public ever identified a female named Cherokee or Chance, and after more than ten years of appeals, Charles Groth was executed, the event attended by a fair amount of survivor anguish, anti-death-penalty second-guessing, and rude hoopla. On the night of the execution, a contingent of pro-death-penalty Greeks—Ray Brittan's frat house brothers—had chanted and marched outside the penitentiary with nooses around their necks.

When I finished at the library, I drove to Magnolia Bluff, to the home of a woman on Bertona Street. Midway through my research that morning, I'd phoned her, figuring she could uncover any details I'd missed. I hated driving through Magnolia, probably because I'd killed a man who lived near the bluff and it brought back associations and emotions I hadn't yet put to bed.

Valerie was a professional researcher with a computer and modem and not nearly enough customers. She had once worked for one of the local newspapers but had married a dentist and now took care of his investments half the day and ran her own research service the other half.

At the front door, Valerie handed me a stack of printouts almost two inches thick, then invited me in for coffee. The offer would have been tempting if I drank coffee and if she hadn't owned five of the friendliest dogs in town, all crowded around her feet, anxious to apply their tongues to my wrists and what they could reach of my shins.

Downtown, I parked and headed straight for my office, where I spread the materials on the floor in a mosaic. Even though it was far from the largest paper in the region, the *Journal American* had the most extensive coverage. Set in Bellevue, the *Journal American* served the bedroom communities on the east side of Lake Washington as well as the growing rural areas between the lake and the Cascade Mountains. Valerie told me the newspaper had a small budget and a rapid staff turnover, yet each of their articles over the seventeen-year span between the crime and the execution had been written by the same person, Elizabeth Faulconer. The name meant nothing to me.

It was almost noon when I buzzed Kathy in her office. "Hey, Sister."

"What's up, Bud?"

"You gonna be busy at lunch?"

"Not necessarily."

"Save an hour for me. I might have something for you to do."

"An hour, huh? What exactly did you have in mind?"

"Come to my office and you'll see. Bring all your lipstick."

"What about my riding crop?"

"That too."

I called Lainie Smith's condo and got no answer, then dialed her office. No answer. The second line was busy too. I called the first line again and Kent Wadsworth answered. I told him who I was and asked to speak to Lainie.

"What's this about?" he said.

"Business."

"I'll have her call you. She's on the other line. By the way, have you heard the one about the three guys on the desert island who find a genie in a bottle?" With little preamble and no encouragement, Kent proceeded to tell an incredibly long joke, which I stayed on the line for in the hope that Lainie would complete her other call while he was talking, which she apparently did not, because while he was still howling at his own punch line, he racked the receiver.

I dropped to the floor on hands and knees and once again went over the materials I'd assembled. The one tidbit Valerie located that I hadn't was something that was first reported by Elizabeth Faulconer in the *Journal American* almost a year after the quadruple slayings. It had been mailed to the parents of Tess Hadlock and appeared to be her last thoughts, written just before she died.

It was a two-page note, and while Hadlock's mother and sister, as well as FBI analysts, declared that the handwriting was not Tess's, some of it included comments and information only Tess would have known. Basically, it was a goodbye note written by a young woman who knew she was about to die. If the killer or killers had untied her so she could write the note, why wasn't it in her own handwriting? And why hadn't it been at the crime scene? But most important, who, other than the killer himself, could have had it and mailed it to her parents a year after her death?

In countless jailhouse interviews, both during the trial and afterward, Charles Groth denied any knowledge of the note, and if the police and FBI experts were able to glean anything from the handwriting, the paper, or the envelope, they did not share it with the public. The prosecutor declared it a hoax.

There was more bothering me than the fact that Nat Bowers had a manila envelope full of clippings about the slayings and that Lainie was close to the right age to have been the mystery woman who called herself Cherokee or Chance. During the blackmailer's last call to Lainie, he made reference to the fact that she could end up on the front page of *The Seattle Times*, a fate easily befitting a missing witness to a quadruple slaying. But one of the blackmailer's phrases stuck out in my mind. He had said Lainie "wouldn't want people to know how cold-blooded you really are."

I was beginning to think I didn't want to know how cold-blooded she was either.

"Just what I love to see," Kathy said, stepping into the room. "A man on his knees."

"A woman on her knees might earn a kiss."

"Or a worse joke than mine," said Kathy, remaining on her feet. "I'm not falling for that old line."

The phone rang before I could reply. It was Elmer Slezak, the private investigator I'd borrowed the walkie-talkies from. While I was conversing with him, Beulah buzzed through another call, this from Lainie, which I accepted after putting Elmer on hold. "Thomas?"

"Lainie, I saw your blackmailer again last night, and we need to talk before this goes any farther."

"Why? What—"

"I thought Kathy might want to be there."

"You saw him? What did he say?"

"I'll tell you about it when we meet. When can we do this?"

"What's wrong with right now? I'll be here if you want to come over."

"Fifteen minutes." I got my jacket and stepped over the newspaper clippings on my way to the door. "Come on, Sister. Or would you rather spend the first part of your lunch hour on the couch with your riding crop?"

Kathy slipped into my arms and we kissed. "You know I would, but I don't want a crowd gathering outside like last time."

"Did I make too much noise again?"

"It's that Apache war cry you let out."

I stooped and picked up a long article written four months earlier by Elizabeth Faulconer of the *Journal American*, handed it to Kathy and said, "Most of what you need to know is in this one."

"We're going to ignore that Apache war cry thing, are we?"

"Until I can think of a snappy answer."

"Would it embarrass you, letting out a war cry once in a while?"

"Not at all. It's the riding crop that embarrasses me."

We were a block away before I remembered I'd left Elmer Slezak on hold.

CHAPTER 10

Instead of lifting, the morning haze had thickened and grown fuzzier around the edges, as if some monster child had mixed all the day's watercolors together until there was no real hue at all. As we drove the short distance to Lainie Smith's condominium on First Hill—sometimes called Pill Hill because of the profusion of hospitals—I watched the bay in my rearview mirror fade into a muddy solution of grays and tans. The air had warmed up but not by much. The sky was a pale, brownish mauve now, although if you looked straight up, you could see a bald spot of robin's-egg blue.

"Lainie?" Kathy said as she finished reading the newspaper article and folded it into her purse. "This business here is about Lainie Smith?"

"I'm hoping it isn't. So far it's only a few clippings and a real bad feeling."

"How could Lainie be involved in this?"

"She was seventeen or eighteen at the time. I'm thinking maybe she knew Charles Groth. Maybe he was her boyfriend or something, and she knew about the crime all along. It's possible she was the girl he claims was with him or that she knows who that girl was."

We parked half a block from Lainie's condo. I picked a chestnut up from the parking strip, broke it out of its green husk, and polished it on my jacket. For some reason, fall days like this in the Northwest always reminded me of my childhood in Tacoma. All I needed was the smell of burning leaves and I'd once again be heaving chestnuts at the side of the nearest delivery truck for the sheer pleasure of hearing the thump.

It wasn't until after we'd walked to the steel-gray condominium on the corner, displayed photo ID for the two security guards in the lobby, and were riding the elevator to the tenth floor that Kathy said, "I hope you're wrong about this."

"Me too."

Kent Wadsworth was standing directly in front of the elevator doors with his hands clasped in front of his brass belt buckle, his thick arms a canvas of veins and pride paid for with hours of pumping pig iron and more hours in a tanning booth. Just as the elevator doors whispered open, a lopsided chestnut went rolling across the floor of the lobby. Wadsworth gave me an indignant look.

Without speaking, he turned and, almost in slow motion, escorted us down a corridor of locked doors, a batch of keys clicking in his fist. I knew from Wednesday's visit that some of these doors led to closets, others into the office portion of Smith's floor, and others into what, for want of a better term, might be called the servants' quarters.

While Wadsworth led the way, I imitated his stiff-spined walk, moving as if I had a raw egg balanced on my head and a pencil clasped between my butt cheeks. For my trouble, I received a bump from behind. The closer we got to what I felt would be a showdown with Lainie Smith, the more infantile I became, but then, a friend once told me if I ever found myself in front of a firing squad, I'd probably ask for a yo-yo.

Wadsworth led us into a small sitting room containing two coffee tables laden with the latest trendy magazines, as well as fresh bananas, grapes, croissants, grapefruit juice, and coffee. The refreshments appeared to be placed for us. We sat, and Kent left without uttering a word, though he wasted a few moments trying to make eye contact with Kathy, who was enthralled with the murky view of downtown Seattle.

Several minutes later Lainie Smith walked into the room, greeted us, sank into the sofa across from the one we'd taken, and put one leg over the other.

"Goodness, I'm so plump I can hardly cross my legs," she said with a nervous giggle. Kent Wadsworth trailed her and stood with his back against the door, his personality invading the small room like the odor of manure wafting off a pair of shoes.

"Uh-uh," I said, looking at Wadsworth.

"You'd like this to be just between us?" Lainie asked, her voice more girlish and less businesslike than during our previous encounters. My feeling was she knew the jig was up and this was her angel act.

"Just us."

"Kent, I'll talk to you later. Thank you." The door closed with the quiet precision of a gun being cocked. "So what do you have?" Lainie asked, staring at Kathy, who turned to me.

"The Deception Pass quadruple murders seventeen years ago," I said, letting some time go by as a helicopter motored past outside the window, probably transporting a patient to one of the nearby hospitals. It must have been a small comfort for Lainie to see somebody else in more trouble than she was. "This guy who took your money has a whole bag of clippings about it."

"How do you know that?"

"Trust me."

Lainie's breath whistled in her nostrils before she spoke. "And?"

"You may remember four months ago on June third a man named Charles Groth was executed for those crimes. He claimed he was innocent. He claimed he had an accomplice who was the actual murderer. A young woman."

"I don't see what you're getting at," Smith said. Her rose-colored dress was not quite long enough to hide her ankle, where I was surprised to see a small tattoo of an azure feather. She didn't seem the type for tattoos.

"Groth claimed all along he'd been with a young woman that night. He said she called herself Chance, or Cherokee."

"Mr. Black, I don't understand any of this."

"It was you or somebody you knew, wasn't it? The woman Groth's lawyers could never find?"

She looked at us both for a long time. Twice she started to speak, and twice she took a breath and did not. Finally, she bowed her head, gazing down at her clasped hands in her lap, and spoke as softly as if she were praying to herself. "If I knew something about those murders . . . what would happen?"

"We have an attorney-client relationship here," said Kathy. "All of us. We're not going to do anything to compromise you."

"If I knew something, wouldn't you have to tell the authorities?"

"We're bound by professional ethics to protect your best interests," Kathy said. "If you tell us about a past crime and you don't want it to leave this room, it won't."

"What makes you think I was part of that business at Deception Pass?"

"Lainie," I said, "the time for games is over. Your big worry is this peckerwood extorting money from you, not us. You want to keep playing dumb, go ahead. But the more you keep us in the dark, the more you endanger your own position. We have to know what's going on."

Lainie recrossed her legs in the other direction, straightened her dress across the span of her thighs, folded and unfolded her hands, then pushed her hair behind her ears. Her eyelids were thick and heavy, the tip of her upturned nose blunt. She licked her lips and blinked back tears. She looked at both of us in turn. "I've never told this to anyone."

"Maybe it's time you did," Kathy said softly.

"It seems even more like a dream now that all this time has passed. I feel so stupid. . . ."

"You can tell us," Kathy said.

"I was a rebellious teenager. Mom was . . . I think, much more patient than she had any right to be. I used to be appallingly rude to her in front of my friends. And Dad . . . he didn't know how to talk to a girl. I lipped off to him so much, he'd hide in the garage and pretend he had to fix the lawn mower or tune up the car. . . . I wish he was alive so I could tell him how sorry I am."

"Please go on," Kathy said.

"They were both afraid of their own shadows, and, I don't know, I guess it used to make me sick. It's only since I've been around the block myself that I understand how much there is to be afraid of. One of the things I did, probably just to upset them, was to have sex with the nineteen-year-old neighbor boy. Dad raised the roof when he found out, which, thinking back on it, I was pretty careful to make sure happened. Because I was four-teen, they wanted him to go to jail, but I wouldn't admit to any-thing. We had loud fights over it, and you have to understand this was a house where I don't ever remember anybody raising their voice before that. Ever. Our neighbor joined the army, and I ran away from home, came back, and ran away again.

"My parents would drive the streets for days at a time look-ing for me, and then when I came back, they grilled me about what I did. I never said anything. On the streets I began drinking and doing drugs—marijuana, sometimes speed or LSD.

"We were out partying one night, and I'd been—I don't know—living on the street maybe a week this time, and an older guy came along and he had some drugs, so we were all doing his drugs, and I ended up in this horrible little motel room with him out on Aurora somewhere. The place smelled like mothballs, mildew, and old linoleum. It was a Thursday night. Actually, an-other girl, Fredericka, stayed there with us. He and I slept in one bed, and Fredericka slept in the other bed, but when I woke up in the middle of the night he was in bed with her. I don't know why I'm giving you all these gruesome details. I'm stalling. And maybe I want you to realize what a completely different person I was in those days. Fredericka called herself 'Today.' I called my-self 'Cherokee.' On Friday morning she took off hitchhiking down Aurora, and I never saw her again. I spent the rest of the day and part of that night with this guy. . . ."

"Charles Groth?" Kathy said.

"He called himself Charlie, but yes, later—five years later—when he showed up on the news, I found out his name was Charles Groth."

Lainie looked at each of us, and when neither of us moved or spoke, she continued.

CHAPTER 11

"We hung around together all day, Charlie and I, and by late Friday afternoon we were looking for someplace to spend the night. Charlie was driving an old black Ford Falcon, which I found out later from the papers had been stolen.

"To make a long story short, we ended up on the beach up there by Deception Pass—I think he knew the area from when he was a kid or something—stumbling around full of beer and pills and chemical mood swings, both of us. It was beginning to get dark, around nine-thirty or so, and Charlie kept trying to molest me, but my period was starting, and I just wanted to get him off my back. . . . I can't believe I'm finally telling somebody this story." She made a face. "It makes me sound horrid, doesn't it?"

"People change," Kathy said. Not knowing what else to do, I nodded. I didn't want to be a part of this secret. It was going to get worse, I could tell, and I was already carrying around enough secrets to sink a ship.

"So then he got this idea to go up to one of the houses along that stretch of beach and steal some cash. It wasn't until we actually got to the house that I realized he was planning to rob the occupants, not an empty house. I thought he'd been talking about a burglary. When the woman answered the door, I should have jumped off the porch and run for my life. Don't ask me why I didn't.

"But he told me he'd done plenty of robberies before and he'd never been caught and nobody ever got hurt. He said he was a pro. I was stoned out of my head. I could hardly walk. I'd drunk half a six-pack, and Charlie had been feeding me these orange pills. To this day I don't know what they were. I thought at the time he might have been wanting to put me out on the street, because he kept talking about that." Lainie stopped suddenly, looked from me to Kathy and back again, and said, "I guess I was lucky to get out of the whole mess alive."

I said, "As far as the world knows, everybody who was in that little cabin that night was either murdered or executed. Did you go in?"

She swallowed and tented the long, painted fingernails of either hand against each other, clicking them with a sound like beetles walking on rice paper. "We walked up to this house, and there were lights on, and these people were dancing to a Three Dog Night album. We watched them for several minutes, and they were really having a good time, and I told Charlie, 'Let's not. These look like okay people.' "

For a moment Lainie looked as if she were going to start crying, her cheeks twitching before they cemented themselves into a stiff pout that was hard to watch in the way it was always hard to watch an adult suppressing tears. "There were two women and a man inside, and when Charlie knocked, one of the women walked right over to the door and opened it. On my deathbed I'll still see the look on her face when Charlie stuck his gun up against her head. Until that instant I didn't even know he had a gun. I swear it. I don't know what I thought we were going to do when they opened the door. I was so out of it."

Kathy said, "According to the papers, when Groth got on the stand at his trial, he said he forced his way in with a knife. There was never any mention of a gun."

"All I can think was that he was so stoned he didn't remember. But it was a gun. He put it in Amy Brittan's face and she backed up into the house, and pretty soon the whole cottage was quiet because somebody turned off the music, and they were all staring at me and Charlie and the gun. He made them sit down in chairs at the table there in the living room where they'd been getting ready to play Parcheesi. Then he told me to tie them to their chairs."

"You tied them?" Kathy asked.

"I thought we were going to rob them and leave. I tried to make the knots loose so they'd be able to get free after we left, but Charlie was checking, so I didn't dare make them too loose. After I had them gagged, Charlie started searching the place. He didn't find much, and it made him mad. Twenty-seven dollars and ten cents. I don't know why he could remember the exact amount at the trial and get almost everything else wrong, but he did. So then he started getting angry, and he took the gags off the women and demanded more money. They offered us watches and rings and a jar full of pennies and anything else they could think of. And then the second man came back."

"Which one was he?" I asked.

"Raymond Brittan, the husband of the woman who answered the door. He came in with a grocery sack in his arms, walked through the back door where he couldn't see us, called out to his friends, and then stepped through the kitchen and saw what was going on. He turned and raced back through the kitchen toward the back door he'd just come through. If he'd just thrown the groceries down, he might have made it, but he slowed down to set them on the counter, and when he did that, Charlie had time to tackle him. By the time I went in, they were rolling on the floor. They must have fought for . . . I don't know how long. Charlie kept yelling at me to get a knife out of the kitchen drawer and stab him."

"Why didn't he use his gun?" I asked.

"I didn't know. At the time, I couldn't see the gun, and I sure wasn't going to get a knife for him. Charlie was big, but he actually wasn't very strong. Raymond Brittan, who was a lot smaller, nearly outwrestled him."

"He didn't, though," I said.

"No. While they were rolling around on the floor in the kitchen, Charlie kept reaching up and pulling out drawers. Finally he flipped the silverware drawer out and it rained knives and forks. But Charlie couldn't find a sharp knife, so he got hold of a fork and stabbed it in Brittan's ear, but that only made Brittan fight harder. Then Charlie grappled around and found a knife, and I couldn't watch anymore."

"What were you doing at that time?" I asked.

"I was in the dining room. Charlie'd told me to watch the others. So, like a dope, I watched them. The other man, Schupp, he was still gagged, so he didn't say anything, at least not anything intelligible, but the two women kept begging me to untie them. They were afraid they were going to be killed, but I kept telling them we only wanted money. I told them Charlie'd committed plenty of robberies and he'd never hurt anybody.

"For seventeen years I've been trying to figure out why I didn't untie them, and I'm still not sure. At first, I thought the fight would take only a minute, that if I tried anything, Charlie would shoot us all. I'd been with him for almost two days, and I knew enough to be afraid of him when he was angry."

"Go on," I said, feeling as if the truth was falling through the cracks. She'd already contradicted herself, saying she thought it would be a simple burglary and then admitting the lights had been blazing and music playing. Surely before the door opened, even before they were on the porch, when they approached the house, Lainie knew it was going to be more than a burglary.

"When the noise in the kitchen stopped, I could hear heavy breathing. After a bit, I realized it wasn't the breathing of two people. Only one. It took a while to get up the nerve to look in, but when I did, there was a black-handled knife sticking out of Brittan's chest. I watched him for a long time, waiting for him to come to life, but he never did. Then Charlie went in the other room and told them there'd been an accident and he was going to have to kill them all.

"I started crying and pleading with him, but he pointed the gun at me and told me if I said another word, he'd shoot, and then he calmly walked over and took a rock from the mantel and hit Jack Schupp over the head with it. No preamble."

"Again, he didn't shoot?" I asked.

"No. Amy was crying and trying to talk, but she was so upset we never knew what she was saying. He bashed her over the head with that same rock. I think the papers said it was a geode."

Kathy said, "He slaughtered them like animals?"

"Until he got to Tess Hadlock. She was the calm one. She said, okay, kill her, but let her write a note to her family first. She wanted to tell them goodbye. So Charlie turned to me and asked if he should let her. I said, 'You're the one with the gun.' So he had me untie her hands, and she took the pencil and started writing real fast. I guess she thought he might change his mind. She wrote a note, and then Charlie asked how she wanted to go, with the rock or the knife, because he had another knife from the kitchen now, and she said the rock. So he looked at her and she looked up at him, and I thought for a moment he wasn't going to do it, but then he reared up and hit her."

We were quiet for a few moments while Lainie gathered her wits, if gathering one's wits was possible after recounting such a history. Lainie wasn't crying, though the story had obviously sapped all her strength, just as it had pulled the color from Kathy's face. I wasn't quite sure what it had done to me.

CHAPTER 12

We sat for a while, and Lainie stared at her hands, the mass that was her breasts and shoulders shifting up and down with each breath. Her dark hair, which had resembled a tight wig or a skullcap the first time I'd seen her, now looked like black paint applied to her skull by a very precise technician.

She certainly wouldn't have been the first person to freeze at the sight of a gun, and from one vantage point, it was almost understandable that she hadn't untied the three victims during Groth's struggle with Raymond Brittan. From another viewpoint, it was a reprehensible omission which condemned her to the same moral dungeon as Groth.

Any defense counsel would argue that the murder of the three bound victims had come after the struggle in the kitchen, and that Lainie had no way of knowing that any killings would occur until that struggle ended, which, coincidentally, also closed her window of opportunity to free the captives. The prosecution would claim that she was a willing accomplice, that she'd tied up the victims and was acting in tandem with Charles Groth.

What she'd neglected to relate during her tale was the viciousness of the crime, details of which had been coming back to me while she spoke. Schupp's skull was battered twenty-three times with the rock; he was stabbed twelve times, then slashed across the face and neck several dozen times, this last after death. Amy Brittan was rendered unconscious with four blows of the rock and then stabbed in the back of the skull and so many times in the torso that an arm was nearly severed, not an easy feat with a kitchen knife.

Only Tess Hadlock was not mutilated, though her death had not been easy either; she was struck in the front of the skull three times with a blunt object, presumably the same geode off the mantel that was used on the others. She was the only victim who had not been stabbed.

What Lainie had admitted to us was enough to result in a death sentence, yet she may well have been minimizing her part in the killings. No wonder she'd given cash to the blackmailer so freely. On the other hand, what sort of blackmailer would ask Smith, one of the richest women in the state, for two thousand dollars a week when he could be collecting hundreds of thousands, if not millions?

One reconstruction of the events postulated that the struggle in the kitchen between the killer and Raymond Brittan had taken somewhere around ten minutes, which, if true, meant Lainie had gone ten minutes with a clear opportunity to free the other victims. Even if the struggle had taken only a minute, surely, had she wanted to release the victims, Lainie could have released them.

"It's understandable," Kathy said, thinking like the criminal defense attorney she was, "that you agreed to participate in a specific crime, and then that crime escalated through no fault or intention of your own; that you, in fact, became a fifth victim of your partner, who misled you from the start. You didn't know he was armed. It's also understandable that a young woman—let's see, you would have been eighteen?"

"Seventeen," Lainie said.

"Okay, it's understandable that a young woman of seventeen could be swayed, threatened, and coerced to stand by and do nothing while a man—Charlie was what? Twenty-five?—eight, nine years her senior, a man with a gun, did what he did."

Lainie was shaking her head while Kathy spoke, as if there

was nothing at all that could exculpate her for her part in the crime, and all I could think about was that the crime reconstruction experts claimed Tess Hadlock had survived for as long as half an hour after the killer left the cabin, having been found on the floor fourteen feet away from the other two. All I could think was that if Lainie had called the authorities, Hadlock might have lived.

She'd consented to rob the occupants of the cabin; under Groth's direction she had tied up Schupp, Brittan, and Hadlock; she stood by while Groth executed them one by one. Any way you stacked it, she was an accomplice to murder. And yet, here she was sitting in front of us, pale and clammy, her dark eyes begging for understanding, amnesty, absolution, none of which we were authorized or impelled to impart.

"What happened afterward?" I asked.

"We went down the beach, and Charlie stole a shirt off somebody's clothesline to replace his, which was soaked in blood. At first I was afraid he was going to try to break into that house too, but there was a dog in the yard and it scared him. We went farther down the beach and crossed through somebody's property to the road, and he stopped again and peered in some windows. I was so numb I just followed him like a lost puppy. . . . Can I ask a question before we go on?"

"Absolutely," Kathy said.

"Doesn't it count for anything that I was a juvenile when all this happened?"

"They would have tried you as an adult."

"What about the drugs? I was stoned on whatever Groth gave me. I don't know what it was, but it wasn't LSD like he said. It made me sleepy, and I was sick for a week."

"Drugs can take away intent, which might bring the charges down from murder to manslaughter, but if you'd been a participant and taken the drugs freely, I doubt they would get you off. If it had been prescription medication taken according to a doctor's orders that had made you do something you wouldn't ordinarily be capable of doing," Kathy said, "that would be different. But you willingly took what were undoubtedly illegal drugs."

"I didn't know what they were."

"All of which puts you in the category of the drunk driver who kills somebody while under the influence."

"But I didn't do anything."

"You didn't stop anything," I said.

Lainie gave me a startled look, perhaps sensing the accusation in my tone.

Kathy said, "This all assumes somebody can build a case against you."

"Somebody's got something," I said. "Somebody's blackmailing her."

Lainie brushed an errant strand of hair off her milky white brow and swallowed. A second strand of hair remained stuck to her forehead. In our previous meetings she had seemed so in control of her life and her thoughts, but now she looked woozy on memories of misdeeds and guilt.

"You didn't finish telling us what happened after you left the cabin," I said.

"We got up on the road, and Charlie was headed for his car when I turned around and went in the other direction. He told me to come with him, but after what happened in the cabin, I didn't want to see him again. That was when he pointed the gun at me. I thought he was going to shoot, but I kept walking anyway. I didn't care. He ran after me and grabbed me. It seemed as though he had gotten weaker after the killings, while I had gotten stronger. Eventually I knocked him down. When he fell, his hand went out with the gun still in it, and the gun shattered into about ten pieces in the street."

Kathy was horrified. "He used a toy gun to go in there and tie those people up?"

"That's why he wanted a knife in the kitchen."

"And that's why he killed them with the rock," I said.

"I was so terrified of that gun. I thought if I untied them, everybody would die because he would shoot us all, when in reality, if I'd untied them nobody would have died."

"This is heartbreaking," Kathy said.

"So you actually had a plan when you didn't untie them," I

said. "You thought you were helping? That if Groth saw them free, he'd start shooting."

"Yes. I was terrified of guns. When my mother was a child, her little brother was accidentally killed by a neighbor kid with his father's deer rifle. She must have told me that story a thousand times."

"So you're up on the road, and you've discovered it was a toy gun," I said. "What then?"

"I ran. He chased me, but there were car headlights approaching, so he hid and I kept running and ended up walking what must have been close to five miles. Later that night, an elderly couple in a Cadillac gave me a ride all the way back to Seattle. Lectured me the whole trip. 'What's a girl like you doing hitchhiking? Don't you know what sort of trouble you can get into?' They said a white slaver was going to get me. In their wildest dreams they couldn't have thought up Charlie Groth." She looked at us both and then tried and failed to draw a deep breath. "So? What do you think?"

"You had seventeen years to bring this out in the open," I said. "Why didn't you?"

"Post-traumatic stress syndrome? Fear of jail? Guilt over my part in it? Inertia? I had it all. I still do. For the first ten days I thought there would be an all-points out on me. I went home and barely said a word to my folks for the rest of the summer. I never left the house. I think for a time my mother was afraid I was pregnant. Dad didn't know what to make of it. I got my GED by the end of the summer and was able to get into Green River Community College that fall. A year later I transferred to the University of Washington."

"You didn't tell anyone?" Kathy asked.

"No. When the bodies were found, I followed every newscast, saved every clipping."

So did the blackmailer, I thought. And then it occurred to me that many of the clippings I'd seen in Nat Bowers's room were yellowed with age, yellowed because they were seventeen years old. Seventeen years ago, Nat Bowers would have been eight.

"Something I kept wondering about for the first year after it happened," said Lainie, "was why the note Tess Hadlock wrote wasn't mentioned in the newspapers. After a while I figured the police were keeping it secret for some reason. And then a year later the Hadlocks got that anonymous letter that was supposed to be a note from their daughter."

"The police never found out who sent it," I said.

"Not that I ever knew."

"You didn't send it?"

"No. It wouldn't have been like Charlie to send it, but who else could it have been? Most of it was reprinted in the papers, and it was all pretty much the way I remembered it, but I know the note the Hadlock family received wasn't the original."

"Why is that?"

"According to all the news reports, the note was on two sheets of paper. But Tess didn't write her note on paper. We couldn't find any, so she wrote it on the face of a Parcheesi board that was sitting out on a card table. The police had to have seen it. I kept waiting for it to come up in the news and then during the trial, but it was never mentioned anywhere. All I can think is that there is some reason the authorities want to keep it a secret from the public."

"Do you remember anything in the original note that could identify you in any way?" I asked.

"Believe me, I've been thinking about that for seventeen years, and I can't think of a thing. It was so sad, that note. She knew she was going to die. Schupp had just been murdered and, while Tess wrote it, Charlie was stabbing Amy Brittan's lifeless body. It was a pretty astonishing document, given the circumstances under which it was written. It was just . . ." Lainie stopped and put her hands to her face. Her red nails looked like tropical berries against her skin.

"Go ahead," Kathy said. "It's okay to cry."

"No," she said, dropping her hands back into her lap. "I've cried too much. Let me finish. Tess had been so composed and so full of poise. She sat down with a pencil and wrote out this wonderful, uplifting letter to her folks and her little sister, and then she signed her name and wrote 'love' all up and down either side of the board, and after that she sat back and waited calmly for Charlie to do whatever he was going to do. All I could think of was what a great person we were about to kill and what total nothings we were, Charlie and me. I don't think he wanted to kill her, because I think at that point even he was impressed. But then he hit her with that rock just the same. And that was that."

"Then what?" Kathy said.

"Then Charlie wanted to dance. If he hadn't been before, all the killing had made him mad. He put out his hands and actually wanted to dance. I couldn't believe it."

"And when Groth was caught and went to trial?" I said.

"Like everybody else, I listened and watched and talked about how horrible it was. I had a nervous breakdown too, but that's another story."

"Did you ever think about stepping forward?" Kathy asked.

"I've thought about it every day of my life."

"And if they'd found you?" I said.

"They didn't."

"They have now," Kathy said. "Somebody has."

CHAPTER 13

Staring hard at Kathy, Lainie said, "What do I do now?"

Kathy crossed her legs, and her hosiery let out a low scream that was almost inaudible. "This is your decision, just as it's always been your decision. I can advise you of your legal rights, but I can't tell you what to do, nor am I here to convince you of your moral obligations. I'm not even sure I know what your moral obligations are at this late date. Legally, unless somebody brings this to the attention of the police and the prosecutors, you're about where you've always been."

"Free and nervous," I said.

"You're not going to turn me in?"

"I'll say it again, Lainie. I'm your attorney. I can't turn you in. The only situation where we're ethically allowed to do that would be if we knew about an ongoing crime or some future crime you were planning. In that case, we'd be obligated as members of the court to bring it to the attention of the authorities."

Lainie's voice sounded like a balloon slowly losing air. "I guess after so many years of pretending this never happened, now that it's come out in the open I'm a little anxious. What would you do if you were in my shoes?"

Kathy said, "To be totally honest, even if I had as much time to think about it as you've had, I'm not sure I would know."

When she looked at me, I said, "What would I do in your place? I did once find myself in a similar situation. A crime had occurred. I was part of it. Nobody knew, and unless I said something, nobody ever would know. In the end, I decided old lady justice was better served by not speaking up."

"You still haven't told me what you would do."

Kathy was looking at me intently. I said, "If I felt innocent, I'd leave it alone. If I felt guilty . . . I don't know. How do you feel?"

Lainie didn't reply. After a few seconds it became clear she wasn't going to. Watching the memories percolate in her dark brown eyes, I began to wonder how she'd kept her sanity all these years.

"I'd be remiss if I didn't advise you to turn yourself in," Kathy said. "If somebody robs a bank and kills a teller, under the law even the getaway driver who was outside is guilty of murder."

"That's not fair," Lainie said.

"It's the law."

"Did you leave fingerprints in the house?" I asked.

"I must have."

For seventeen years she'd been carrying this sarcophagus of memories around, and now that it had been exhumed, she wanted us to tell her there was nothing ghastly inside, that it was all right, that we understood and forgave her. Neither of us was going to tell her that.

"Lainie," I said, "we're not God, and we're not a jury. I told you what I did in my situation. Same as you. I cut and ran. There's not a day goes by that I don't think about it, but that's what I did."

"But you didn't kill anyone."

"Thomas has said too much already," Kathy interjected.

"Besides," I added, "blackmail is a complication I never had. Now let's get down to it. What does your blackmailer know, and where might he have gotten the information? We heard the third phone call. What was said in the first two?"

"The second call was almost like the third. He said he knew about me, and then he told me where to deposit the money. It was the first call where he mentioned Amy and Tess by name. I didn't cry, but I must have gone to pieces in some way because he asked for money right then."

"So he didn't necessarily know anything more than the fact that you got nervous after he made some vague accusations?"

"They were more than vague accusations. He knew the gun was plastic. That scared me. Nobody knew the gun was plastic."

"And Groth never admitted to having a gun, plastic or otherwise. He testified that the two of you forced your way in with a knife. In fact, a gun was never mentioned during his trial, was it?"

"Not to my knowledge. I think he really forgot. I think he was so drugged out he forgot."

"That's how you knew you were in trouble?" Kathy said. "Because they knew about the toy gun?"

"Yes." Lainie nodded quickly. Again, it was hard to watch the subtle quivering in her cheeks. Kathy leaned forward in her seat and took Lainie's wrist, but when it became clear Lainie took no comfort in the contact, Kathy sat back and clasped her hands around the knob of one knee.

"Charles Groth knew about the gun, and he knew about you," Kathy said. "As did anybody he told the story to over the years, and he might have told any number of people. After all, he originally became a suspect after talking about the murders to another inmate in the Pierce County Jail."

"Well, yes, Charlie," Lainie admitted. "But Groth only knew me as Cherokee. If he'd had any clue to my actual identity, his lawyer would have tracked me down at the time of the trial. Don't you suppose?"

"You're making two assumptions," said Kathy. "That his lawyer believed him. And that his lawyer had the resources to seek you out. Not all defenses have money."

"What if Groth's lawyer tracked me down and didn't let anybody know?"

"That's highly unlikely," Kathy said. "It wouldn't have been in her client's best interest, since his claim was that you were the one who committed the murders. Besides, if that's what happened, they waited twelve years to contact you. Why?"

"Did you have money twelve years ago?" I asked.

"No."

"Maybe that's the answer."

Lainie kneaded either side of her face with her pale knuckles, pushing her cheeks into various shapes. When she removed her hands, she looked steadier.

Lainie's feet barely touched the floor, so when she shuffled them, they swung freely under her like pendulums. She steepled her fingers and tapped her long nails together. She looked at me and then glanced away, as nervous as a used-car salesman watching for last week's snookered customers.

"You haven't kept a diary, have you?" I said. "With all this in it?"

"Of course not."

"Ever been hypnotized, been to see a psychiatrist, blacked out drinking, talked in your sleep, been under Pentothal?"

"None of those things. And I haven't slept with anybody in ten years."

"Does the name Nat Bowers mean anything?" Knowing I wasn't inclined to give that sort of information to a client, Kathy shot me a look. When a man hired you to find his runaway wife, you didn't tell him where she was without more information. Maybe he was a wife-batterer and needed you to find her so he could kill her. The same with Lainie. She was being blackmailed, and it was my job to stop it; it wasn't my job to give her a name so she could hire a hit man. But I gave her the name anyway.

"Is that who was in that picture you showed me?"

"Yes. Does the name mean anything?"

"No. Nothing." She tilted her head toward the floor to one side of her chair as if readying herself to vomit, but even before she looked down, I could see from the look of fury in her deep brown eyes that telling her had been a mistake.

"Just one last question," I said, glancing at Kathy, who moved to the window for a last peek at the smoggy panorama that was Seattle's skyline.

Lainie didn't look up from the carpet.

"This Fredericka who spent the night with you and Groth? Did she know your real name?"

Lainie looked up, her brown eyes wide and glassy. She took

a deep breath and sat upright. "No. She called herself Today, and she used to write all these insufferable poems about horses. A big blonde with muscular legs and a foul mouth. I hardly knew her."

"How many people saw you with Groth around the time of the murders?" Kathy asked.

"Nobody saw us after," Lainie said. "Dozens saw us before. Nobody I knew, but it could be any of those people, couldn't it? If their memory is good enough that they could recognize me as Cherokee."

I said, "Promise me you won't try to contact Bowers."

"Of course not."

As she escorted us down the hallway to the elevator, Lainie made small talk. "You two get along so well. It's like you're not married at all, like you're best friends."

"I'll consider that a compliment," said Kathy.

"I meant you're so comfortable with each other."

"We were best friends from the minute we met," Kathy said, giving me a quick look as the elevator light came on and a bell chimed. "But we were never romantic until recently."

"I was romantic from the first," I said, but neither of them paid attention to me.

"I'm sure you'll be able to get this straightened out for me," Lainie said as we stepped into the elevator.

"We will," said Kathy. "Don't worry about it. Thomas is the best."

Alone in the elevator, I said, "I was romantic."

"Poor Lainie," said Kathy.

CHAPTER 14

As we walked outside the building along sidewalks ruptured by tree roots, Kathy leaned against me and said, "You shouldn't have told Lainie the blackmailer's name."

"The devil of it is, I'm not even sure Bowers is the guy. When I spoke to him, he didn't sound all that much like the man on the tape. If we get the time, we should do some voice analysis. But he did have the money and the newspaper clippings, and he certainly had the attitude."

"I don't know where Bowers got his information, but I have a feeling he's running the show. Asking Lainie for two thousand dollars a week?"

"The amount seems like Bowers."

"You never should have told Lainie his name."

"I thought if she recognized it, everything might click into place."

"It's all so pathetic. If only Lainie had had the sense to tell Groth she wasn't going to rob the house. If only one of the victims had realized it was a toy gun. If Brittan had been a little stronger or quicker and taken Groth in that fight. Or if he'd come back earlier, before they were tied up. Or later, after Groth and Lainie were gone."

"Or if Lainie had not tied them up," I said flatly. "Or if she'd untied them when she had the chance. Or if she'd helped Brittan wrestle Groth."

"You blame her, don't you?"

"If her story's true, Groth was a nut case. But Lainie . . . she stood there and watched them beg."

"He had a gun."

"A plastic gun."

"She didn't know that."

"We don't know what she knew. We only know what she tells us she knew. And what she tells us is bad enough that I don't have much sympathy for her."

"Of course she didn't know about the gun. It must have looked real enough or those three people wouldn't have let themselves be tied up."

As we walked along the cracked sidewalk, the heavy autumn air smelled of wet leaves, city buses, and, for some reason, hot coffee. From time to time I stooped and picked up chestnuts for the stockpile in my pockets. "I'm suspicious of everything. I don't think she was telling us half of it."

"How can you be suspicious, Thomas? She was like a rose in an oven. She opened up and wilted right there in front of us."

"All this charity bullshit? She's acting like the queen of the Northwest, but all the while she's had this dirty little secret under her pillow with her jammies. She's a quadruple murderer."

"She was afraid for her own life. Groth did the killing. Legally, she's culpable, but I'm not so sure she is morally."

"She didn't even have the foresight to leave out the parts that incriminated her."

"All I know is, for half her life she's been doing penance like a cloistered nun. First, she went back and became a devoted and dutiful daughter. Then she went to college and worked her butt off. No dorm parties. No dating. She worked at night and went to school in the day. Then she got a job at Globe Xenotronics and worked without a paycheck for three years. She bought that place out in Gig Harbor for her mother. Even you called her 'Mother Teresa with a bankroll.' Don't you see what's going on here? She was so devastated over what happened at Deception

Pass, she's been trying to make up for it ever since by being some sort of saint."

"Oh, come on. I bet you think she shits strawberry pop too."

"Didn't you see what telling that story did to her?"

"A saint with a full-time staff of four to take care of her, a condo most people would die for, all the do-gooder prestige she could ever hope for. She's got the moon with a fence around it. I don't call that penance."

"So the question you're asking is, who's the real Lainie Smith? The one the public knows, the one we saw upstairs—or the scared street kid from seventeen years ago who got herself involved in one of the ugliest murder scenes this state has ever seen? Or someone else. A killer, maybe."

"I think they're all the real Lainie. And I think they're all a little bit devious and a little bit manipulative. I think when you scrape away all that nice-nice she's got painted on, you'll find a liar and a killer. She wants us to believe that story has been festering inside her for seventeen years. She was on drugs. Groth had a gun. She didn't know it was going to be a robbery. She didn't think there was time to get them loose. Seventeen years to concoct alibis, and that was all she came up with?"

"You're judging her too harshly. And I think her life has been courageous."

"About as courageous as a spelunker in a basement."

"Look, Thomas. Two guys decide to rob a liquor store. They go in, and suddenly one of them pulls out a gun his friend didn't know he had and starts shooting people. The letter of the law says they're equally culpable. There are even cases where two people go in to rob a store, the store owner kills one of them, and the other is charged with murder. It may be right legally, but there are times when common sense tells you something else. And maybe I shouldn't say this, but people in glass houses shouldn't throw stones." Kathy was angry; her cheeks were beginning to flush.

"I don't like Lainie, and I don't like this case. If she didn't do it herself, she helped murder four people. Incredibly brutal murders. Glass houses? You're talking about Philip, aren't you?

You're talking about the fact that I accidentally killed your fiancé."

"Please don't call him my fiancé."

"What should I call him? You two were engaged when he died. What are you going to do? Throw this up in my face every time we have a disagreement?"

"No, but I thought the situations were somewhat analogous. Forget it. I'm sorry I opened my mouth. I don't want to talk about this, Thomas. I'm really sorry. What happened with Philip was an accident, a complete accident, and we both know it. The two situations are not comparable. I'm sorry I ever brought it up."

"I'm glad you brought it up."

"I shouldn't have said it."

"Sure you should." I stalked across the street to the car and unlocked it.

"Thomas? I *am* sorry." She followed me quickly, afraid I would speed away without her, which, to my own surprise and chagrin, I found myself considering. After the car was moving, she looked across the seat at me and whispered, "I didn't mean what I said. It just came out. Forgive me?"

Maybe Kathy had a point. Maybe I'd come down hard on Lainie because she reminded me of myself, not that I'd killed four people, but I killed one, albeit by accident. It was possible Lainie considered her situation an accident too. Maybe Kathy's remark had stung because I knew how similar our situations actually were. Lainie's blackmailer could just as well have been *my* blackmailer, although as far as I knew, Kathy and I were the only ones who knew the details of Philip's death. Kathy's fiancé, Philip, and I had been in a deserted house with a sociopathic killer. After Philip sustained a head injury, I sent him away while I searched the unlit house for the killer. Eventually, I fired six bullets through a plasterboard wall and killed a man with a gun—the bad guy, I thought. Later, I found I'd shot Philip by mistake—Philip, who had come back with a gun, presumably to help me. The killer had fled.

It had been an accident, though an accident one could not prove. Had the deserted house not caught fire and burned to the ground, I would have turned myself in. At least, that's what I told myself. However, with no evidence except a razed house and a badly charred corpse, I did not tell the authorities and still carried enough guilt over it that on the anniversary of the death I arranged to be out of town by myself.

When we got back to First and Yesler, I stopped and idled the Ford in front of Trattoria Mitchelli. "You aren't going to come in?" Kathy asked, climbing out of the passenger seat.

"I've got things to do."

"Are you still mad at me?" She leaned below the roof of the car to look in my eyes. "Just tell me if you're mad."

"I'm mad." We stared at each other for a few moments, and she shut the door. I drove a couple of blocks toward the water, then took a right on Alaskan Way, meandering north without aim or ambition. Kathy's comment had robbed the strength from my limbs, so that the steering wheel felt like it was half buried in sand.

After a while I found myself parked in Myrtle Edwards Park facing Elliott Bay and watching lunchtime joggers bounding past the front of the car. After forty or fifty joggers, I got out and began walking north. It was some time before I realized I wasn't wearing an overcoat.

Gulls sailed over Elliott Bay, which was pyramided with chop. The thought kept coming to me that I might easily find myself in Lainie Smith's predicament, one day picking up the phone to confront a blackmailer.

How easy it was for us killers to decide we'd gotten away with it.

Lainie had spent seventeen years assuring herself nobody knew about her. In fact, for all of the blackmail and the payoffs and all of her worry, Lainie was *still* sure nobody knew of her involvement at Deception Pass. She had repeatedly said the whole thing was impossible, and she seemed to believe that.

What bothered me the most about Lainie's case was that Tess Hadlock had survived after Groth and Lainie abandoned the cabin. I wondered whether Lainie had suspected she was still alive and, if she had suspected, why she hadn't done anything about it. If her only concern was to ensure her own escape, Lainie would hardly have stopped off at the nearest pay phone and made a call to the local ambulance service. If that wasn't murder, what was?

Lainie was full of compassion for the victims now, but it was easy enough to recall all the nice things I'd said about Philip after he was dead—Philip, a man who, when alive, I'd detested and called the F person. That sort of compassion and limp-wristed exhortations of innocence had never dragged anybody up out of the ground or breathed life into a wormed-out corpse. And now Kathy and I were squabbling. This whole case was making me miserable. I felt like sewing myself into a sack and waiting on the end of a pier for somebody to kick me into the water.

CHAPTER 15

Friday night I flew to Dayton, Ohio, for the wedding of a friend who'd spent the last five years troubleshooting software for a computer company in the Netherlands. In Amsterdam, Herb Lattimer had met and wooed Julie Haversham, a young technician stationed with him in that city.

The wedding was slated for Saturday evening in Beaver Creek, outside of Dayton, but it wasn't until the entire wedding march had been played three times that I, along with the two hundred other guests and the bewildered groom, began to realize something was amiss.

Ohio was suffering an autumn heat spell. After many long minutes, the churchload of sweaty, would-be celebrants watched a cabdriver with a cowlick that stuck up at the back of his head like weeds on a widow's lawn stumble in, march down the aisle, and thrust a note at Herb, a note scrawled on the back of what turned out to be a receipt for a six-pack of beer. Herb was so dumbfounded he read it aloud. "Cold feet? Fine. See you in the next life. P.S. I'm taking Moochie." Moochie was the cat that had been with him since high school.

After the dust had cleared and the majority of guests had departed, an elderly gentleman approached Herb and admitted he also had once been abandoned at the altar. Herb, who had always been an indecisive sort, confessed that he had volunteered to mail the wedding invitations from the post office the previous month. When he got there, he had a last-minute paroxysm of panic and went home with the invitations in the trunk of his car, assuring Julie they'd been posted. He mailed them in the end, but it took him two weeks to do it.

On the morning of the wedding, after talking with guests who had all inexplicably received last-minute invitations, Julie confronted Herb, who laughed sheepishly and confessed the invitations had ridden around in his Toyota for two weeks while he debated whether he was doing the right thing.

For Julie, this was only the last in a long train of offenses, minor and otherwise, the worst being that he remained in contact with most of his ex-girlfriends.

During the long and awkward lull before the cabdriver arrived with Julie's message, the best man and minister sheepishly questioned Herb, who assured everyone repeatedly that he had no idea what was going on. The pitiful part was, he *had* no idea.

We found out the next morning that Julie had taken a plane back to Amsterdam, where, according to her sister, she was planning to give herself to the first man who caught her fancy.

Monday morning, after making love to Kathy, a pleasure enhanced by the knowledge that there were plenty of others on the planet, including Herb, who didn't have brides to shower their love on, I bathed, breakfasted, and was abandoning Kathy to a drowsy languor when she said, "You're just going to do me and leave, huh, Tarzan?"

"Tarzan? Whatever happened to the Big Unit? I liked it when you called me the—"

"That was you?"

"Who else?"

"Is that why you had that tape measure out the other day?"

"I was measuring for a new cycling helmet."

"Didn't you just buy a new helmet?"

"I gotta go."

"Thomas?"

"Yeah, Sister?"

"I'm sorry I said what I said Friday. I'll never mention it again."

"You had every right to mention it."

"Maybe so, but I shouldn't have used Philip's death as ammunition in a quarrel. And Lainie's situation isn't really comparable to yours."

"I *was* hard on her."

"Maybe you had a right to be. After all, a lot of people are dead. Including Charles Groth."

"And she's sailing along leading the good life," I added.

"Right."

Finding a place to park on East Republican took five minutes. As I was heading down the sidewalk, I found myself a hundred fifty feet behind a man, who, from the rear, looked suspiciously like the Shaolin priest who'd wrestled with us Thursday. He wore a tattered coat and old work boots. When he stopped in front of Nat Bowers's rooming house and turned to survey the neighborhood, I knelt quickly and began fumbling with a shoelace, presenting the top of my head and little else. By the time I looked up, he'd disappeared into the house.

I waited outside.

The day was full of promise, students hustling to school on the sidewalks, an old man leaving the apartment house next door with a jangle of keys and a spring in his step. He tipped the bill of his knit cap at a stocky young woman on a mountain bike. A car cruised down the street and left a perfume of automobile exhaust in the still air.

Eighteen minutes later the Shaolin came out cradling his raggedy jacket as if it held a litter of kittens. He was wrapped in his own thoughts and ducking his head like a boxer walking down the ramp to the ring—or an ex-politician being led into the courthouse in handcuffs and sunglasses.

Feeling a flood of adrenaline wash into my stomach, I stepped out from behind a laurel hedge and said, "Hey, guy. Funny meeting you here."

He stopped and reached into his coat as two crisp twenty-dollar bills spun in quick, sloppy spirals to the sidewalk. I would

have commented on the loose cash if he hadn't been holding a
nickel-plated revolver just inside the folds of his jacket, his blunt
thumb tipping the hammer back.

"Whoa there, buddy," I said, showing him my palms. "I'm
only trying to be friendly."

"Back off, asshole."

"Just what I was planning to do." I stepped into a yard in
front of a narrow, three-story apartment house, my heels sinking into the freshly mulched dirt of a dahlia bed.

Rounding a corner in a fast, hopping gait and then breaking
into a run, the Shaolin disappeared before I could gather up the
juice to spit. I snatched up the twenty-dollar bills from the sidewalk and pulled on the ends, which made sharp little reports
like far-off .22 shots.

I don't know why I accosted him, since he was meaner than
a half-drowned skunk, had come close to killing me in our scrap
the other day, and I had no reason to think he wouldn't have
done the same again.

On the wooden porch of Bowers's rooming house, I rang the
bell and stood tall when the same young woman who'd let me in
Thursday night answered the door in a robe.

"Oh," she said, failing to recognize me. "I thought you were
John."

Holding out a counterfeit Rolex, I said, "Do you think this
belongs to Nat Bowers?"

"I'll go ask him for you."

"I think I'd better show it to him myself."

"Sure," she said, swinging the door wide. I wanted to tell her
the Rolex was a fake and she was a dope to let a stranger into
her building, but I followed her meekly up the stairs and rapped
on Bowers's door while she went into her room and threw the
bolt. When nobody answered my knocking, I twisted the knob
and found Bowers's room unlocked.

"Yo! Anybody home?" I pushed the door wide.

The room was a shambles.

There was a small hole in one of the windows above his
desk, a hole that looked as if it had been shaped by the passage

of a bullet. Another hole marred the wall at the junction where the two windows met.

Bowers was in the corner on his back.

He was pale, eyes filmed over, one leg cocked like a mannequin waiting to be tilted up and put on display.

I went over to him and didn't bother to take his pulse. He wore a white T-shirt and a pair of dark socks, nothing else, although somebody had placed a bedspread over him from the waist down. The T-shirt had two holes centered in the chest, blood tattooing the rim of one, nothing on the other. I reached under the spread and felt his bare knee; it was as cold as the ground outside. He'd been dead for hours, probably all night.

A carpet of magazines was spilled across the floor. His bicycle was on its side like a wounded deer. Blankets had been pulled off the bed and strewn across the center of the room like a taffy pull gone awry. The drawers of his desk had been emptied onto the floor, and his closet looked as if it had imploded, most of the hangers and clothing on the floor.

My search was a little less than thorough since I was trying not to move things, but it appeared that both the manila envelope containing the Deception Pass clippings and the second envelope containing the cash were missing.

On the desk where I'd seen it when I'd searched the place Thursday night was a closed game board. I opened it and saw that it was a very old Parcheesi board. The penciled note was hardly faded at all:

Dear Mom and Dad and Cindy and all my friends,
    Don't be sad for me. I'm not scared. Life is an adventure that ends the same for everyone. I'm lucky in a way. Not everybody knows when their adventure will end. Not everybody has a chance to tell the people they love how much they mean to them. Cindy, I love you, you little sweetheart. Grow up strong and stay just as cheerful as you are right now. Go to vet school! Mom. Thank you ever so much for all your care and for all those mornings you got up early and drove me to swim practice. You've been the greatest. Dad. I

know you can't always show it, but you love me as much as Mom and I know that. Don't feel bad for me. I had a happy life! I did what I wanted! Tell Bill I'm sorry. Tell Jack's favorite catcher all is forgiven. Say hi to Cheryl. I wish her well with her new baby.

Your loving daughter, Tess

She'd scrawled along the sides of the Parcheesi board in handwriting that steadily deteriorated, writing the word *love* a couple of dozen times along the edge.

"Is he dead?" It was the girl who'd let me in, dressed now in torn jeans and a hooded sweatshirt, the hood up, her lips thickened with black lipstick, her hair wild and black as motorman's grease. Either she'd gotten made-up very quickly, or I'd been in the room a whole lot longer than I thought.

"Yeah, he is. You got a phone here?"

"What? You want to call the police?"

"I was thinking you could."

"It's a pay phone." I dropped a quarter into her palm, and she looked at me and said, "Are you crying?"

"You better call them."

She walked away with the coin before I remembered pay phones provided free 911 service.

Alone again, I reflected on the awkward position I was in. Friday, Lainie Smith learned Bowers was blackmailing her, and Monday he was dead. On top of that, Tess Hadlock's farewell note was here, and had been here Thursday night when I'd searched.

"How long's he been dead?" asked the girl, back in the doorway now after her call. She was more curious than frightened.

"Did you hear gunshots last night or this morning?"

"No, but we were out last night until late."

"Did he have visitors?"

"Oh, lots. Mostly guys. He was—you know . . ." She showed me a limp wrist.

"Gay?"

"I never saw him up here with a girl, at least not one his age."

"Remember any of his visitors?"

"I don't think I ever saw anybody twice."

"You said you hadn't seen him with any women his age?"

"He had a couple of older women visit. I think one was his mother. The other one I just caught a glimpse of as she was going into his room a month or so ago. All I remember is she was tall. I just saw her backside."

"Can you describe her? Heavyset? Thin? Hair color?"

"I don't remember."

"Long hair? Short hair?"

"I really don't remember."

"Was anybody here last night?"

"We were out last night. I'm not sure anybody was in the house. But there was a black guy here earlier this morning."

"I know. Had you ever seen him before?"

"No. But he was scary."

"Yeah. That he was." On the floor near the doorway I spotted a small black-and-white photograph, a head shot of a young man and a young woman, the male's arm draped over the female's shoulder, the type of photo you could take of yourself at a fair in a booth. I must have stepped over it on the way in. I squatted and studied it until one of the teenage faces began to take on some familiar contours: an upturned nose, a pair of heavy-lidded eyes, poreless skin—Lainie Smith sixty pounds and maybe twenty years ago. Using a thumbnail, I turned over the snapshot. Written in faded pencil on the back was the word *Cherokee*.

CHAPTER 16

By the time I exited the house past the incoming uniforms, a knot of neighbors and passersby had gathered on the sidewalk.

"This is kinda cool," said the girl with black lipstick as she stared at the people, the police cars, the whirling blue lights. We were pals now, Shanarra and I, confidants tossed by the waves of fate up onto the same bizarre beach of circumstance. In two hours we'd forget each other, but we were pals now. Her name was Shanarra Rosenblatt, and she was nineteen. She said, "Wait'll I walk into class and tell everyone I was late because there was a murder in my building."

Shanarra looked up and noticed a pair of plainclothes detectives approach the house from the sidewalk. I knew the shorter of the detectives. His name was Arnold Haldeman, and he tried to stare through me just as he always did. Built like a cartoon figure, he had tree-trunk legs, balloon arms, sausage fingers, and puffy lips I had a hard time looking at. His round, bald head with the fringe of hair around the edges only added to the cartoon effect. It was my belief that Haldeman suspected he cut a comic figure, which was why, as he proceeded through life with his badge and gun, he attempted to wreak revenge wherever and whenever he could.

"Black, what the hell are you doing here? Chasing ambulances again?" He looked Shanarra up and down. "This a little friend of yours?"

"I found the body. This young woman happens to live across the hall from the deceased."

Haldeman always paid more attention to the women I was with than he did to me, his disposition leering and greedy. Today his staring embarrassed Shanarra. I'd always been puzzled by his relatively open lust, for I was convinced it was faked.

"You found the body?" he asked, looking at me.

"Yes."

"What were you doing here?"

"Looking for a witness to an accident."

"Like hell you were. What were you really doing?"

"You probably remember. It was a car wreck on the Spokane Street Viaduct. Last winter, two children and their mother got killed in a five-car pileup on the ice. Our office is handling it." It was an ongoing case, and I frequently used it as an excuse to question people, to access addresses and phone numbers from citizens who otherwise would have been reluctant to hand them over.

"You're so full of shit, Black. If I find out you're lying, I'm going to lock you away in the darkest cell we've got, and I'm going to leave you there until the sight of daylight gives you nosebleeds."

"Will I be allowed conjugal visits?"

Ignoring my crack, he cast a long, wayward, and vaguely distrustful look at Shanarra, then, moving like a wobbly bowling ball down a lane, he followed the other detective up the steps to the house and through the front door. As usual, Haldeman's suit and footwear were impeccable.

"God," said Shanarra. "What a creep."

"A fair enough description," I said, though over the time I'd known Haldeman, I'd decided his real problem was that he was intensely afraid the world would not mark his passing. His jibes and insolence, I had decided, were scratch marks on the downhill slide of life, anything to keep from going into the great beyond without having been noticed.

"Excuse me?" A couple of inches taller than me, the man on the walkway behind us was six-three or six-four and had a large pale face with blush spots from the cold morning air in the center of each cheek like applied makeup. Long, tweedy eyebrows peeked over the rims of a pair of thick glasses. His hair, which looked as soft and fine as a baby's and was mostly gone from the front portion of his head, was styled in a casual brush cut and was just starting to go gray at the temples. He wore pleated gray wool slacks, dress shoes, and a button-down green shirt with a tie under a shiny black windbreaker.

A woman maybe five years his junior, possibly in her late thirties, stood behind him.

"Yes?"

"Has something happened? Is there some problem here?" His voice was too soft for his physique in the same way his hair was too soft for a man's head.

"And you are?"

"I, uh . . . I know somebody who lives here."

"A dude named Nat Bowers took two hard ones to the chest," said Shanarra, dramatically clutching her breast. "The cops are up there lookin' him over right now."

"Is he . . . well, how is he? Is he going to make it?"

"He's dead," Shanarra said.

"My God. Are you sure it's Nat?"

"Honey?" His woman companion stepped forward and grasped the tall man's arm. "What is it?"

"They're telling me Nat is dead."

"We're not telling you he's dead," Shanarra said. "He *is* dead. And he's not wearing any pants either."

"I came to visit him," the man said. "We were on our way to work."

"Are you a friend?" I asked.

"I'm not sure you'd call us . . . actually friends." The murder frightened him, but worse than that, it diluted his will to the point where he couldn't leave. "He's really dead, huh?"

We chatted for a while, the four of us. The man's name was Corliss Dootson, and it seemed to fit. The woman's name was Ione Barocas, and she looked to be of Greek extraction, undoubtedly a beautiful woman in her youth, but toughened over time.

"What do you think happened?" Dootson said, turning to me.

"Hell if I know," I said.

"Who shot him?"

I shrugged.

Shanarra said, "Somebody tossed his room."

"I met him in an art class over here at Seattle Community College," Dootson said softly. "I like to keep growing, so I take an occasional class over at the college. He was a nice guy. I wonder what—"

"I want to know who took his pants off," Shanarra said. "They put a cover over him, but he died with his pants off."

"It was a sex crime?" asked Dootson.

"Danged if I know," Shanarra said, looking at me.

It might have been a money crime. It might have been that the Shaolin went up there and took all of Bowers's cash and shot him. Except he'd been dead for hours when the Shaolin went up. It might have been a dispute over the blackmail operation. It might have been a botched robbery.

After listening to Dootson and Barocas tell their story to several passersby, it occurred to me that they were crowing because they knew a murder victim, in the same way people crowed because they'd met a president or a celebrity. In the same way Shanarra was crowing because she'd seen the body.

Barocas said she and Dootson both worked for the same small architectural firm downtown. She was a personnel manager, and, judging by her smart brown suit, her watch and rings, she was well paid. As far as Dootson went, I'd seen his kind before. He belonged in a home for the bewildered, the kind of shaky personality who borrowed his opinions from people more certain about life. He was a big man, but he looked fragile and diffident.

According to Dootson, he and Bowers had become friends in a drawing class at the community college. In local cafés they'd sipped coffee while discussing art, movies, and regional politics. When they discovered they were both aficionados of old-time Hollywood flicks, they began going to films together at The Egyptian, The Harvard Exit, and the Broadway Market. Dootson said they had been casual friends for about six months.

Pushing her way to the front of the crowd on the sidewalk, a tiny woman in men's clothing, close-cropped graying hair, and no makeup identified herself as Nat's mother. She wore black jeans and a gray sweatshirt and had a chain running from her belt to an oversized wallet in her rear pocket. Though she clearly had an idea something was wrong, it wasn't until one of the uniformed policemen spoke to her that she began crying. Within moments she grew hysterical, and a police officer escorted her into the house where the onlookers and riffraff like me couldn't gape.

Still, from my vantage point on the front porch, I could see just a sliver of the common room where they'd taken her. She was sitting on a run-down sofa, and it was from the porch that I watched her cry so hard she began puking. I'd never seen anyone take a death so hard. The manager of the house, an unshaven, seedy-looking man in pajama bottoms and a shrunken T-shirt, a cigarette dancing off his lower lip, held a wastebasket in front of her. Nat, I heard her explain tearfully between eruptions, was her only child, the product of a six-week failed marriage when she was twenty-seven.

Blaming his death on a homosexual she claimed Nat had been living with until just a few months previous, she vowed to find him and kill him. She cried and then got an extraordinarily violent case of the hiccups. After a while, her stomach now empty, she began dry heaving. She claimed not to know the name or the address of the man her son had been living with.

"Tell me, why would an ex-lover want to harm your son?" Haldeman asked.

"He had a thing for Nat, but Nat was sick of him."

"And you can't give me a name?"

"Kevin. I think his name was Kevin."

A minute later Arnold Haldeman came out, pinched my elbow hard, and took me aside. "Black? What the hell are you doing here?"

"You told me to wait."

"No, what were you doing here at this house?"

"I told you. Looking for a witness to an accident."

"You know who did this, don't you?"

"I don't know anything," I lied. I knew why I was here. I knew what Nat had been doing with his time. I knew what the Parcheesi board upstairs meant. "His mother in there thinks an ex-lover did it. Maybe that's why he wasn't wearing any pants."

"Let's just forget about what his mother said, okay? And whether or not he was wearing any pants. And who told you to eavesdrop, anyway? You ever see a young woman or a young man, maybe eighteen to twenty who looks like either of these two?" He held up a small plastic evidence bag that contained the photo I'd spotted on the floor in Bowers's doorway.

"Eighteen or twenty, who looks like that? Nope."

"Tell me exactly what you did this morning, from the time you opened those big brown eyes right up until this moment. And if you want to land with your buns in the butter, you better not leave anything out."

I left out plenty. I left out making love to Kathy. I left out Lainie Smith, and I left out the blackmail. I told him what I'd seen that morning: the Shaolin priest, the gun, and the money, and then I told him about the Rolex. When I was done talking, Haldeman said, "You know anybody named Tess?"

"I know a Beulah."

"Beulah's your goddamned receptionist. Quit playing games with me, Black. We're thinking maybe this kid knew somebody named Tess. She mighta committed suicide."

"Did you ask his mother?"

"I'm not asking for tips on how to investigate, bean brain. I'm asking if you know anybody named Tess who might have committed suicide."

"Bean brain? Did you call me bean brain? Is that harassment? Are you harassing a witness?"

"Fuck you. Hey, Black," he said, after I'd turned my back and was proceeding down the steps. "Know how to paralyze a woman from the waist down?"

I turned and said, "Did we miss the last couple of sensitivity training sessions? Can't they reschedule you?"

"Screw you, Black."

When Haldeman moved on to Shanarra, I approached Corliss Dootson and Ione Barocas, wondering how a man who looked as soft-centered as Dootson could have ended up with such a hard-edged woman.

"What have they found out?" Dootson asked. "Do they know who did it?"

"Not that I know of. They'd probably like to talk with you, though. You know somebody named Kevin? Did Nat ever mention a man named Kevin?"

"He might have. It does kind of ring a bell," Dootson said.

"Did you know he was gay?"

"Nat? Well, that was something we didn't discuss. I always assumed it, but it never came up in conversation, if that's what you mean. Why should it?"

"Did he know an older woman?" I said. "Somebody who might have visited here recently?"

"As far as I knew, most of his friends were men," Corliss said, touching the centerpiece of his glasses with his middle finger. "I don't remember any names. What is it about the woman? Is she a suspect?"

"I couldn't tell you."

"It's really such a shame," Dootson said. "He had a lot he could have done with his life."

CHAPTER 17

It was almost noon when Kathy buzzed me. "Thomas? Can you come in here for a moment?"

"Sure."

Maybe she could cheer me up. I'd been feeling lousy all morning, not only because of the murder, which was depressing enough, but because Bowers's death had pulverized his mother right down to her essence and would continue to pulverize her forever. Judging by her dress and manner, she had little education and less money, and I had an intuition she didn't have many friends either, so losing Nat had probably knocked out the single pillar of support in her life. It would be some time before I would shake myself loose from that brief glimpse of her crying in the common room of her son's rooming house.

As I approached Kathy's office door I saw Kent Wadsworth sitting stiffly on a sofa in the anteroom reading a copy of Martha Stewart's *Living* magazine. He made a point of not looking up.

Clad in a long, black coat, hands folded primly in her lap, Lainie Smith was seated across the desk from Kathy. She looked nervous, if not sick, in stark contrast to her air of command and propriety the last time she'd visited. Outside the window, the yellow foliage in the peaks of the maple trees across the street was dulled by an overcast sky that was slowly closing down on the planet and threatening to develop into fog. Most of the cars and buses in the street were running with their headlights on.

"Thomas," Kathy said after I'd closed the door. "Take a chair. The three of us have several items to discuss." I pulled a chair close to Lainie and sat. Kathy, who had spent a good portion of the morning listening to my theories on what had happened on East Republican Street, looked at me calmly and said, "Why don't you go first?"

"Nat Bowers is dead," I said, watching Lainie, who suddenly became so rigid she might have turned to marble. "Somebody shot him. My guess is it happened either early this morning or late last night. It might sound like good news, but it's nothing like it. The police are involved, so now we've lost ultimate control over keeping your name out of the news."

What I didn't tell her was that Haldeman, once he found out she was involved, would make a game out of taking her apart notch by notch. The rich and powerful were special enemies to Haldeman, and his weapons of choice would be carefully worded "leaks" to the press.

"Do they know who killed him?"

"When I left his apartment this morning, the police didn't seem to have any solid leads. He had a visitor right before I found him, the same man who'd been to Southcenter with him when he picked up the money. If he did it, he didn't do it on this morning's trip. Bowers was cold when I found him."

"Aren't dead people always cold?"

"Not right away. It takes hours. I told you there were materials about Deception Pass in his room? They're gone now, except for a game board. A Parcheesi board. The one with Tess's note on it."

"Is this a joke?"

"It's no joke. She wrote in pencil? On the left-hand side of the board?"

"Yes. Oh, my God. It was in this man's room? What was he doing with it?"

"I was hoping you could tell me."

"How would I know? Maybe . . ." Lainie put her head in her hands for a few moments, then looked up. "Maybe it's a policeman. Maybe somebody from the investigation is black-mailing me."

"I didn't tell the Seattle police what it was, and they didn't seem to know, but the man in charge is pretty thorough. I'm thinking he'll figure it out sooner or later."

"Surely you're not thinking of telling him?"

"I don't know. I'm pretty uncomfortable holding as much back as I'm holding. After all, this is a homicide investigation."

"So where do we stand? I don't understand what this does. Did you tell the police about me?"

"I didn't tell the police diddly."

"Thank you."

"Which doesn't mean they won't find out. And it doesn't mean I won't tell them later. Like I said. Holding all this back makes me real uncomfortable."

"I know you think I had something to do with this, but I didn't. I haven't done anything since Friday but stay home, watch ball games, and read novels."

"As far as I can tell, all the materials I saw in Bowers's room the other day are missing. The money is missing too, but I know who took that. I'm worried about who might have been in on this scheme besides Bowers and his friend."

"So the police didn't get the newspaper clippings? They don't know it's about Deception Pass?"

"I don't know what they know. And even if the police have the game board, even if they have all the rest of the material, I don't see how they would know you were involved. There's one other thing, though. I found an old photo on the floor in his room. One of those photos you pay a couple of bucks for in a booth? You were younger. You had a feather in your hair. The name Cherokee was written on the back in pencil. There was a young man in the picture with you."

Staring at the floor in front of her feet, Lainie was quiet for a while. Finally, she said, "That picture was in my office. I've kept it there for years. I had it tucked in the corner of the frame on my college graduation picture. One day I noticed it was missing, and I thought it had fallen out and ended up in the trash. But now I realize somebody must have seen it in my office and taken it. They must have known me back then or seen me on the street, and when they saw that snapshot in my office, they connected *that* me with *this* me."

"How long ago did the picture turn up missing?" I said.

"Maybe six months. I never thought much about it."

"Who was the young man in the picture?" Kathy asked.

"Somebody I was very fond of at one time. I guess you could call him my first real boyfriend. It was the only thing I kept from that period in my life. I just couldn't let it go."

"Who might have picked it up in your office?" Kathy asked.

Lainie shook her head. "It could have been any one of hundreds of people. We hold charity auctions up there. Funding parties. All sorts of meetings. Just a week ago we threw a private party for the symphony. So many people go through that floor in a given year."

"Is your office usually locked?" I said.

"It's *never* locked. My living quarters are. They're separate. You saw that. But anybody could have wandered into the office and found the picture."

"What I'd like you to do," I said, "is try to pinpoint the approximate time it turned up missing. Then draw up a list of people who visited around that time. To be safe, do a month or two before, and a month or two after. Is that possible?"

"I'll have Kent get on it this afternoon."

"It would be better if Kent didn't know about this."

"Okay. But there are guest lists, and there are drop-ins, and then guests bring guests. I'm sure we won't have a record of *everybody*."

"We'll work with what we get."

Kathy scooted her chair forward, placed both elbows on her desk and flattened her forearms across her appointment calendar. Sitting in front of the window, her hair appeared to be almost black, and she looked sunless and pale. "Now there's something Lainie has to tell *you*, Thomas."

Lainie glanced at Kathy and then at me. "I got a phone call this morning. I was in the other room and wasn't expecting one of those calls, so I guess it caught me by surprise. He said there would be no more penny-ante stuff. He said I was to get as much cash together as I could manage and we'd finish this off once and for all. When I told him I didn't know what he was talking about—you know, the ostrich strategy—he said, 'It was too bad the whole thing happened over a plastic gun, wasn't it, honey?'"

"Those were his exact words?"

"Yes."

"He say how much cash he wanted?"

"As much as I could manage."

"Did you answer the call on the phone that has the recording machine on it?"

"I've been answering all my calls there like you said."

"Good. What about the trap?"

"We got a number, and I called my friend at the phone company with it, and she said it was a pay phone on the first floor of the Westlake Center downtown."

"I wish you wouldn't do any more detecting on your own," Kathy said. "The fewer people who can connect you to any of this, the better."

"I guess you're right. It already seems like everybody and their mother can connect me."

"Did it sound like the same person who called before?" I asked.

"I don't know. There was a large dog barking in the background, though."

CHAPTER 18

From my office I called Bruno Collins and asked him if he could drive or take a bus to the Westlake Center at the end of the monorail line to look for a shopkeeper, a coffee vendor, or a beggar with a cardboard sign hanging around his neck, anybody who might have seen a man loitering near the pay phone Lainie's newest blackmailer had used.

I telephoned the Skagit County Prosecutor's Office and spoke to a man named Bradbury who said that, because of the recent execution, they'd been getting plenty of calls on the Groth murder case, mostly from newspeople and kooks, a few from relatives of the victims. I could tell from his voice he'd already inserted me into the kook category.

Bradbury said if I wanted more background, the person to speak to was the man who'd done virtually all the prosecutor's legwork for the trial, Melvin Sternoff, now retired and living on the Washington coast in Grays Harbor County. Sternoff, whom he called a dogged investigator, had maintained voluminous notes of his interviews.

When I dialed Melvin Sternoff's number, a very slow-talking woman answered. I told her who I was and what I wanted. "Melvin can't come to the phone," she said.

"Could I call later?"

"He won't come to the phone then either."

"Can I come to see him?"

"Sure. That would work."

"What about today? Could I come out today?"

"Whenever. Don't matter none. We had the news here every week all summer. Just bring a bottle of wine." She gave me the address and rough directions, all of which I dutifully wrote down. A bottle of wine? From the back of the cupboard over the kitchen sink, I got a dusty bottle of St. Francis chardonnay given to me a couple of years earlier by a client who didn't realize I was a nondrinker.

To reach the Washington coast from Seattle you drive south on I-5 through Tacoma, past McCord Air Force Base and Fort Lewis, through range land to the state capital, Olympia, where you detour west on a narrow, mostly evergreen-lined highway that takes you to Aberdeen and Hoquiam, twin towns haunted by dead wood mills. From Aberdeen you follow signs past the cranberry bogs to the ocean beaches. It's a long drive, a little over three hours.

In their infinite wisdom, the state fathers had allowed most of the forested land near the coast to be clear-cut, so that what greeted the vacationer closing in on the ocean beaches was a hodgepodge of rolling hills covered with tree stumps and stacked-up dreck from years-old logging operations, all of it about as pretty as a crusty booger. If any of it had been replanted, it hadn't taken.

Highway 109, which paralleled the Pacific waters for many miles, was empty except for the occasional out-of-state motor home or, once in a while, a local pickup truck. It wasn't raining, but the roads were wet. The directions I had were imprecise. I was to take a right-hand turn in Copalis at Johnson's Mercantile. She'd said to drive four miles from Johnson's and then start looking for three blue houses to the left. After the blue houses, there would be a yellow trailer on the right.

It turned out to be a double-wide trailer scabrous with rust and pocked with small, round holes I couldn't identify. The trailer might have been yellow at one time. It was positioned on concrete blocks at the end of a long, sloping, dirt and gravel drive. Moss clung to the shallow roof and dripped off the broken gutters like icing. The clear plastic sheets taped over the windows were tattered and cracked from sun and incessant salt-laden winds.

As I parked in the muddy grass of the driveway and got out of my car, a logging truck roared past on the road, the first moving vehicle I'd encountered in ten minutes, proof that when the nuclear war cleared most of the planet of civilization, these people weren't going to know the difference. A moist ocean breeze chilled me.

In the driveway sat a green Thunderbird with primer on the driver's door and a broken spring on the passenger side causing it to sag to the right. Flower pots, most of them chock-full of weeds, dotted the property, along with six more Thunderbirds of various vintages, none looking road worthy. The Thunderbird I'd parked behind had a trunk latch made of twine and a missing rear window, yet it had been driven recently, as evidenced by the fresh divots it had flung out into the yard. A curious visitor could count—as did I—thirty-eight sets of antlers nailed over the doorway to the trailer, along a wooden fence running to the back of the property, and across a ramshackle brown outbuilding destined to collapse in the next good windstorm.

Despite all the flower pots, it had been years since anybody had done any work in the yard, which was filled with thistles gone to seed and huge, rangy rhododendrons you probably couldn't kill with neglect or even raw gasoline.

The door knocker was made from what appeared to be a bobcat's paw wrapped around a rock. A Band-Aid was dangling off the door, a loose patch over what appeared to be a bullet hole from a small caliber weapon. Suddenly I knew what the holes in the walls were.

I knocked three times, but it wasn't until a man inside began bellowing that the door opened a crack, just a crack, as if she'd been standing there all along but was too timid to open it.

Even before the gust of sickish warm air kissed my face, I could smell the dogs. Through the narrow opening I was greeted by a small, hunch-shouldered American Indian woman with long gray hair braided on one side and not the other, no life at all in her dark eyes. She appeared to be in her late fifties or early sixties and wore coveralls with a black T-shirt underneath. She was barefoot, her toenails painted carefully. Her front two teeth were badly chipped, and all of her lower teeth were higgledy-piggledy.

"I've come to see Melvin Sternoff. Thomas Black. Do I have the right place?"

"Hung the bastard!" cried a booming voice from inside that was so loud it made the woman jump and tremble like a wet cat in a wind. "Let him in, Melody. Let the poor man in out of the weather, so he can give me that goddamn bottle. You brought a bottle, didn't you? You bastard. You don't come in here without a bottle."

Melody disappeared behind the door as I entered. The smell that hit me was a cross between the inside of a state park urinal and a trapper's longjohns at the wrong end of a long, hard winter. I waited until Melody had closed the door and handed her the chardonnay.

She was staring at it when he said, "You gonna open that fucker, woman, or am I gonna . . ."

Melody scrambled into the kitchen area behind me while I stepped forward over a large yellow dog who wasn't going to move until the war began. He lay there and, without budging his head off the floor, followed me with his eyes. Two smaller, rat-like dogs, inspired by my visit, were ricocheting around on the main piece of furniture in the room, an enormous bed.

On top of the bed, head propped up with six or eight dirty pillows, was the largest man I'd ever seen. My first guess was four hundred pounds, but further calculation snowballed that to five, maybe six hundred pounds. Aligned perfectly with the man, a soundless television was perched precariously high on a stool at the end of the bed.

"Come on in here, you fucker," he said. "What'd you say your name was?"

"Black. Thomas Black."

"And you're a private dick?"

"Investigator, yes. I understand—"

"Melody! Where the *fuck* is that wine?" She was in the room almost before I saw movement, handing the opened bottle to Sternoff along with a small wicker basket filled with taco chips and a bowl of mayonnaise. While she held it out, Sternoff took three chips from the basket, scooped up a big dollop of mayonnaise, and downed the concoction. He took the wine bottle from her and swigged from it, then offered it to me. I shook my head, and it was all the encouragement he needed. He drank again. Holding the basket of chips, the woman waited beside him like a piece of furniture. I noticed she stood as far away from his reach as possible.

She avoided my eyes.

When one of the small rat-dogs leapt up onto Sternoff's chest and licked at the snout of the chardonnay bottle in his hand, Sternoff smacked the dog away as casually as a man shooing a fly. The dog flew across the bed, rolled over two times and got up all in one motion, licked his hind end, and meticulously sat down as if it happened to him every day and he didn't mind in the least. The second rat-dog on the bed eyed Sternoff patiently. The large yellow dog on the floor in the doorway still had not moved.

"What the fuck are you looking at, woman?" Sternoff said.

She put the basket of chips down alongside Sternoff's humongous left arm and went back into the kitchen area. It was pretty clear she didn't have anything to do in the kitchen except hide or read the Bible or maybe slit her throat.

Sternoff drank from the bottle again. Even from where I stood, his breath smelled of alcohol. He wore a T-shirt that covered only the top half of his enormous paunch, and pajama bottoms that left most of his shins and what appeared to be a knee exposed. His crotch was folded away in rolls of fat, or it would have been exposed too. A twisted sheet lay across his legs. His toenails, yellowed and cracked, were too long to fit into shoes. A pair of crutches with cloth pads crudely taped around the arm pieces leaned against the wall across the room, where he couldn't get to them without yelling at Melody.

Despite the smell and the fact that everything within reach of Sternoff was a pigsty—the wall at the foot of his bed had layers of splotchy food stains like a painting—the kitchen area had been well policed. She kept her own territory tidy, if not clean.

Sternoff's every breath was audible.

"You tell me what, boy," he said, looking at me. "What is it you want?" He was clean-shaven but had bushy eyebrows with stray strands curling down almost to his cheek. Though combed, his gray hair was unwashed. I'd watched him lift his ponderous arm to eat, and wondered if he could actually reach the top of his head with a comb or if Melody did it for him. Even his scalp was fat, and his gray eyes were pinched small by his bloated cheeks. Because he had no wrinkles, it was hard to know how old he might be.

"I'd like to know anything you can tell me about the murders at Deception Pass seventeen years ago."

"And why is that?" he asked gruffly.

"I have a client who has information about the missing witness."

"You're a little too late to be bringing witnesses around, buddy. We hung the fucker. Hung him June third." He laughed loudly. It was a mean, braying laugh. "I wish I could have been there."

"I still would like to know what you could tell me about Deception Pass."

"Missing witness? Fuck the missing witness. You believe that shit? There wasn't no missing witness. That was rabbit piss Charlie Groth was spraying out trying to distract all of us from the God's honest truth, which was that he butchered those poor kids with a bread knife and a mantel rock. There wasn't no missing witness. I looked all over hell. If there'd been anybody, I would have found them."

"Were there unidentified fingerprints in the cabin?"

"Of course there were. Every crime scene will have a few unidentified prints around."

"It was just a question. I have a client who swears there was a witness." Sternoff looked at me for a few seconds and then stared ahead at the wall across the room before tipping the green bottle to his lips.

"We had some sloppy work out there at that cabin," he said breathily. "Skagit County never got enough big-time murders to practice on, so we were not as efficient as the big boys processing all that stuff. I'll admit that. Those extra prints come off some ambulance driver. A coroner's assistant. Whatever. I'm sure of it. We checked everyone we could think of, but we never kept no crime scene log, and I'm convinced there were people who went in and contaminated the scene that we never got on our lists."

"Groth said he had an accomplice."

"No. What he claimed was somebody else did all the killing. He was trying to put it off on this woman. But I couldn't find her and the defense couldn't find her. Because she didn't exist."

"It took long enough to produce Groth. Five years. If he says he wasn't, how can you be sure he was alone?"

"When Charlie confessed to Luther Clampett down at the Pierce County Jail, one of the things he told Luther was where he'd hidden the bloody shirt he wore that night. We never told anybody we found it under a log at a parking area up the road. But Charlie pegged it. He knew because he put it there. Plus, he left his fingerprints all over that damn cabin. Hell, he left prints on the knife we pulled out of Brittan. There's no doubt in my mind and there shouldn't be any in yours. He killed 'em."

"The question on the table is whether he was alone."

"Well, now . . . I have to admit . . . if there was somebody else, I'd like to find them. To my own mind, there's questions still haven't been answered."

"Such as?"

"Why on earth did he let that Hadlock woman loose and then go and kill her after? She wasn't molested. What was the point?"

"Did any of the victims leave a note?"

"A note?"

"You know. Like a dying declaration?"

"Hell, they didn't have time for no notes. Charlie went in there with a knife, tied 'em up, and killed them. Nobody had time for any notes."

"What about a Parcheesi board?"

"Now what the hell do you know about a Parcheesi board?" Sternoff snapped. "You know something about a Parcheesi board, mister?"

"I know it was probably missing."

"That was never common knowledge. We found the box and the pieces all out on the table, but the board was gone. Never figured out why. Where'd you hear that?"

"I don't remember. People feel freer to talk now that Groth's been executed."

"I suppose they do. That Parcheesi board didn't bother me at first, but then I got to thinking. Why on earth would it be gone? I'm convinced Charlie killed them, but I'm not convinced we know what went on in that cabin. At least, not all of it.

"Even today I keep seeing those four kids. Hell, I drove to Montana on my own dime to track down a hooker who'd been shooting her mouth off about it. She didn't know shit, but she thought she did. On my own hook I flew up to Ketchikan twice on bogus tips. Spent almost a year in downtown Seattle looking for some broad named Today who was supposed to have spent time with Charlie around the week of the killings. That's where I met Melody, and that's how she broke up my marriage. All I knew was this broad I was looking for, Today, had been with a pretty hard man the night before the murders and had gone around telling some people he'd been planning to go up to Deception Pass and commit a robbery. We weren't even sure if it was the right weekend."

Sternoff tipped the wine bottle to his lips.

If Charlie had told Today the night before the murders that he was planning to commit a robbery at Deception Pass, then he'd probably told Lainie also, so that her version—that it was done on a whim—was a lie. Despite my initial reservations, I wanted to believe Lainie Smith. I *wanted* to believe all the best parts of her story and none of the worst, but once again I was beginning to wonder if I could believe *any* of it.

"You ever find this Today person who was with Groth the night before the murders?"

"Never did. She's either out of state or she's dead."

"Where'd you get the tip about her?"

"Street kid. Name was Chuckie something or other. He died of hepatitis a few years back. I didn't always live out here in the sticks with a squaw, you know. It was that year I wasted in Seattle bumming around with all those freaks that cost me my family. I had three boys and a wife who cared about me. Donald comes out once in a while. The others . . . You see, Black. I never went to sleep without seeing those dead kids. Tonight I'll see those kids. A thing like that gets under your skin and rots."

"I know it does," I said.

"You find this 'missing witness,' Black, you bring her here. You listening? You bring her here, and I'll skin her. I'll skin her and hang her out back with the other skunks. That was part of it, Black. People talk about the death penalty being revenge, but revenge'll heal a lot of sores. Charlie died, and I felt better right away. So did a lot of other good people. Those kids were having a cheap little vacation in a borrowed cabin one minute—living their worst nightmare the next. You find this other killer Groth claims was with him, I want you to bring her to me. I think he called her Cherokee, or something like that."

"The prosecutor in Skagit County said you had notes from the case."

Sternoff took another drink from the wine bottle, emptied it, and tossed it across the room, where Melody quickly scooped it up and left. Sternoff reached under a pillow on his right side, took out a .22 revolver and aimed it at the wall at the end of the bed. It was only then that I realized how many holes he'd put into the walls. The molding at the edge of the kitchen, the same niche Melody was hiding in now, had forty or fifty holes, dents, and nicks in it.

"So you think there's another person involved?" Sternoff mused, cocking the pistol repeatedly and then easing the hammer down. His hands were so fat they looked like rubber gloves blown up like balloons. The gun looked like a hunk of licorice.

"I do. You have any idea how Groth got into the cabin?"

"That was no secret. Knocked on the door just like any other citizen. That's what he said he did, and that's what I had to conclude. When one of the women answered, he put a knife to her throat."

"And then he tied them all up?"

"There were only three people in the cabin when he showed. Tess Hadlock, Amy Brittan, and Jack Leroy Schupp. The only one of those three he probably had to worry about was Schupp. He had one of the women tie up Schupp. She then tied up the other woman and then he tied her. Later on, Raymond Brittan showed up with a bagful of groceries, and they fought in the kitchen. In fact, that's how we fixed the time of death, from talking to the store clerk."

"What about the neighbors?" I said. "Did they see anything?"

"Zilch. Nada. Normal activity on Friday night, the cars arriving and some unpacking and whatnot, and then nothing until Monday morning when we showed up with the coroner and the dogs."

"Were there any promising leads that never panned out?"

Finished with the wine, Sternoff returned to the chips, taking each with a slab of mayonnaise. "We didn't have squat. We had fingerprints, but we had nobody to match them against. We had a stolen car down the road, swiped in Puyallup, but there were no good prints on it. We never were sure it was even related to the killings.

"My own pet theory at the time was that it was a payback. That one of the kids had pissed somebody off, and they came and took them all out. I was thinking an angry boyfriend. A pissed-off husband. Maybe one of the guys had been banging a married broad. Something like that. I made a list of everybody who knew those kids. Must have talked to four hundred people. Ex-roommates. Current roommates. Sorority sisters. Jack Schupp had been on the U.W. baseball team two years runnin', and for a while we thought we had a lead there because one of the other players and him got into it a few times. It's all in the other room. All my notes. I still got it all."

"Could I see it, do you think?"

"Not a fucking chance. That's private shit."

I took a fifty-dollar bill out of my wallet and stuck it in the chip basket. "I drove all the way from Seattle."

"You drove all the way from Seattle?"

"Yes."

"Just to talk to me?"

"Right."

"You must think you're really on to something."

I put another fifty into the basket. "I think there's somebody else who knows what happened. I think if you let me look at those notes, we might find more of the truth."

Sternoff nodded his head, which for him was a rocking motion on his pillows. "It's in the other room there. Melody! Melody! Get in here!" Fleeting and soundless, she moved like a ghost. "Show this fucker where my work stuff is. The boxes are all marked, Black. Show him, Melody. And don't either of you mess it up."

Leaving him to his own manufactured crime scene—spilled food and bullet holes—Melody took me into a back room and turned on a light in the center of the ceiling. It was almost too dim to read by.

CHAPTER 19

Barefoot, Melody stood next to me as I knelt in the dusty room and sorted through stacks of dark brown cardboard boxes with deep lids and handle holes sawed into the sides. Off in a corner by themselves, I found three boxes labeled DECEPTION PASS.

The middle box was heavily stained along the outer edge, and, since the room smelled strongly of dog piss, I assumed the boxes and their contents had absorbed their share of the pungent bouquet. Those little rat-dogs in the other room undoubtedly took their vengeance promptly and often, roaming unseen in here to piss all over a lifetime of work whenever the mood struck.

I'd been going through the records for five minutes when Sternoff yelled, his voice harsh enough to peel paint.

"Woman? What the fuck are you doing? You get in here, or you'll be sorry."

As she scurried away, her bare feet making a scuffing noise on the worn carpet, I tried to give her a sympathetic look, but it was a wasted effort, as she was concerned only with the bellowing in the other room.

To my surprise, Sternoff's materials were neat and pretty much in chronological order. The first box represented the early years: interviews with neighbors, the statement of the meter reader who'd discovered the bodies, statements from Tess Hadlock's roommate in Seattle and Jack Leroy Schupp's guilt-ridden girlfriend, who'd been planning to meet the foursome that Sunday morning but failed to show up because she'd fallen behind studying for an oceanography final.

One envelope contained the crime-scene photos. Suddenly the four victims were no longer an intellectual exercise, an accident of history, but four once-living, once-breathing people. I looked for a clean spot on the floor and knelt, arraying the photos around me. Even in death they looked like nice people.

The first photo was of the kitchen, destroyed and strewn with blood, Raymond Brittan sprawled in a corner, his head against the wall, neck bent at an acute and unnatural angle, the black handle of a kitchen knife jutting from his chest. He had blood and cuts over both hands and arms. Of the faces that hadn't been mangled, his was the only one that looked angry.

The two bound victims were shown together in most of the pictures. Amy Brittan was slumped backward, while Jack Leroy Schupp's head was resting on his chest, his features unrecognizable. The top part of Amy's head and face had been caved in.

But, just as her letter had done, Tess Hadlock's photo put tears in my eyes.

After she'd been bludgeoned, her death of choice, she'd fallen over with the chair still tied to her legs, her arms free, and had crawled almost fifteen feet across the hardwood floor, large smears of blood trailing her. She had been heading in the general direction of the kitchen, so my guess was she was going to see if she could help Raymond Brittan, or was on her way to get a utensil to free herself from the strips of sheet binding her ankles to the chair.

She had blue eyes and a large mouth with full lips in a wide, round face bisected by a trickle of blood that had run down from her scalp. She had the strong shoulders and body of a swimmer. Had she lived, she would have been a little older than Kathy, a little younger than me. She probably would be married. Probably would have kids by now.

Our client, Lainie Smith, had been part of this. The pictures, combined with what I remembered of Lainie's story, made it too real. I could visualize Tess Hadlock pleading for Lainie to untie her. I could visualize the wild eyes of the three bound victims as they listened to the fight in the kitchen. I could almost see the look on Tess Hadlock's face when she asked to write a goodbye note. How could anybody have stood by and let this happen?

Along with other information, the first box contained several long lists of people the victims had known in the three years prior to their deaths. Additional names that had cropped up during the interrogations were listed at the top of each interview sheet. Sternoff's handwriting was small but precise, most everything written in the same fine-tip blue-ink pen.

I skimmed some of the interviews, none of which revealed anything of interest. Twenty minutes later, long after the shouting in the other room had ceased, while I was halfway through my preliminary look at box number three, Sternoff called.

"Black, you fucker! Get in here! Black! Black? What are you doin'?"

Glancing through the remainder of the materials, I stood up, knees popping, stretched my arms and back, and replaced the covers on all three boxes. Then, in an effort to thwart the rat-dogs, I piled the boxes on top of another row of boxes against the far wall.

In the main room Sternoff had a fresh bottle of wine in his grip. The basket of chips had been consumed, the bowl of mayonnaise empty and clean. One of the small dogs was curled up next to his huge thigh, a ring of mayonnaise around the dog's snout. If Melody was somewhere in the residence, I couldn't see her. I was beginning to get the feeling Melvin Sternoff was either unwilling or incapable of leaving his bed, that Melody was his lifeline both to the kitchen and to the outside world. Far from his reach, the phone was mounted on the wall near the front door. I wondered how he used a commode without shattering it, how he even got to it.

"Black, what the hell were you doin' in there, writing a how-to manual for jerk-offs?"

"Naw, I'm too lazy for that." Sternoff laughed like a steam train getting stuck on a hill, in a series of hoots, each weaker than the last.

"You're a funny fucker."

"Don't have a heart attack."

He laughed again. "You know, had I run into you back in the old days, I would have chewed you up and spit you out. You big-city fucks came up to our neck of the woods all the time trying to act like you knew everything."

"I don't know shit," I said. "I'm here to learn. Any little thing I can."

After he decided I wasn't making fun of him, Sternoff said, "What'd you find?"

"Some names I'd like to talk to you about." I flipped open my notebook. "Luther Clampett. Elizabeth Faulconer. Aldrich Russell. The way I understand it, two of them are dead."

"Now don't go getting your shirttail caught up in any conspiracy theories. Conspiracy theories'll drag you in and suck you under. You take a hundred people, come back in five years, some of them will be dead. That's only natural. Come back in twelve years, and more will be dead." Sternoff stopped to swig from his half-empty wine bottle, then to breathe—as if he might smother himself with too long a drink. His own body weight must have made breathing a singular chore. "You want to talk about the jailbird who ratted out Groth? Name was Luther Clampett? Used to break into small businesses at night and steal cash registers; sell them on the black market. Groth told him he knew who killed those kids up at Deception Pass. The only reason Clampett even ratted him out was because Charlie kept saying he was going to make him ride the whip. You know what that means, Black?"

"I think so."

"He wanted a different cell, was what he wanted."

"How did Clampett die?"

"He was parked in his pickup out by Snohomish or some-place when a logging truck came around the corner and lost a whole shitload of logs on top of him. The other gent you mentioned . . . who was it?"

"Aldrich Russell."

"Big Al. He prosecuted. Pussy-whipped is what he was. Moved to New York because his wife wanted to be near her family, and then she ended up leaving him anyway. Smashed his Volvo into a freeway underpass. Dead on arrival. Person you should really be speaking to is Charlie's attorney. I can't recall her name just now."

"Priscilla Penick?" It was a name I remembered from the newspaper clippings.

"Right. Groth's defense attorney. She was a cute little twitch. I don't know what they were doing, finger-fucking under the table or what, but they got awful neighborly during the trial. Who was the third person you wanted to know about?"

"Elizabeth Faulconer."

"The reporter. Now there was a strange duck. I actually dated her a couple of times after my wife left, but I still couldn't figure her out. All she would talk about was her dead ex-husband who I later found out wasn't dead at all, and she never would let me touch her. She and Charlie had some sort of relationship. I don't know what it is with killers and women, but he had them two, his lawyer and that reporter. Somebody sent me some articles she wrote this spring before they got rid of Charlie. I could have Melody look."

"Thanks. I've seen most of the newspaper stuff. One last question, if you don't mind. Why do you think three of the victims were mutilated and the fourth not?"

"Killing people the way he was killing them is hard work. He ran out of steam. He was in a frenzy, and he got tired. It's common enough in a mass murder."

When I left, the yellow dog rolled his eyes around watching me, never once picking up his head from the floor. Outside, in the wind and the rain, I thought I heard a sharp crack that might have been a gunshot from inside the trailer. For a moment I debated going back to make sure everything was all right, but then I heard Sternoff yelling, the phone ringing, the phone not ringing. Melody had picked it up. It was clear Sternoff was on his deathbed, the promise of which was probably what kept Melody and the three dogs going.

I wasn't sure what I'd learned in Grays Harbor County. Sternoff had collected hundreds of names. After all these years it would take a team of investigators a year just to locate all those people; and a lot of them would *never* be found.

When I got back to Seattle, the hustle and bustle of the University District seemed tranquil and reassuring in some strange way. I fed L.C. on the back porch of our dark house, changed into sweats and Adidas basketball shoes, wrote an I-love-you note to Kathy, put an excited L.C. on a leash, got my Wilson ball, and walked several blocks to the school, dribbling with my left hand and struggling with the taut leash in my right. A cross between a Chihuahua, a collie, and a small mule—though not as smart as any of them—L.C. had followed me home from Safeway one evening, deciding to stay only after sampling the chow.

It wasn't raining, but the court was wet, so the ball stayed wet through all of our games. They were from Cambodia and Vietnam and the Philippines, or their parents were, and in heavily accented English they called me Shaq, probably because nobody else on the court came even to my shoulders. Because of the height disparity, we usually played with one less member on my team, and tonight we played with two less, working like demons to make up the deficit. It was almost ten o'clock when I cooled down alone shooting hoops at the far end of the court, letting L.C. chase the rebounds with me. There was nothing like a little exercise to burn off stress.

Twenty-five minutes later, as I stepped out of the shower, I heard Kathy rumbling around in the hallway. When I poked my head out of the bathroom door, she came over and gave me a kiss, her lips cold, her face chilled.

"My my," she said, leering at me through the half-open doorway. "Where is that darn tape measure when you really need it?"

"I can go get one," I said.

Slipping into her Mexican bandit accent, she said, "Tape measure? What tape measure? We don't need no steenking tape measure." She laughed, kicked off her shoes, and hung her overcoat in the closet. "We'll just lay it out on the table and pace it off."

After I'd toweled off and found my robe, I ate some leftover enchiladas at the kitchen table while Kathy sat across from me and sorted the mail. "How was your day?" I said.

"Aside from the fact that our client lost one blackmailer and picked up another within hours, just ducky."

"Ducky, huh? Now that you've had some time to digest it, what do you think about Bowers?"

"I think it was no coincidence the blackmailer phoned Lainie about the same time you and the police were standing over his body. Aside from her telling us, it's just about the only thing that convinces me Lainie wasn't involved."

"Oh, she was involved."

"I meant she didn't kill anybody."

"Don't forget we only have her word there is a new blackmailer. Maybe she killed Bowers and made up a second blackmailer to divert suspicion from herself."

Kathy sighed. "Telling her his name was a big mistake, Thomas."

"A lot of stuff I did last week was a mistake. I won't do any of it this week."

"I know you won't. The question is, who killed Bowers, and who's blackmailing Lainie now, or is anybody blackmailing Lainie now? And if they are, are the killer and the blackmailer the same person?"

"If they are the same person, and the police catch Bowers's killer, the whole world's going to know Lainie's secret."

"There's no doubt about that."

CHAPTER 20

The next morning, I called John Bowers, Nat's uncle, who didn't know any of Nat's friends, who didn't have a clue who the Shaolin was, and who told me Nat's mother was in the county hospital under sedation.

Over the phone, a source with the Seattle Police Department confirmed there hadn't been any progress on the Bowers murder, the current theory being that it had been a lovers' spat. They were compiling a list of the dead man's friends, acquaintances, and sexual partners, a compendium that would, according to my source, because of Nat's reputed promiscuity, "be about as thick as the Gig Harbor phone directory."

Bruno Collins was in his office in the back of the shoeshine shop when I reached him by phone.

"Thomas, my man," he said. "I looked all over downtown for somebody who might have seen a man using that pay phone, and you know what?"

"What?"

"I didn't find stink."

"Thanks for trying. Put it on the bill."

"I did run into a man who's looking for divers to help salvage a Spanish galleon off the Florida Keys. I thought about flying down with him, but I'm afraid of them Cuban women. For some reason they go nuts around me. It seems like that part of the country's full of Cuban women."

"I didn't know you were a diver, Bruno."

"Three years in the navy. I go out a couple of times a summer, just to keep my feet wet." He laughed.

Priscilla Penick worked out of an office in Lynnwood just off Highway 99, which was a four-lane atrocity running through a gauntlet of car dealerships, muffler shops, taco stands, billboards, cemeteries, junkyards, and drive-in banks shrouded by car exhaust. Every year, several pedestrians were killed walking alongside or trying to cross Highway 99, a misdemeanor clearly not deserving of death.

An assortment of strip malls abutted the roadway, and it was in one of these quieter malls that I found a storefront with a one-word sign over it: ATTORNEY.

Despite the reflections off the picture windows from the sunny street, I could just make out a slender woman in a white suit sitting at a desk, erect and seemingly implacable.

Although there were two other desks, Penick's was the only one occupied when I went through the front door. There was a small law library in the far corner on the wall behind Penick's desk. Everything in the room was in its place, including the woman in the white suit who rose as smoothly from her desk as if she were on pneumatic jacks instead of stick-thin legs.

"Ms. Penick?"

"You must be the investigator who telephoned. Mr. Black?"

I nodded.

"Have a seat. What can I do for you?" She didn't walk around the desk to shake hands, and I had the uneasy notion I was large enough and unfamiliar enough that being alone in the office with me made her edgy.

The office was as neat and cold as an ice cube, the only personal touch a pot of rather sickly cacti at the other end of the room. Although she had been working when I came in, all I saw in front of Penick was a phone and a closed folder that might have been centered on the desk by a surveyor.

Priscilla Penick's hair was short and tight to her scalp, and the shiny gloss on her red lips stood out like a harlot's smile on her otherwise bare face. There was something about her strict diction and the immaculate manner in which she was dressed that made me think she didn't have any lint in her house, her car, or even in the toes of her socks.

She was a pretty woman, or had been before she'd lost all the weight. She had birdlike hands, unvarnished nails chewed down to the quick, and the bony, fleshless skeleton of a high-fashion runway model, although she wasn't tall enough to be a model. I could see the cords in her neck and larynx as she spoke. I could see the veins through the skin around her eyes. I wanted to stuff a Snickers bar into her mouth.

I took a wooden chair, sat, and smiled, even though the look she gave me didn't invite smiles. I said, "I understand you represented Charles Groth."

"That's common knowledge."

"I'm looking into the murders up at Deception Pass, and I was wondering if you might answer a few questions."

"My uncle's looking into the murders at Deception Pass. He's thinking about writing a book. Everywhere I go, somebody has something to ask me about it. A week ago, a woman came up to me in the grocery store and told me she'd been the girlfriend of Jack Schupp's roommate their sophomore year at the U. She said her husband had once worked with a man who'd dated Brittan's first roommate's sister in high school. My grocer's looking into the murders. My librarian's looking into them."

"You run into anybody at the grocery store who might turn up the missing witness?"

The bored look on Penick's face was replaced promptly by the most artfully blank expression I'd seen in a long while. Penick knew how to conceal her emotions, and if it hadn't been for the clenched jaw muscles in her face, I would have believed her next statement. "We looked all over the West Coast and couldn't come up with anybody. Charlie's gone. It's too late to change that. Who have you been talking to?"

"Melvin Sternoff."

"I thought he was dead."

"He's doing his best to get there," I said, thinking she was too. Sternoff had gained something on the order of a quarter of a ton, while the woman in front of me had starved herself so close to the bone that she didn't look as if she had the strength to pick up a cough drop.

"What do you want, Mr. Black?"

"I want to know what Charles Groth told you about that night at the cabin."

"There's a trial transcript. You're free to—"

"I want to know what he told you that you were afraid to let out at the trial. And why you couldn't find that witness."

Her voice rose just a bit. "We couldn't find her, but that didn't mean she didn't exist, and it certainly doesn't mean we were hiding anything during the trial. It means we couldn't find her. And I don't see any reason to tell you one word of what Charlie said."

"Not even if I can turn up the missing witness?"

"The missing killer, you mean."

"That would be for the courts to decide."

"I got to know Charlie better than I've known any client before or since, and I believed him when he told me he didn't kill those people." For the first time since I'd come through the door, a trace of emotion crept into her voice, a voice that cracked on the high notes and was as thin and reedy as her physique. "But I'm not going to help you with your fishing expedition, Mr. Black. My time is valuable, and the case is over."

"You don't want to hear what the missing witness has to say?"

Penick chewed it over for a few moments. Outside in the parking lot, a red Firebird swung into a space beside my Ford. A Hispanic man in a black leather jacket got out, locked his car doors, and walked past Penick's office. She watched as if she knew him, as if she wanted to shout out that he was heading for the wrong door, but she didn't move.

"In the last week I've run into a number of individuals who have information about Deception Pass they shouldn't have," I said. "I'm trying to figure out where they got their information."

"You believe there was a woman in that cabin with Charlie, do you, Black?"

"I do."

"And why is that?"

"I just do."

"Because she's your client? This woman?"

"Did Groth tell you anything that was said inside the cabin?"

"I'd have to review my notes. He told me some of it."

"Did he give you the particulars of the killings?"

"My notes are at home. He said Hadlock begged to be allowed to write a note to her family. He wanted to let her, but the girl refused."

"So there was no note according to Groth?"

"There was no note."

"And then he killed Hadlock?"

"Then *she* did. According to Charlie, she killed them all."

"He put all of it on her?"

"Of course in court nobody believed a word of it. I don't know. It was the first time I'd ever had a case like that, and I really didn't have the experience. I'd only been out of law school a year and a half. Charlie deserved a more experienced trial lawyer, and I told him as much, but he wouldn't have it. It had to be me."

"If she killed them, why didn't Groth stop her?"

"He told me in confidence that she had a gun, but he wouldn't let me use that information in his defense. He was convinced that if he admitted either one of them went in there with a gun, he wouldn't stand a chance in court. I guess he didn't have much of a chance anyway."

"So, what was his story, the way he told it to you?"

"She had a gun. They went up to the house because the girl said she was getting her period and was feeling sick. A woman opened the door, and the girl pushed a gun into her stomach and made Charlie tie them all up."

"Raymond Brittan died in the kitchen after a fight the police estimated lasted between five and ten minutes. Are you saying a girl wrestled Brittan for five or ten minutes?"

"She'd already killed the others when Brittan came into the cabin and saw the bodies. He went berserk. He ran into the kitchen and got two knives out of the drawer and, thinking Charlie had killed them, went after him."

"Why didn't the girl just shoot Brittan?"

"She thought it was funny. She thought the whole evening was funny. She was on drugs, and she wanted to see people die."

"Why did Brittan go for a knife if she had a gun?"

"I told you, he saw his wife and his friends dead, and he went berserk. According to Charlie, she stabbed Brittan to death as they wrestled, and then she left. Charlie crawled out of the house, cut so badly he almost bled to death himself."

"Explain to me why she didn't use the gun, if she had one. Why bludgeon and stab them when she could have more easily shot them?"

"It was summer. The windows were open. She didn't want the neighbors to hear the shots. Personally, when I took the case, I thought Charlie killed them. Even so, legally they were both responsible."

"Did you ever get a name for her?"

"All Charlie had was a vague description and her street name, Cherokee, and he wasn't even certain of that. Sometimes he called her Chance. She would have been twenty-five or twenty-six at the time of the trial. We checked out every hooker and drug addict on the West Coast, but we couldn't find her. Charlie was no brain surgeon, Mr. Black, and he was certainly no angel—he had a record of petty theft and shoplifting—but I'm not convinced he was a killer."

"It was a man's crime."

"Or a woman on drugs."

"He wasn't on drugs?"

"Not like her."

"What about the bloody shirt the police found up the road? It was a man's shirt."

"It was Charlie's. Most of that blood was his. He almost died that night. Brittan cut him a dozen times."

"Did your investigators find *anything* at all on the missing girl?"

"No. It was a blank wall."

"Did he talk about the case to anybody besides you?"

"Betty Faulconer. It's interesting you should ask, because I heard from her just last week. Guess who's writing a book."

"How did a reporter end up getting close to Groth?"

"I'm not the first person to say it, but there was something unnatural about their relationship. You see, Charlie never really had a mother. The woman they talked about in the papers, the woman who raised him, she was his grandmother. Charlie's father committed incest with his own daughter, and Charlie was the result. He only found out during the trial when the newspaper people were poking around. The woman he thought was his mother was his grandmother. The woman he thought was his sister was his mother. Faulconer's had family troubles herself, and they used to talk about it."

"So it's possible Elizabeth Faulconer knows things about Deception Pass nobody else does?"

"I doubt it. Betty was on a mother trip, not a fact-finding excursion."

"You said she was writing a book."

"I told you. Everybody's writing a book."

CHAPTER 21

Faulconer's editor, who sounded like a milksop, told me on the phone Faulconer was in but couldn't be disturbed. I took the 520 floating bridge and got off I-405 on Northeast Eighth in Bellevue, where I pulled into an eye clinic parking lot and plopped my King County Thomas Guide across the steering wheel. Ten minutes later I found the *Journal American* buildings in a neat little wooded business park. The main building was a two-story gray structure surrounded by sixty-foot Douglas firs.

Walking past a UPS driver manhandling a large brown package out of the back of her truck, I went through the main doors. There was no receptionist in the lobby. A sweeping staircase behind me led up to an open area. A woman with short, gray hair and tortoiseshell glasses came down the staircase with a sheaf of papers in her arms.

"Can I help you?" she asked.

"I'm looking for Elizabeth Faulconer."

"Betty's right over there." She gestured with her head toward a large room to the south. "Is she expecting you?"

"She will be," I mumbled, striding through the wide doorway. There was another receptionist area inside the large room, this one occupied by a pudgy man in a sweater vest and a button-down shirt. "Could you point out Betty Faulconer, please?" I asked.

"The big lady over there with the hat."

He nodded at a corner cubicle about forty feet from the main doorway. It was a large room partitioned off with chest-high walls, eight or ten heads visible over the walls. Private glass-walled offices lined the corridor to the right.

She was a large woman in a flower-print dress, broad-shouldered, tall, with a mane of hair dyed almost white, and a face that reminded me of a baby's butt, both in its paleness and its lack of expression. She had a broad face and bright red lipstick. Black-rimmed glasses with lenses like plastic coffee coasters. A black, snap-brimmed fedora was pinned on top of her white hair. It didn't go with the dress, and it didn't seem to go with the woman either. When I looked around the room, the man at the receptionist's island was watching me, a wicked little grin the only residue of our earlier exchange.

She was madly typing on a laptop computer.

"Elizabeth Faulconer?"

The coldness with which she looked at me was accentuated by her large, flat, expressionless cheeks. The thick lenses of her glasses made her eyes look as if I were seeing them from the wrong end of a microscope.

"Do I know you?" she asked, her voice pinched and milky, as if she'd just drunk something and hadn't yet cleared her pipes.

I told her who I was and said, "I understand you were close to Charles Groth?"

The name induced her to look up once again from her laptop. She spoke as if making an announcement at the beginning of a class lecture. "I know all about Charlie Groth. I know more about Charlie than Charlie knew about Charlie. My series on him won just about every major journalism award except for the Pulitzer, and I happen to have it on good authority I was short-listed for that."

Her statements seemed to be challenges, and each time she looked me in the eye, I had the feeling she was measuring herself against me. We were in a competition here, but I couldn't figure out what that competition was about or why it was happening. It didn't help that her tiny eyes seemed never to blink.

"What on earth do you want with Charlie Groth?" she said.

"I'm a private investigator. His name has come up in a case I'm working. I'm trying to find out some of the particulars of what happened at Deception Pass. Some of the stuff that wasn't in the papers."

"Well," Faulconer announced grandly. "I'm writing a book about it. When it's finished, you can buy a copy. If you drop by, I'll even autograph it for you."

"I'll look forward to that, but I wonder if you might answer a few questions today."

Faulconer turned back to her laptop and began hammering the keys in what appeared to be an effort to make as much noise as possible. I wondered why she was working on the laptop rather than the larger computer on her desk. The walls of her cubicle were papered with articles she had written on Charles Groth, the murders, and the trial. Interspersed with the clippings were a number of photographs, mostly of her.

Turning back to her keyboard, she said, "You'll have to excuse me, Black, but I have a very important deadline. A young man was murdered on Capitol Hill yesterday morning, and as it turns out, I knew him. If I don't get this piece done, my editor will kill me."

"Nat Bowers?"

Faulconer pushed her chair away from the desk, stood ponderously, and stared at me for a good long while. For a moment or two I genuinely believed she was getting up to use the rest room and was offended that I hadn't yet left, but then she touched her glasses—her hand as white and unwrinkled as her face—and said, "How on earth did you know I was writing about Nat Bowers?"

"It was a wild guess. I found the body."

She continued staring until I thought she'd gone to sleep on her feet. "That is just godawful spooky. You are a spooky man. Come in here and take a load off. I didn't know you came for that."

"I didn't," I said as she wheeled another chair into her crowded cubicle. I walked in and sat. She was a tall woman, but that didn't stop her from wearing what I assumed were the highest heels she could comfortably get away with. The too-small fedora made her seem taller yet.

When she was seated and had her notebook out, she said, "I've spoken to all the neighbors. In fact, I think I have your name on a list here somewhere to call." She swiveled around and pawed through a stack of notes on her desk, looking as if she'd birthed the entire Green Bay Packers front line.

She turned back to me, pen in hand, and said, "It's somewhere here. I'll find it before you leave. Now. How is the murder of Nat Bowers related to Charlie Groth?"

"It isn't," I lied. "It was a total coincidence. I had no idea you were writing that article."

"Why shouldn't I be writing it? I'm the crime reporter for the *Journal American*."

"I went up there to see Bowers on a personal injury case." I regurgitated my lie about the car accident.

"I don't understand."

"Like I said before, I'm here to talk to you about Charles Groth and Deception Pass. I'm particularly interested in how the killer gained access to the house, who the missing mystery woman might have been, and anything else Groth might have told you."

"Charlie told me *everything*," Faulconer said. She settled farther into the chair like a colossal hen on a nest. "I know everything there is to know about it."

"About the mystery woman?"

"That's going to be one of the surprises when my book comes out—my book, incidentally, that all the New York publishers were too unenlightened to buy. I've had to do it with a regional press. But I'll have my revenge. With what I know and the way I can write, it will naturally be a best-seller. I'm going to buy a ranch in Wyoming with the money."

Faulconer proceeded to tell a story about being picked up by a regional press, replete with praise quoted word for word from her editor and publisher and her mother. I had never heard of the publisher, and had a feeling the book was coming out of somebody's garage. I let her ramble until she began to assume we were a team, she and I, amazed at how quickly she fancied we'd formed a compact against those "filthy" New York publishers.

Faulconer suddenly changed the subject. "Charlie wasn't a bad man, Black. He was a small-time punk and a petty criminal, but he wouldn't hurt a fly."

"A jury of twelve disagreed."

"Twelve fools. Despite what we did for him here at the *Journal American*, he was tried in the press, and he had an incompetent lawyer. Penick was about as worthless as tits on a boar hog."

"If he didn't kill them, who did?"

"The girl, of course. There was so much that never got into the trial. For instance, did you know Charlie's father was also his grandfather?"

"I was wondering if you knew how they got into the house."

"It was quite simple. She had a gun."

"In his statements, Charlie said they got in with a knife."

"The police coerced those statements out of Charlie. He told me after the trial that she had a gun."

"It wasn't Charlie who had a weapon?"

"No."

"What makes you think he was telling the truth?"

Her eyes focused on me from behind the thick lenses the way a kid focused sunlight through a magnifying glass, and I felt like a squirming ant with smoke coming out of its hind end. "Charlie wouldn't lie to me, Black. We had an understanding. He knew I was going to write his story, and he knew he was going to die. There was simply no reason to lie. I know he made a statement early on that he forced his way in with a knife, but she had a gun. Why Penick never had him retract that statement about the knife is beyond me."

"Who was the girl?"

"That will be in the book."

"But you know who she is?"

"You bet your patooties I know who she is. And you would be surprised."

"She's still alive?"

"Very much so."

"Living in this area?"

"Very much so."

"Somebody I might know?"

"You knew Bowers. By the way, I spoke to Bowers's mother. In fact, I got the feeling from her that she was the one who discovered the body. At least, that's how I've got it in my article."

"I was the one, but write it however you want. I don't need my name in the paper."

The phone rang and Faulconer picked it up. "Oh, hi. I was wondering when you would call." She waved me away with a flick of her fingers, swiveled her chair around until her back was to me, and kicked both large legs laboriously up onto the counter. I had been dismissed.

I might have waited her out, but I was beginning to wonder how much of what she said could be trusted. There was a grandiosity in the way she spoke that seemed to contaminate her words.

On the way out, the man in the sweater vest pigeonholed me in the outer foyer near the front doors. His broad face and pleasant, rounded features were common enough that five minutes from now I wouldn't remember what he looked like. When I questioned him, he said, "Betty's been writing a book ever since I've worked here. It's always different. Right now she says it's about Charles Groth. It's the one project she might actually get published. Much as we hate to admit it, she did make a name for herself with those articles."

"How long has she worked here?"

"I think they might have put this building up around Betty. I'm not sure. You do realize she's a pathological liar, don't you?"

"Really?"

"She writes the crime blurbs. You've read them. Somebody's mailbox gets blown up with a cherry bomb. A dog bites some kid, and the parents get into a fistfight. Bones are found out by North Bend. She's our crime reporter basically because cops are the only people who can stand her. She goes out to interview anybody else, she gets into her Empress of China mode. We've had people who wouldn't talk to *any* reporter after a visit from her."

"What about the Groth case?"

"She lucked into that. Groth lived right here in Bellevue for a while with his sister—in fact, just a few blocks from here. The same apartment complex where a woman was raped and murdered. They never caught anybody for that one, but we all know it was him. Because he was from Bellevue and because his sister lived here for so many years, the managing editor wanted more than just the news-wire stories. Then Betty turned it into some sort of cause célèbre. She actually thought he was innocent."

"She didn't write her articles as if she thought he was innocent."

"They wouldn't let her. Her only kid's a double murderer. Did you know that?"

"Faulconer's son?"

"When he was seventeen, he got tanked up on amphetamines—her diet pills actually—and ended up killing a couple of homeless guys on some railroad tracks. This was a few years back. When the *Journal* tried to print something about it, she went upstairs and threw a tantrum. I don't know what she threatened them with, but they didn't run it. I think he's out already; living down in New Mexico near Truth or Consequences with his father."

"We didn't get to that."

"You're lucky. She'll call the managing editor from her phone over there and disguise her voice and tell him what a wonderful article Betty Faulconer wrote that morning. She'll do this two or three times a week. The weird part is, everybody knows she's doing it, and she must know we know. Some weeks she'll bring in selections from her fan mail to pass around. We checked one of those letters once. It had a dummy return address. She calls the Groth thing the 'worst miscarriage of justice since Patrick Henry was hung.' "

"I believe Patrick Henry died of natural causes."

"Really? That'll be good to know the next time she brings it up."

"But she really got close to Groth?"

"There's no doubt on that score. On the night he was executed, she was the last person to speak to him. She's got a picture of the two of them taken two hours before he bought it. It's going to be on the cover of her book. You see the jar on her desk? Somehow she got his ashes. She's planning to promote her book with them. You buy a book, you get a little plastic packet containing a pinch of Charlie Groth. She plans on cutting Charlie with ash from her wood stove to make him go further. She figures she can get packets to the first fifty thousand lucky book buyers."

"Charming."

"Isn't it, though?"

CHAPTER 22

In Seattle, at Twenty-third and Jackson, I described the Shaolin to the clerks in Welch's hardware and asked if they knew him. Nobody did.

After testing the waters at two other businesses on Jackson— a flower shop and a ribs place where the smell of baked beans was almost overpowering—I dropped in at the Wonder Bread thrift store on Twentieth and bought a box of Hostess Baseball cupcakes. Though they were marked at two bucks, the heavyset woman behind the counter gave them to me for twenty cents and winked when I left. She hadn't seen the Shaolin either.

I canvassed the Jackson neighborhood, then drove north on Twenty-third past Garfield High School and Ezell's Fried Chicken. After I'd been at it an hour, I found a pay phone and thumbed through the yellow pages to lawn mower repair. Both times I'd seen the Shaolin, he'd smelled of freshly cut grass.

At Fourteenth Avenue East near Madison, just across the street from a gay bar, I walked into a lawn mower repair shop and waited behind two Asian customers. When the place had cleared, I asked the wiry black man behind the counter about the Shaolin. He took off his glasses and rubbed the bridge of his nose with two fingers.

"Real tough guy? Head shaved with stripes down the sides and the back?"

"That's him."

"First of all, most tough guys, it's my belief, aren't tough at all. They're unhappy. And the more unhappy they are, the tougher they act. It's all a comedy. But yeah, he comes in all the time pushing a Toro he beats all to heck. I already put four sets of wheels on that dang machine this summer."

"Do you have a phone number or a name for him?" He slipped his glasses back on and acted as if he hadn't heard me. "I'm not out to hurt him, and he'll never know who told me."

"What'd he do?"

"He may be a witness to a crime."

"You a cop?"

"I was. I'm not anymore." I slid twenty bucks across the counter.

After thumbing through a handwritten receipt book, he gave me a name and phone number and watched me leave. I drove to First and Yesler, parked at a meter, ran upstairs and used the computer on my desk to translate the number into a street address and a name: Helvittia Dewitt. He was living with somebody.

Ten minutes later I stopped and honked outside the shoe shop at Second and Cherry where Bruno Collins kept his makeshift office. Moments later Bruno came out, unbuttoned his double-breasted suit coat, and climbed into the Taurus.

Smiling affably, he said, "What's up, boss?"

"I wish you wouldn't call me that."

"I didn't mean anything by it. You know I love you."

"Have a Baseball." Using one hand, I offered him the box of cupcakes and then gnawed the cellophane off one for myself. We drove up the steepest part of Yesler and crossed over the freeway, heading out of downtown.

Bruno took a bite of his Baseball and peered down at the jammed lanes of I-5 below Yesler.

"I got the Shaolin's address."

"How'd you do that?"

I told him.

"Don't worry," Bruno said. "He's not going to fight. You know what the trouble with him was? We got off on the wrong foot communicationwise. Mind if I have another Baseball?"

"Go ahead, but more than three will make you thirsty."

According to the man in the lawn mower shop, the Shaolin's name was Leslie Petty. When I told Bruno, he said, "Leslie? No wonder he's so rough. My mother hadda named me Leslie, I'd be rough too."

Petty's address was near Twenty-fifth and Columbia, within walking distance of Garfield High School and the business areas I'd canvassed earlier. I wondered how many of the shop owners and restaurateurs had recognized my description without saying anything. I wondered if Petty had been warned.

"You have a gun on you, Bruno?"

"We won't need a gun for this guy. Not for somebody named Leslie." Bruno grinned.

I laughed. I hoped he didn't kill us.

It was a tidy little neighborhood with two- and three-bedroom bungalows lined up on either side of the street. We parked a few doors down and walked back to one of the few houses on the block that didn't quite measure up, a faded turquoise unit with two of the four numerals missing from beside the front door.

A tiny, hunched black woman, who appeared to be in her seventies or eighties, answered the door in a light blue nightgown, peering at us through wire-rimmed glasses and the broken screen door. Milky cataracts dimmed her eyes. The air pushing out of the house smelled of toast and hair products, and we could hear a TV running. She wore a plastic cap over her head.

After she'd admitted she was Helvittia Dewitt, I asked her, "Does Leslie Petty live here?"

"My grandson's not in," she said, looking Bruno over now that she'd finished with me.

"Do you know where he is?" I asked.

"Out cuttin' grass, I 'spect. Leslie's been working every day. He hardly drink 'cept for the weekends."

Displaying my fake Rolex, I said, "I need to ask him if he knows who this belongs to."

She gave me a suspicious look and then left us at the door for a minute before coming back with a wrinkled envelope on the back of which was a list of addresses written in tiny script. While Bruno made small talk, I copied the addresses into a notebook. I noticed a battered, tan Maverick parked in her yard.

"What kind of car is Leslie driving, ma'am?"

"Leslie's hard on wheels. I can't be letting him have mine."

"He's in a borrowed car?" Bruno asked.

"On foot."

"Thank you for your time," I said.

There were six addresses on our list, two just a few blocks north of Union. The lawns at the first three addresses had freshly trimmed turds of dark green grass littering the sidewalks. The fourth address was just around the corner from the Sally Goldmark Library on Union. We heard the growl of a mower as we drove past. I parked out of sight around the corner, opened the trunk, and took out a length of two-by-four.

"Want one?" I asked Bruno.

"I don't need no chunk of firewood for this clown."

"Why not? Your fists are boards?"

"No," Bruno said, peeved. "Because he's not going to give us any trouble."

"He did last time."

"I told you that was poor communication."

Petty was laboring in the yard of a shabby, beige, two-story house where all the water-stained shades were drawn in the windows. The grass was peppered with foot-high weeds. Across the street, an elderly black man in a gray windbreaker and tan slacks fussed with a pile of leaves.

Petty emerged from the side yard pushing the rickety, smoking Toro through the grass to the sidewalk, then back again.

Watching him, it was clear that all he had was a room at his grandmother's, the lawn mower, his haircut, and a whole lot of rage. Yesterday morning as he left Bowers's rooming house, there'd been a peculiar look on his face, but it hadn't been rage then; it had been a combination of fear and sorrow. To my way of thinking, he'd felt almost as badly about Bowers as the rest of us, and remembering it put me in touch with the humanity of the man.

Even so, I kept the two-by-four pressed against my thigh, where it would be barely noticeable to Petty, though it was fully evident to the man across the street, who stopped what he was doing and leaned against his rake to watch.

Petty turned around at the end of the yard and noticed us, though he didn't slow, nor did he give us a second look. Walking the noisy mower in our direction, he gave no sign that he knew who we were, so it wasn't until he was within ten feet of Bruno and had tipped the machine up that we knew his intentions. He walked the now-exposed, whirling blade directly at Bruno's legs.

I threw the two-by-four hard onto the sidewalk, where it bounced under the Toro and made a clunking noise as it jammed the blade and stopped the engine. The neighborhood was suddenly as quiet as a church on a Monday.

"You fucked up my job, man," Petty said angrily, tipping the lawn mower to one side and attempting to jerk the two-by-four from where it was wedged between the blade and the cowl.

As he worked with the board and the dead mower, Bruno patted him on the back. "Don't worry about it, pal. It's just stalled."

Petty set his mower down carefully on the sidewalk, turned, and threw an elbow into Bruno's paunch, quickly followed by two open-handed slash cuts at his neck with the heels of his hands. The elbow connected, but Petty hadn't taken into account Bruno's girth, which pretty well absorbed the blow. Much to my surprise, Bruno agilely dodged both slash cuts to his neck.

Cat-quick, Bruno grabbed Petty's torn jacket at the shoulders, one of his hands diving deep into a tear, and began wrestling with him in a stylized, almost comic manner, the two of them walking each other around and pushing hard against each other's shoulders. While this was going on, Petty attempted to kick Bruno. Bruno outstepped him.

Tugging the two-by-four out from under the lawn mower, I turned around and found Petty had managed to get Bruno into some weird stranglehold. I stood behind Petty and swung the board like a baseball bat. It connected with his ribs, but there was no visible damage and he did not let go of Bruno. I hit him in the ribs again. Bruno's eyes were bulging and his neck veins were beginning to look like garden hoses.

I whacked Petty's back and ribs two more times with even less result, then took a low, cricket-style swing from the ground and hit him in the crotch. He dropped to the sidewalk and veed his hands between his legs, eyes closed. Ten feet away, Bruno clutched his throat and gagged.

"You okay?" I said.

After some seconds of sputtering, Bruno said, "He was trying to crush my windpipe."

"That's sure what it looked like to me."

Putting a knee into the center of Petty's back, I held him and searched for weapons. His left jacket pocket contained a seven-inch switchblade that was so battered I couldn't get the blade out on my first few tries. Then I couldn't get it back in.

"You fuckers," Petty said as I pressed his face into the sidewalk.

"We only wanted to talk," I said. The solid musculature of his back began rolling around under me so that it felt like I was holding down a snake with a plastic fork. He got out from under my knee and began rolling away, collided with Bruno, wrapped himself around one of Bruno's legs, and sank his teeth into his calf. Bruno let out a howl.

I picked up the two-by-four and brought it down edgewise on Petty's shoulder.

Curling into a fetal position, Petty said, "You broke my fucking collarbone."

"That's what happens to slow learners," I said.

"I'm out here trying to make a goddamned living, and you two assholes show up and break my collarbone. First you fuck up my machine, and then you—"

"We came here to talk," I said. "You're the one who ran at my friend with your lawn mower."

"What do you fuckers want?"

Whatever we wanted, it was going to have to be quick, because, leaving his rake beside his front door, the old man across the street had gone in to use the phone. In a moment or two we'd be hearing sirens. Once Arnold Haldeman and the City of Seattle got their hands on Petty, I'd probably never see him again.

CHAPTER 23

"I wonder if dry cleaning will get teeth marks out of trousers," Bruno said, stepping forward with negligible fear and less caution.

"I wasn't hurtin' so bad, you'd be bouncing down the street on your fucking heads," Petty shouted.

I knelt beside him. "We didn't come here to fight. The scrap was your idea."

"And you brought that goddamned board 'cause you're building a fence."

"I had a feeling about you."

"Your feeling better call me a goddamned ambulance, is what it better do." Straining to get comfortable, he cradled his left arm against his chest with his right. "Who's going to pay for my lawn mower? I oughta sue your ass. That's what I oughta do."

Bruno said, "You were supposed to be clipping the grass, pal, not my toenails."

"Listen, Leslie," I said. "It would be better for you if you talk to us before the police get here."

"Talk about what?"

"Nat Bowers." Petty opened his eyes and squinted up at us, and it became clear he did not recognize me. "Yesterday morning

outside Nat Bowers's rooming house, you pulled a gun on me."
When he still didn't recognize me, I added, "It looked like a
nickel-plated .38. Your jacket was crammed with money. Afterward, I went upstairs and found Bowers dead."

"I didn't do nothing."

"You don't start answering questions, I'll sure as hell make it
sound as if you did."

"Why are you doing this to me?"

"Because I don't like people who beat up on women," I said.

"What woman? I never—"

"The woman the other day on the motorcycle."

"That was a woman?"

"Who killed Bowers?"

"How should I know? He was supposed to come over Sunday night and pay me, but he never showed. That's all I know."

"Did you call to see why he didn't come?"

"I was busy watching a ball game."

"What happened yesterday morning?"

"Some guy let me in the door—he was scared. I scare white
folks. I went upstairs and found him like that."

"And you took the money."

"What money?"

"Okay, let's skip the money. What were you and Bowers
into?"

"Nothing. We weren't into nothing."

"Don't play stupid, Leslie. You do, and I'll tell Homicide I
heard shots while you were inside."

"You didn't hear no shots."

"I'll tell them I did."

Realizing he was cornered, he began to collapse like a school-
yard bully who'd just been collared by the principal. "Ah, shit."

"I don't want to mess with you, Leslie. I just want to know
what arrangement you had with Bowers. What was going on between you and him."

"He paid me to be his bodyguard—two, three weeks in a
row. Last week I got tangled with that bitch. I thought she was a
dude. No shit. I was about to put her lights out when these two
assholes showed."

"That was us," said Bruno. "We're the assholes."

"Listen to these lips, man," Petty said. "I didn't kill nobody. Goddamn it. I've been working my tail off. I'm even paying Gramma rent."

"Tell me about your deal with Bowers."

"He would drive out to the mall once a week, and I'd go with him. That was it. I never had to do nothing."

"Except last week," Bruno said. "When you ran into those 'two assholes.'"

"Except last week. Yeah."

I said, "What did he tell you he was doing at the mall?"

"He never said."

"You must have had an idea."

"It never bothered me one way or another."

"Besides the money, what'd you take from Bowers's room?"

"I didn't take shit."

"Don't play games with me, Leslie. You lifted a couple thousand dollars." I pulled two crisp twenties out of my pocket and popped them in front of his face. "These fell out of your coat. What else did you take?"

"Just that gun. It was on the floor."

"Tampering with a crime scene, huh?"

"It wasn't the piece that did him. I smelled it."

"And who's going to take your word for that?"

"Fuck you."

"Who do *you* think killed him?"

"Probably whoever I was protecting him against every Friday."

"And who was that?"

"He never said. But I had a feeling it was a woman."

"Why was that?"

"I don't know. I just did." The sirens were getting closer.

"What excuse did Bowers give you for the bodyguard bit?"

"He didn't give no excuse. The first time, I did it as a favor. I didn't know there was money involved until he forked over a hundred bucks."

"Where did you know Bowers from?"

"Met him through a friend of a friend."

"Can you get more specific?"

"Where do you think I met him? At the Sea Wolf."

It was the gay bar across the street from the lawn mower repair place where I'd gotten Petty's phone number. "Did you have a sexual relationship with Bowers?"

"No relationship. We didn't hit it off after that first time."

"Tell me you're not gay," Bruno said.

"Fuck you! And fuck your ugly sisters too!"

"Come on, Bruno. Stay out of it," I said. "What else did Bowers have you do?"

"He asked me to work over some guy."

"What do you mean? Beat him up?"

"Yeah."

"Did you do it?"

"I thought about it, but I don't mess between couples."

"Who was the guy?"

"I met him once, but I forget the name—some dumb-ass name. An older white man with baby-doll hair. Real tall."

When the uniforms arrived, Petty did his best to convince the two officers, a man and a woman, that Bruno and I had assaulted him while he'd been mowing the lawn. After the officers ran all of our names through the computer and spoke to the old man across the street, they came to the conclusion we were telling the truth and Petty was lying.

"Is anybody going to prefer charges here?" the male cop asked.

Without looking up, Petty grew quiet. Like most bullies, when he finally made the switch to victim he was pathetic.

"Not us," I said.

As the woman cop helped Petty into the backseat of her vehicle for the ride up to Harborview Hospital, where he would be met by Arnold Haldeman, he shouted at me. "Dootson. I told you it was a funny name. Tall white dude. Baby-doll hair. Nat wanted me to mess him up. His name was Dootson."

"Thanks."

"I told you he wasn't going to give us any trouble," Bruno said as I tossed my car keys at him. I gathered up the yard tools and righted the lawn mower, which had spilled a balloon of gasoline onto the sidewalk.

The lawn was less than half finished—and that, not in any

particular pattern. The random stripes in the tall grass and weeds seemed to reflect some of the disorganization in Petty's brain.

After we'd loaded the tools, the Toro, and the empty gas can into the trunk of my car, Bruno said, "He isn't gay."

"What makes you think that?"

"Everybody knows there aren't any gay brothers. And even if there were, they would automatically lose their minority status."

CHAPTER 24

It was almost three o'clock by the time I visited Trattoria Mitchelli and went back to the office with a Skid Road chicken pie pizza, rushing it through the office before too many pieces got hijacked.

On the computer, Leslie Petty was relatively easy to track down. Six months earlier, just months before Charles Groth was executed in that same institution, Petty had been paroled from the Washington State Penitentiary in Walla Walla.

It was doubtful Petty and Charles Groth had known each other or that there had even been any contact between them. Groth had been on death row, and Petty, most likely, had hung out in the general population. Yet it was an extraordinary coincidence, being incarcerated in the same penitentiary at the same time, and even though I knew coincidences such as this happened often in complex cases, it made me uneasy.

Was it possible Petty had heard something about Groth's crime while in prison, and, through some peculiar litany of circumstances I couldn't even guess at, his information had led to Lainie Smith?

Petty was thirty-three, five feet ten inches tall, two hundred eighteen pounds, and had served eight years for drug charges and assault. He'd been in the county lockup eight times, state prison twice, and Western State Hospital, a facility for the mentally ill, once. As far as I could tell from what I found on the computer, he'd had no run-ins with the law since his parole last spring.

I phoned Lainie Smith and asked her to free up her schedule for tomorrow, which she agreed to without asking why. She was trying so hard to be cool that she was heading in the direction of comatose.

After twice searching my desk and files, I looked in my wallet and found the business card Corliss Dootson had given me yesterday morning. He worked downtown in an architectural firm in the Rainier Tower just west of and across the street from the Olympic Hotel.

As I was leaving the office, Beulah stopped me. "Phone call, Thomas." Reaching down past the high counter, I picked up a handset, and Beulah connected the line.

"Black? What the hell do you think you're doing?"

"Detective Haldeman. So nice to hear your voice."

"Black, you don't interview a suspect in *my* murder investigation. You don't go around tracking down *my* witnesses. You don't mess in official police business. You do, I'll run you in for obstruction. And when I do that, even your pretty little lawyer won't be able to save your bacon. Even if you *are* sleeping with her."

"I resent the implication that we're only sleeping together. It's a fully committed relationship, Arnold. We're married and happy to be so." Beulah looked up, a note of curiosity dancing in her Technicolor blue eyes.

"Are you mocking me, Black?"

"You know I would never do that."

"Maybe you would. Maybe you wouldn't. What did you talk to Petty about?"

"Is that his name? Petty?"

"He says you busted his lawn mower."

"I did, but I took it to a shop up on Capitol Hill to be fixed."

"Smart-ass. You better open your eyes. I don't know what happened between you all, but when he was in Walla Walla, your friend Petty killed a man with his bare hands. Before that he was sent up for turning some U.W. jock into a paraplegic. He's not somebody you fool around with. Black, what's going on?"

"Sir?"

"Don't give me that *sir* crap. What's the link between Bowers and Petty? How did you know Bowers? And don't give me any more of your bullshit."

"Petty didn't tell you?"

"Petty told me he went up to Bowers's room, found him dead, took ten dollars off his desk that he claimed Bowers owed him, and went on home. Now, Black, supposing you tell me how you got into all this."

"All I know is they met at a gay bar on Capitol Hill."

The line went quiet for a few seconds. "Black?"

"Yes, sir."

"Stay out of my hair."

"Sir?"

"What is it?"

"You have hair now?"

Whether it was because of the overcast skies or because I'd just been chewed out by a homicide detective I didn't care for, I found myself somewhat depressed. The sky was gray, the air cold, traffic heavy, and the exercise brisk as I walked up First Avenue and then up the hill on Union. The jaunt cheered me.

The Rainier Tower was a forty-two-story building with a tapered base smaller than its body, so that it looked a bit like a huge pencil standing on its squared and sharpened tip. When it was first built, there was speculation that it would tip over during the first good windstorm, but the engineers assured us it was stable, and after countless windstorms, it was still standing.

I walked in through the east entrance, strode past the shops and the bookstore, and rode the elevator to the thirty-fourth floor.

Spader and Associates took up most of the southwest corner of the floor.

After passing through a pair of blond, wooden doors, I encountered a large man wearing a phone set on his head. He directed me across a narrow office to a cubicle at the end of a row of similar cubicles, many of which were unoccupied, a coffee cup or Walkman and earphones awaiting the owners. Much like the news building where Elizabeth Faulconer worked in Belle-vue, it was an open office with partitions and a ghetto of desks.

Dootson's space was against the windows and sported a dizzying view of Elliott Bay over a haphazard pattern of down-town buildings.

Dootson, who was moving about his space with a large white sheet of paper in his hands, his sleeves rolled up, a pencil tucked behind a winged-out ear, seemed startled to see me. His quizzi-cal look, along with his silence, might have lasted all afternoon.

"Corliss Dootson?" I said, smiling and extending a hand. "We met yesterday."

He glanced over the neighboring partitions, unwilling to share his personal business with the rest of the office. A brown-haired woman in a checkered skirt walked past us and stared at me. I had the feeling visitors were scarce at Spader and Associ-ates. Dootson was larger than I recalled, three or four inches taller than me and a whole lot beefier, although from the look of his flesh, he wouldn't be a threat on a basketball court. His eyes were blue, and he had a pleasant, good-natured aspect to his fea-tures. Petty's description of his baby-doll hair fit perfectly.

He was in his forties, and the brow line of fluffy, brown hair was creeping toward the back of his head in an even half-moon. He wore khaki slacks, a loosened tie, and a dress shirt open at the neck. His shoes were in a corner. The argyle socks on his big feet looked new.

The corkboard walls of Dootson's workspace contained a couple of Dilbert cartoons, a birthday card, a newspaper article about a commercial building project in Seattle, and several photo-graphs: Dootson sitting in front of a Christmas tree with an older couple, presumably his parents; a glossy black-and-white photo of a high school baseball team, Dootson on the far left in knee pads; another of a high school basketball team, Dootson wearing number twelve; and a snapshot of a woman in a bathing suit sit-ting on a sandy beach. Dootson wasn't in that one.

"Sit down. Sit down," Dootson said. I took one stool while he took another, and we perched beside each other like a couple of talk-show hosts waiting for the band to strike up a tune. "What can I do for you?"

"I'd like to ask about Nat Bowers."

"I've already spoken to the police about him. You're not with the police, are you?"

"No."

"I didn't think so." He sat back.

"I ran into a roughneck who claims Bowers tried to hire him to mess you up. Why would he have wanted to do that?"

"No," Dootson continued, as if the question hadn't been asked, "I didn't think the police said anything about you being with them."

"Why would Bowers want to mess you up?"

Curiosity suddenly overwhelmed discretion, and he said, "Are you sure about this?"

"I spoke to the man he tried to hire."

"Nat and I were friends."

"Is that why you went by his place yesterday morning?"

"Yes. We were just dropping in to see how he was getting along."

"At eight in the morning? What sort of relationship did you have with Nat?"

"Nat lived with me."

"When?"

"Last spring. He had some money problems and needed a place to crash, so I let him bunk with me."

"How long did that last?"

"It started sometime in the winter and went on until May. It ended in early May."

"You have a pretty large house, do you?"

"It's an apartment. It was my fault he moved out, really. I had a bad spring. I was going through some emotional problems."

"You were lovers?"

Dootson glanced around the office. Even though I had spoken softly, he was clearly nervous about people eavesdropping under cover of the Muzak. "He lived with me."

"Where did you meet him?"

"I met him winter quarter at Seattle Community College. He kept a room in that house the whole time he was living with me. Now I know why."

"Why?"

"Nat was running around on me. From the word go. I don't mind that sort of thing so much if that's the original understanding, but that wasn't our understanding. Nat was a tramp. I don't like tramps."

"So he wasn't staying with you because of money problems. You were lovers?"

"He had money problems too."

"But he kept his own place at the rooming house. I assume he was paying for it."

"Well, I don't know what kind of problems he had."

"Did you tell any of this to the police?"

"They didn't ask."

"You and Nat, did you part on amicable terms?"

"Nat and I were still speaking to one another, if that's what you mean. You don't think I had something to do with his death?"

"It's occurred to me that if *he* wanted to mess *you* up, *you* might have wanted to mess *him* up."

"Why would I want to hurt him?"

"I don't know. Why?"

"We broke up because I was going through some emotional problems. There was no animosity. We were still friends."

"You ever hear of a man named Charles Groth?"

"Who?"

"He was hanged by the state in June."

"The man who killed all those people up in Island County?"

"Skagit County, actually."

"Everybody's heard of him. I certainly never met him. Why?"

"Did Bowers ever talk about him or the murders at Deception Pass?"

"No. Why would he?"

"You know a man named Leslie Petty?"

"I might have run into him. I think he was a friend of Nat's, but I don't know him."

It was clear that I wasn't going to get any more out of him.

I was almost out the door when a woman said, "Hey."

At first I didn't recognize her. She'd been with Corliss Doot-son on Monday morning outside Nat Bowers's rooming house. Ione Barocas was sitting on a stool in a cubicle within sight of the main doors, so I'd probably passed her on my way in. She snapped her fingers twice and walked toward me in what I thought was a rather provocative manner, as if she were trying to look sexy. She was prettier today, her hair long and loose, her navy suit snug and trim. She had a rich, expensive, neurotic look. Her nose was slightly hooked, and her skin was as smooth as white chocolate. Her liquid-brown eyes held me like a baby's lips held a nipple. "I'm sorry, but I forgot your name."

"Black," I said. "Thomas Black. I didn't recognize you at first. I'd forgotten that you and Corliss both worked here."

"Oh, yes, we've been here for ages. Funny running into you."

"Yeah, funny."

I realized now that the woman in the bathing suit in the picture on the wall in Dootson's cubicle was Barocas. It was hard to tell what their relationship might be, unless she was a front Dootson used to pass for heterosexual when circumstances deemed it prudent.

I broke off eye contact and said, "Well . . ."

"Yes . . ."

"I'll see you sometime."

"Will you?"

"Yeah. Maybe."

As I walked back to the office, I kept thinking Petty had been paroled from Walla Walla last spring at about the same time Dootson broke up with Bowers. I wondered if the events were related.

CHAPTER 25

Tuesday night the weather pattern changed, and by Wednesday morning a heavy fog blanketed the Northwest from British Columbia to Portland.

The public radio station announced all the freeways were snarled and one of the bridges would be tied up all morning due to a fatal accident involving thirty vehicles, all of which, from what I gathered, had been tailgating in the fog.

"A field trip!" Kathy said, turning away from the mist outside our living room window. "What sort of field trip?"

"Only if you have time."

"But I do. There's almost nothing on tap for today." After I explained, she headed for the spare bedroom where most of her extra clothes were stored, emerging fifteen minutes later in a beret, knickers, long navy socks, wooden clogs, and a white blouse with a little green ribbon tie. There was no telling where she'd gotten such an outfit or why she chose to wear it now. I could only be grateful it wasn't any goofier.

I said, "You look like a leprechaun," and goosed her as she walked past the kitchen table.

In the dense fog, we drove to First Hill and pulled into the small passenger load circle in front of Lainie Smith's condominium. Kent Wadsworth, who was standing resolutely in the lobby, watched us pull in and vanished in the direction of the elevators. A few minutes later he came down with Lainie, who wore a long black coat buttoned to the neck, black slacks underneath.

She looked as if she hadn't gotten much sleep, her normally neat hair mussed, a thin slice of pale scalp showing through in front where it had parted accidentally. She wore no makeup.

Kathy had climbed into the backseat so Lainie could sit in front, but Lainie, accustomed to having chauffeurs, got in back with Kathy, plunking down with a sigh and a roll of her eyes and a look that was all surrender.

"How long?" Lainie asked, looking from me to Kent, who was shivering in shirtsleeves beside the car.

"Five or six hours. We can call. I've got a phone."

"I've got a phone too," she said, touching her purse. Kent nodded and closed the door for her. "I got another call."

"What did he say?" I reached across the seat and accepted the cassette even though I didn't have a player in the car that would accommodate it.

"He told me to get one point five million dollars and wait. That he'd be in touch. He told me Tess Hadlock was still alive when we left the bungalow."

"Was Hadlock still alive?" I asked.

"I don't think so. I would have called an ambulance. But the blackmailer talked as if he knew she was."

I said, "Even the police speculated Hadlock might have been alive after the killer left. He's going to have to do better than that."

"What do you mean?" Lainie said.

"So far, he hasn't put forth anything more than guesswork about your connection to Deception Pass. Bowers knew the gun was a toy. He hasn't even said that."

"But he did," said Lainie. "He said the gun was plastic in the first call. Don't you remember?"

"That's right. You're right. I'm losing the threads of this thing. What else did he tell you?"

"That was it."

"When did you get this call?"

"Just after nine this morning."

The dash clock said it was nine-forty. "Are you going to get the money together?"

"The bank is bringing the cash over even as we speak. Do you think I'm doing the right thing?"

"It's up to you, Lainie," I said. "*I* wouldn't do it, but I don't have that kind of money either. The way I see it, it might be a million and a half this week. A million and a half next week. And then, the week you don't pay, they go right ahead and tell the world what you don't want the world to know. When is he going to call back?"

"He didn't say."

We'd been idling in the circular drive in front of her building. I pulled out into the street, went south to James, rolled down the hill, and entered the freeway a couple of blocks later. Inching along at five and ten miles an hour, all we could see was fog, brake lights, irate drivers grumbling over their coffee cups, and, at one point, an ambulance snaking its way up the emergency strip on the outer perimeter of the roadway. We had plenty of time to talk.

"It's actually . . . it's actually nice to be with you two," Lainie said. In the rearview mirror she looked as if terrorists had just kidnapped her. "You're the only people who know what I'm going through. I find a noticeable relaxing of tension when I'm around you."

"I'm glad," Kathy said. "Maybe you should spend more time with us."

"How about all day today?" said Lainie, offering a feeble wisecrack to go along with a feeble smile. "By the way, Thomas, I'm certainly willing to go anywhere you feel is necessary to get this straightened out, but you never told me where we were headed."

"Lainie, the way I figure it, this case is a lot like a garden hose with a marble in it, our goal to find the marble. At one end of the hose is you and me and Nat Bowers and everything else that's been going on. At the other end is the night of the murders, the search, the trial. There are two ways to work on this, Lainie. From the present, or from the past."

"And somewhere in the middle is whatever gave me away to the blackmailer? The marble?"

"That's the way I see it. What I'd like to do today is drive up to Deception Pass and look around. Seeing the cabin might jog your memory. Or Kathy or I might notice something. There's got to be something going on here that we don't know about."

"I can't," Lainie said, her voice quivering. "I can't go."

"Why not?" Kathy asked.

"I've never been back. Not since it happened."

"You've never had a reason to go back before," I said. "This is important."

"I'm afraid I'll . . . have some sort of panic attack like I used to. I'd get so my muscles would cramp, and they would have to give me shots."

"Why don't we do this?" Kathy said. "We'll drive up, and any time you feel the least bit panicky, we'll turn around."

"But that would mean you both wasted your time."

"Nonsense. We're working for you."

"Is the cabin still standing?"

"According to Elizabeth Faulconer's articles, it is," I said.

"Okay. But I don't think I can do it."

We nudged along to Mountlake Terrace, where the gloom lifted enough that traffic sped up to fifty-five miles an hour. We took Highway 525 down the hill into Mukilteo, a tiny town known mostly in connection with the ferry that crossed Possession Sound to Whidbey Island, the largest island in the state and the island with the longest coastline in the continental United States.

On the long downhill into Mukilteo, we passed a teenage boy beating on a bus shelter with a stick. I said, "It must be nice to have your head so empty you can spend your time like that."

"Believe me, it isn't," Lainie said. It was the first sentence she'd uttered in twenty minutes.

We bought tickets from the woman in the kiosk and parked in one of the ferry traffic lanes, resisting the temptation to queue up for a cup of clam chowder under the blue and white rowboat on the roof of Ivar's Fish Bar. After the ferry had disgorged the traffic from the island, we were ushered on and directed to the front of the boat, which appeared to be one of the oldest in Washington State's fleet of twenty-five working ferries.

Twice during the twenty-minute crossing, we saw sea lions fishing for salmon, each sighting signaled by a platoon of gulls hovering for discards.

As we disembarked at the town of Clinton, a bank reader board informed us the temperature was forty-seven degrees Fahrenheit.

Driving north through the rolling countryside of Whidbey Island, we passed a winery, a vineyard, a hog farm, a sheep ranch. The fog blurred our occasional glimpses of the sound.

Reading a highway sign, Kathy said, "Useless Bay Road. Wouldn't you love to live in a place called Useless Bay? That would suit me just fine."

It was a long drive, nearly fifty miles, and the closer we got to Deception Pass, the more desperately Kathy and I filled the car with small talk. Yet Lainie, sitting in the back alone now, remained silent and pensive, peering out the window, occasionally clearing her throat as if she were planning to speak, but never speaking.

After crossing the first leg of the 976-foot steel bridge over Deception Pass, I swung off the roadway and pulled in next to three parked cars on Pass Island, a tall, rocky outcropping. Pass Island was a cone-shaped anchor in the middle of the narrow strait and served as a natural support for the two spans of the Deception Pass Bridge. Built in 1935, the bridge, now a national historic monument, was a Public Works Project constructed by workers from the Civilian Conservation Corps. To the west was the sound. To the south, the deep cut with the water channel running through it.

"I thought we might want to take a break and gather our thoughts," I said.

The three of us walked over the gray rock outcroppings until we could see the southern span of the bridge we had just crossed and the beach of Deception Pass State Park far below across the narrow channel. The brilliant deep green waters were boiling furiously as they raced through the narrows below us.

The smooth rock was laced with trails that led down the slope to a sheer cliff that dropped another thirty yards to the water. Slowly, we hiked down the hillside, gaining a better view of the bridge and waterway with each step. The breeze had turned Lainie's cheeks bright. A sightseer on the hillside stared at Kathy's outfit, ignoring the spectacular view.

I kissed the tip of Kathy's nose. "What's that for?" she said.

"Every once in a while I like to kiss a schnoz."

"I hope it's usually mine."

"Usually. Sometimes it's just the first schnoz I get to."

We walked down the rocks until the tourists peeking over the railing of the bridge above us were mere specks, until we could have thrown pebbles into the kelp massed in the deep green pools along the cliffs. Car tires thrummed over the bridge decking.

On the hike back up the hill, I forged ahead while Kathy politely lagged behind with Lainie. It was a long wait. When they got to the monument and plaque off the roadside, Lainie was breathing hard and had tears in her eyes.

"Too steep?" I asked.

Kathy looked at me soberly and said, "We better do this in the car."

Lainie got in back, Kathy and I in front. Lainie was crying freely, something she had not done until now.

"What is it?" I said.

"I didn't tell you everything," Lainie said. "The night before it happened, there were four of us, not three. Me. Charles Groth. The girl who called herself Today. And my boyfriend."

"Who?"

"Robbie Pedersen. The boy in that picture you found. He wasn't like the rest of us. Robbie wouldn't even have a beer. I think that was why Groth didn't like him."

"What happened to him?" I said.

"In that motel room I was with Robbie. I know I told you I was with Groth, but Today was with Groth. Groth kept making lewd suggestions, you know, that we switch off. It never happened, but the next morning Today left first thing, and then Groth and Robbie and I were driving around. We got as far as this bridge, where we stopped and Groth and Robbie quarreled.

Robbie went over to the road, and the first car that came along picked him up. I never saw him again."

"This was before the killings?" Kathy asked.

"Yes."

"And then you went with Groth down to the cabin, and all the rest happened?" I said.

"Basically. Yes."

"Why didn't you tell us Robbie was here?"

"I didn't . . . I didn't really forget, but I didn't really remember either. It just wasn't there when I told the story. I can't explain it. I thought if he was the one doing this, you'd find him."

"You think he's blackmailing you?"

"I have all along."

"And you didn't want us to know about him?" Kathy said.

"I guess not."

"You're still in love with him?" Kathy glanced at me.

Sniffling, Lainie blew her nose and said, "If you can be in love with someone you only knew for a few weeks seventeen years ago. I guess I am."

"Why did you tell us you slept with Groth?" Kathy asked.

"I did, once, but not that night. I guess I wanted you to think I was as worthless as I feel."

"He wasn't at the trial, was he?" I asked. "Pedersen?"

"Not that I could ever find out. As far as I know, the police never spoke to him."

I wondered if the name Robbie Pedersen would show up in any of Sternoff's files. I wondered if Pedersen even realized what happened after he left Groth and Lainie. Maybe he didn't know about the murders, or hadn't connected them to Lainie. Why should he? Five years passed before the police found Groth.

"Pedersen never contacted you afterward?" I said.

"I don't know if he remembered my last name. He was such a straight arrow compared to the rest of us. I don't even know why he was on the street."

"And you never tried to contact him afterward?"

Lainie had her face in her hands now, a Kleenex squeezing out between her fingers like a hernia. "I hid out. I thought Groth and I were going to be arrested any minute. I went home and I went to college. I straightened out my life. There wasn't anything else to do."

"And you've never run into him or seen him or gotten word from him?" Kathy asked.

"No."

"Are you sure you want to go through with this?" Kathy asked.

Perhaps because she could no longer trust her voice, Lainie nodded. I was beginning to wonder if I trusted her voice or any other part of her. Maybe Groth had told the truth. Maybe *she* had killed them and *he* had been the bystander. It was hard to trust witnesses whose stories kept changing.

We headed north, traversing the second span of the bridge, which took us to Fidalgo Island and from Island County into Skagit County.

CHAPTER 26

It was past noon, and most traffic was still running with head-lights.

As we drove, a lake appeared to the left of the highway, a body of mirrorlike black and green water rimmed with fir trees, an odd little lake with stumps in it. It was startling, not only because of how quickly it had come up but because it was almost at highway level near a point where, just a minute earlier, we'd been looking hundreds of feet down at the water. It reminded me of one of those mystery houses where steel balls roll uphill and a man with gaps in his teeth and long underwear showing under his shirtsleeves comes out and charges you five dollars to see it, two-fifty for the kids.

"Do you remember any of this?" I asked Lainie, swinging off Highway 20 onto the first side road, a right-hand turn that took us down a gradual slope into an area with houses. Moments later we came upon an intersection, Yokeko Drive to the right, Deception Road to the left. Navigating by a half-remembered map, I swung left and kept our speed down.

"It was almost dark," Lainie said. "I was beginning to realize I'd made a mistake not going with Robbie."

"Why *didn't* you go with Robbie?" Kathy asked.

"I was mad at him. We'd had some silly spat. He wanted me to go back to my folks."

The road continued downhill, a smattering of houses on either side, an odd mixture of double-wide trailers, two-story bungalows, ramblers, and, on the water side, the occasional mansion with private tennis courts.

"I don't remember all these houses," said Lainie.

"They look new," I said.

We swung onto Gibraltar Road, which roughly paralleled the bay, and I drove beyond the address. Lainie didn't stop me or seem to recognize the house, and for a split second I wondered if her entire tale was hogwash.

After another few minutes traveling the two-lane road, she said, "I think we've gone too far. I don't remember any of this."

We turned around, and this time I drove directly into the driveway and down a steep, graveled lane into a small parking area behind a tiny house that was maybe a hundred and fifty feet from the water. Huge chunks of driftwood were piled up along the shore as if there'd been a recent storm, though I knew there had not.

"This *might* be it," Lainie said, growing suddenly talkative. "We walked in from the water side. Groth ran that stolen Falcon into the ground—I felt sorry for the owners—and it finally quit up there somewhere. This looks like it could be the house."

The house was a small, two-story brown clapboard with a tiny front porch made of concrete, with brick planters on either side. A small pickup with a fishing pole in the gun rack was parked in front. The lawn had been usurped by sea grasses, salt air, and blown sand. The nearest neighbor was barely within hailing distance. Although the crime had occurred in August, when windows might have been open, unless there had been closer houses seventeen years ago, it was hard to believe Groth, or anybody else, would have been concerned that anything inside the house would be heard by neighbors.

Without any prompting, Lainie got out of the car.

"Have you thought about this?" Kathy whispered to me. "These people aren't likely to want three strangers snooping through their underwear drawers."

"I had the impression there was a beach," I said, speaking through the car across Kathy to Lainie.

Lainie was too stunned to talk.

The house didn't look as if it could have changed much.

"Look familiar?" I said, but once again Lainie failed to reply.

"How are we going to work this?" Kathy whispered. "We can't very well tell them we're here about the murder, and, oh, by the way, here's the missing witness."

"I was thinking about a film crew. We're scouting sites. If their house is chosen, we'll give them forty thousand dollars. We're doing a remake of *Barbarella*." I handed Kathy a business card that read THOMAS BLACK—MEDIA SERVICES, DIRECT HOLLYWOOD LIAISON.

"*Barbarella?*" Kathy said, getting out of the car. "You've been watching too much TV. Nice card. At least you spelled liaison right this time. Let me do the talking. You always choke."

"I've never choked. What are you talking—"

"Yes?" A man in a cowboy hat and a woman with dyed-black hair were standing at the door, both past retirement age, both looking vigorous and far too discerning for our purposes. The woman did the speaking after the man winked at me and said, "You can't come down that gravel drive without us knowin' about it."

He had gray hairs growing out of his ears, a mat of gray swelling up over his V-necked T-shirt, a smaller bouquet sprouting from his nostrils.

Kathy said, "Hello, folks. We hate to bother you, but we do have a little problem. I'm a psychiatrist. This is my assistant." She gestured at Lainie Smith. "And this gentleman is my patient." I must have given her a cockeyed look, because the man laughed.

"We're making a movie," I blurted, too late.

"Have you folks ever heard of multiple-personality disorder?" Kathy said.

"We're making a movie," I said. "We're going to film it around here somewhere. We're looking for a house."

"My client here has a real bad case of multiple-personality

disorder," Kathy said. "Right now he thinks he's Preston, the film director. This morning he was a twelve-year-old boy named Curtis who shoplifts at JC Penney. Part of his therapy involves helping him revisit scenes where he spent time as a youth. We've been driving around Fidalgo and Whidbey Islands today."

"Oh, where'd you grow up?" the woman asked. "Jay is from Anacortes."

"China," I said obstinately. What irked me was that I'd used the film crew gag so many times I knew it was foolproof.

"See," Kathy said. "It's so strange, this multiple personality business, that it almost looks like he's pretending. But heeeeee's not. I think he's Harold right now. Harold thinks he's a private investigator. Are you a private investigator?"

"You know I am."

"Harold," she said confidently.

Lainie ignored our chatter and stared through the door at the interior of the house.

"Well," the man said, tipping back his cowboy hat, which looked as if he kept it outside on a post at night, "I could see he was crazy as a shithouse rat when you first got out of the car. Why were you lettin' him drive?"

"We really can't discuss the details of this case. It's against our professional code, but I had to give you enough background so you wouldn't be worried if he turned into Fred and started sucking his thumb. We would like to offer you fifty dollars, though, just to spend some time inside your house. Maybe fifteen minutes?"

"I don't understand," the woman said.

"Ma, when this fella was a pup, he lived here. He's trying to remember something that happened to him. I seen it all on TV."

"I don't like it," she said, but Kathy already had fifty dollars in her hand, and then it was in the man's hand, and then we were being introduced all around. The man in the stained hat was Jay. The skeptical woman beside him was Peggy, his wife. Kathy was Kathy. Lainie was Jane. I was Harold, Fred, Curtis, Preston, and God only knows who else.

As we stepped through the front door into the intensely warm living room, Jay's eyes lit up. "Well, now, we don't want to scare you folks, but this place was the scene of a murder a few years back. People say it's haunted."

"It ain't haunted," Peggy said, as if she'd deflected this line of talk more than once. Peggy was watching me closely for signs of abnormality. I smiled like an idiot in the bumper cars. Lainie moved close and grasped my elbow so that the veins in my arm began noodling. She was stronger than she looked.

"You walk around as much as you want," Jay said.

It was a tiny house—what some might call a cottage—and, while it had appeared to be two stories from the outside, once we got inside we saw there was no second floor. The ceilings in the living room were low enough so that if you tried to jump rope it would brush the stucco business above. The rooms had hardwood floors and knotty-pine walls. The living room and dining room overlooked Skagit Bay, where, in the distance, several tiny islands peeked out of the fog. The kitchen was open and led to the back door.

Jay's cowboy boots and Kathy's clogs made almost identical sounds as Jay escorted her through the small house, explaining what he'd done to it in the eight years they'd occupied it, while Peggy, arms folded, stood against a wall behind an easy chair and stared at me. Each of her battered blue slippers had a huge Minnie Mouse head on the prow. To Kathy's credit, neither Jay nor Peggy had given Lainie a second glance.

Jay stood staunchly behind a protruding stomach that looked as hard as stone. Peggy remained against the wall like a shadow waiting for the light.

It was not hard to visualize that August night seventeen years earlier. Knocking at the kitchen door, they'd forced their way in, then tied the first three victims to chairs. There probably had been no tattletale gravel in those days, and my guess was, if Lainie and Groth hadn't heard Raymond Brittan coming, it was because he'd coasted his car down the hill. It was just the sort of trick a young man might play on his friends. It wouldn't have been until he walked through the kitchen that he would have seen what was going on.

Two bedrooms. Two couples. Logically, Raymond Brittan and his wife would have taken one bedroom, and either Tess or Jack Schupp would have taken the other, the remaining person to sleep in the common room on a sofa or on the floor.

When Lainie and I walked back to the two bedrooms and peered into the closets, one of which was bristling with shotguns and rifles, Lainie whispered, "I know what you're thinking. Somebody else was here. Hiding. I'm telling you he looked. He looked *everywhere*. There was nobody."

While all of us but Peggy went outside and circled the house, Jay entertained Kathy with a story about a pesky skunk he'd trapped and gotten too close to: despite his protestations, Peggy had quickly locked him out of the house, forcing him to strip and plunge into the ice-cold bay before handing him a box of matches through the window and telling him to burn his clothes in the burn barrel. As we circled the house, Peggy watched me out various windows, then tracked me with her alert eyes as we came back in through the kitchen door. I said, "This place got a basement?"

"No," Peggy said. "I thought you were here before."

"I'm Thomas. Harold was the one who was here before."

"Who's Thomas?" Jay asked.

"He's a carpenter," said Kathy. "Also, a shameful alcoholic. If you have any cooking sherry, you better hide it."

"I got whiskey," said Jay. "But he better not touch it."

"Don't worry," I said, stumbling through the living room and down a small hallway toward the bedrooms. "I'm not drunk. A little tipsy, maybe, but I'm not drunk. Jay? I don't get it. From outside it looks like two stories. I don't see any stairs."

"We moved in here, Peggy took one look at the heating bill and she was hot enough to fuck. I took out the stairs when I lowered the goddamn ceiling. You should have seen what they had before. Let me show you."

He led me down the hallway, where he picked up a flashlight, then outside and around to a small garage he said he'd built. He carried a wooden ladder around the house and leaned it up against the clapboard siding beneath a small, louvered door under the peak of the roof, climbed the ladder, and snaked through the door like a cat burglar. A moment later, still wearing the cowboy hat, he poked his head out and said, "You won't believe what they had up here."

I wasn't sure I wanted to climb into an attic with Jay, but if he was game to climb into it with Harold, Fred, Curtis, Preston, and Thomas, I wasn't going to be a party pooper.

It was a cramped attic space that ran the length of the house with a jog to the right over the front porch. None of it was finished, wooden rafters, bare floorboards, and an old shingled roof for a ceiling, no insulation anywhere. I tried not to inhale any of the filthy black dust our movement stirred up.

"See that there?" Jay said, shining his flashlight at the floor. "See all them cracks? That used to be the ceiling downstairs."

We were standing on a rough-hewn plank floor made up of one-by-fours that looked as if they'd been nailed down by kids, bent-over nails pounded flat and smooth. Through cracks in the floor I could see insulation on top of the ceiling Jay had installed. Anybody who'd been up here earlier would have been able to look directly down into the house and see everything that was happening. It would have been a Peeping Tom's delight.

Using the tiny mag light I kept in my coat, I discovered a stash of toys over in one corner, more toys hidden in a natural cubbyhole formed by the wall studs: boy toys—plastic race cars and a whole passel of cap guns, squirt guns, even a huge red rubber derringer that shot Ping-Pong balls. It looked like the secret cache of a boy whose family had banned toy guns. The toys, according to Jay, predated his ownership of the house. Looking at the styles of the guns and cars, I had a feeling they predated the murder as well.

In the middle of the floor was a trapdoor.

"Don't worry about that," Jay said. "I screwed that down tight. That ain't gonna open on you."

"I didn't see anything from below."

"Like I said, when I redid the ceiling, I covered the whole goddamn business over."

The possibilities suddenly seemed endless. Could some child have been in the attic when the four vacationers showed up that

Friday afternoon? Had some errant neighborhood kid watched the dancing and the Parcheesi from the attic, hoping for a chance to escape unnoticed? What sort of trauma would the massacre have inflicted on a young mind? I wondered.

"What about the ghosts?" I said, looking at Jay, who'd followed me and was standing against my shoulder. His scruffy cowboy hat was held together at the crown and brim with staples.

"Years back, some college kids got killed downstairs."

"You didn't own the house then?"

"Relatives of one of the kids owned it. Had about three more owners before we got our hands on it."

"What was it like back then?"

"Was bein' bought and sold as a summer cabin. All they had was some broken-down old beds and a table in the living room. A beat-up old sofa. Wasn't nothin' up here but a cot and some old clothes in trunks. After we bought it, the Salvation Army came and hauled it all off."

"They didn't haul off those toys."

"No. We didn't bother with them goddamn toys."

CHAPTER 27

Eschewing the ferry, we drove north toward the Texaco refinery with its towers and flaming stacks jutting up through the murk like the backdrop in a sci-fi movie. Highway 20 took us off Fidalgo Island, which was actually a peninsula, and east through the empty tulip fields of Skagit County. The afternoon had deepened, and the entire landscape was cloaked in an eerie gray that tented distant objects and kissed lights with a blurred and melancholy ring of lavender.

As we passed through the town of Mount Vernon, I told Kathy and Lainie about the attic. "Did Groth go up there?" I asked, watching Lainie in the rearview mirror.

"I didn't even know about it until today." There was no animation in her face, and if she hadn't spoken, you might have thought she wasn't breathing.

"Did you remember anything new while you were there?" Kathy asked.

"Everything. Every second of it."

"Your blackmailers knew it was a toy gun," I said. "Did Pedersen know Groth had a toy gun?"

"He *might* have seen Groth with it."

"What about that attic?" Kathy said. "What if somebody'd been up there?"

"That would mean somebody else had a chance to help and didn't." Lainie began crying.

"There were children's toys up there," I said. "Maybe when nobody was around, one or two of the neighborhood children went there to play."

"That would have been horrible," Lainie sobbed.

"I'll ask the detective in charge when I see him next."

"If it was a child," Kathy said, "it could have been Nat Bowers. He would have been . . ."

"Eight," I said. "Or it could have been somebody Bowers knew."

"But wouldn't their folks have told the police?" Lainie asked.

"Not if they didn't know about it themselves," I said.

"It would be interesting to know exactly where Bowers grew up," Kathy said.

We drove through Mount Vernon to I-5 and south toward Seattle. It didn't occur to us to stop for food or anything else. Lainie was sitting in an uncharacteristic slouch, staring dully at the back of Kathy's head like a mental patient testing some new medication while waiting for sanity to dawn on her.

By the time we entered the city limits, visibility was down to just about twice the distance a car headlight would throw, and traffic was slower than a three-legged race at a nursing home picnic.

It was almost four o'clock when we dropped Lainie off at her condo. "Are you going to be all right?" I asked.

Standing outside the open door of the car, she spoke through Kathy's open window, her brown eyes as alert as mud. "I think Robbie's doing it."

"We'll know soon enough," Kathy said.

She nodded and forged her way through the mist to the lighted lobby. One of the security guards gave her a big smile which she didn't return or acknowledge or even seem to notice.

"Thomas, did we have to take her to that place?"

"It was worth it."

"To *us* it was. She took it pretty hard."

"All murderers should be required to return to the scene of their crimes."

"That's a little harsh, isn't it?"

"I keep thinking about her story of having sex with Groth in the motel room and waking up to find him screwing her friend in the other bed. Who would tell that on themselves if it didn't happen? And now she claims it didn't. The more facts we throw at her, the more her story mutates. I'm beginning to wonder if she hasn't been lying all along."

"She's confused, Thomas. But I can see why she left Pedersen out of her original story. She wanted to separate the memories in her mind. She loved him and didn't want to think about that in conjunction with the murders."

Back at the office, Kathy and I listened to the tape cassette Lainie had given us. "You recognize the voice?" Kathy asked.

"To me it sounds like Haldeman."

"It does a little, doesn't it? Wouldn't that be a trip? You could get lucky and put the jerk in jail." We looked at each other and laughed.

As I put the tape in the office safe, Kathy slipped her arms around my waist from behind. "Is this bothering you, Thomas? This case?"

I stepped away, grasped my head, scrunched my face up, and screamed, "Shut up! Shut up! All of you in there shut up! Curtis, Preston, Fred. Shut up, I tell you!"

Kathy laughed. Beulah opened the door, looked at each of us humorlessly, and finally said, "Scream therapy?"

"Kathy was smacking me around with her quirt."

"Thomas!" Kathy said, giving me a playful swat on my rump. "She might believe you."

"I always do," Beulah said, closing the door.

I wanted to drive out to Sternoff's to look at his records again, which he'd indicated would be acceptable, but after all the highways I'd had under me today, I couldn't stand the thought of six more hours on the road.

When I phoned the next morning, Melody answered, said they were both up and Sternoff had instructed her that I was free to copy whatever in his files would be useful. After carrying one of our small office copiers to the Allright Parking garage and loading it into the trunk of my car, I gassed up and drove to the coast, listening to NPR until the signal faded. For the rest of the trip I crooned along to my secret stash of Rick Nelson tapes. Maybe Lainie wasn't going nuts, but I was. It was one thing to read about it in the papers, quite another to visit the crime site with somebody who'd been there, a woman you were fairly certain would never be taken to task for her iniquities.

The site hadn't bothered me. Lainie had bothered me. Yesterday's trip had transposed a gray-on-gray case into bloody Technicolor.

Except for a row of sun-dappled white clouds out over the ocean, it was clear and windy on the coast. When Melody let me in, I stepped over the yellow dog on the rug and handed Sternoff a bottle of cheap wine I'd picked up in Aberdeen. Both Melody and Sternoff were wearing the same clothes I'd seen them in the other day. Sternoff's body occupied the same spot and position on the gargantuan bed. Next to one of his legs the sleeping rat-dogs were curled up around each other like spoons.

"You mind if I set this up in the other room?" I asked, nodding at the copy machine. I had already dropped a hundred dollars in twenties onto his bed.

"Be my guest."

It took more than an hour and a half to duplicate everything I wanted. While Sternoff watched TV in the other room, Melody—having provided him with fresh wine, a basket of chips, and a bowl of mayonnaise—stood over me and watched me work as if she'd been charged to make certain I didn't pilfer any of his papers.

"Just a couple of questions?" I said to Sternoff two hours later on my way out the door.

"Fire away, young man."

"At the time of the trial, when Groth said there had been another person involved? Did you launch a search for that person?"

"Hell, yes."

"And?"

"If there had been a woman, we would have found her."

"At the murder house, did you go up to the attic?"

"Are you kidding me? Even then I was too big for that shit. I don't recall who went up. But they didn't find anything."

"What about evidence that somebody else had been in the house that weekend?"

"We had sixty-six unexplained prints."

"From sixty-six people?"

"Sixty-six unidentified fingers, anyway. No telling when they were made."

"What about Jack Schupp's girlfriend? She was supposed to go up and meet them Sunday. What happened?"

"Her alibi was good. She was studying with some other girls all weekend."

"How tight was the security on that house?"

"Boy, you just want to know everything, don't you?"

"Everything you know."

"You won't know everything I do if you live to be a hundred. Groth didn't need to be no locksmith. He knocked and went in with a knife."

"What kind of locks?"

"I don't recall. But they weren't much."

"Ever hear of neighborhood kids playing in there?"

"We did hear that. Never thought much about it."

"You ever talk to any of those kids?"

"No reason to."

Three hours later at the office, after a sandwich, an apple, and a can of Hires root beer, I sorted the materials into some semblance of chronological order and studied what I had not been able to study with Melody Sternoff hovering over my shoulder. Sternoff had compiled lists of people who had known each of the four victims.

On Tess Hadlock's list, along with classmates, people from her father's company, old high school chums who'd remained in contact, two roommates from the previous year, and six young men who had dated her, I noticed Hadlock's next-door neighbor at Hansee Hall on the University of Washington campus two years before the killings: Priscilla Ann Morton. Of the hundreds of names on the four lists, only this and a man who'd gone on to become a TV actor leaped out at me. Pedersen did not show up, but then, I hadn't expected him to.

When I looked Morton up in the interview sheets, there were

only a couple of notes jotted behind her name, all of which I took to mean she had been contacted, interviewed, and had provided nothing of significance.

Priscilla Ann Morton.

Priscilla Ann was not a popular name and probably hadn't been any more fashionable thirty-some-odd years ago when it had been inked on her birth certificate. I wondered if Priscilla Morton had married a man named Penick.

When I called Penick's office in Lynnwood, a deliberate woman who paused carefully before each statement told me Penick was out of town. It gave me an idea.

"It's a real mess here," I said. "I'm at the home office of Trenton Security Systems. This is the work number for Priscilla Penick, isn't it?"

"Yes, it is."

"The police are out there—they've been out twice already—and they're plenty P.O.'ed because her system keeps tripping, and we can't deactivate it from the main office without verifying her maiden name, but we had computer problems earlier in the week that wiped out some of our files, so we don't have her maiden name. I was hoping Ms. Penick could tell me, so we could get this straightened out."

"Oh, dear."

"Maybe I should send the police over. Would that be better?"

"Oh, don't do that. Let me see. When I first started here, her last name was Scott. But that was a married name. Before that it was Gunnel, I think. Yes. Gunnel. Let me think. Penick was the name of her husband when she got out of law school, so it's been her business name all along. But before Gunnel . . . I know her mother's name is Laura Morton, because she came in here a few times. But she might have remarried. Her mother lives in Mountlake Terrace."

"Are you sure her mother's name is Morton?"

"Oh, yes."

I thanked her and hung up.

The odds of these being two different people were decreasing rapidly. The CD phone records in my computer listed a Richard and Laura Morton in Mountlake Terrace. After I dialed the number, the woman who answered confirmed her daughter was Priscilla Penick.

"Mrs. Morton, I understand your daughter was the attorney for Charles Groth."

"We told her not to get messed up with that."

"Did your daughter also attend the University of Washington and room in Hansee Hall next door to one of the victims?"

"Richard was so upset. I begged Priscilla to go through rush and pledge at my old sorority, but she just wouldn't do it."

"Priscilla knew Tess Hadlock, and she went ahead and became Charles Groth's attorney anyway?"

"What are you getting at?"

"Didn't she know she had a conflict of interest?"

"Priscilla's in Canada on business, but I see her most evenings during the week. Would you like me to give her a message?"

"Thanks. I'll get in touch myself."

CHAPTER 28

Hilda, my primary researcher, had been running background checks, and some of them had come across on my fax machine while I was on the coast.

Kent Wadsworth had flunked out of the University of South Carolina and, though he was only thirty, had already been married and divorced twice. He'd been hauled into court as recently as three weeks ago for failure to pay child support. His résumé included living in a cult in eastern Oregon, analyzing urine samples for a large drug-testing lab, environmental work for a PAC in Washington State, and volunteering for a group dedicated to saving the sea lions at the government locks in Ballard. He rented an apartment in Bellevue, was buying an expensive Japanese sports car on the first year of a six-year contract, and owed $11,000 on his credit cards.

Priscilla Penick carried almost $38,000 on credit card balances. At the time of the murders, she was a student at the University of Washington. After graduating, she attended law school at the U.W. and took third in her class. She'd been married and divorced five times, and, except for the last coupling, which lasted eighteen months, each union had been terminated in less than a year; her first marriage had fizzled after only two weeks.

She leased a Lexus. A previous leased car had been confiscated after she'd run behind on the payments.

Nat Bowers, an only child, had been raised by a single mother in rural Skagit County, not far from Fidalgo Island and Deception Pass, but not so close it was likely Nat would have been in the attic on the day of the murders. When he was twelve, he and his mother moved to Shoreline, where Nat was eventually booted out of high school for possession of drugs. Recently, he'd been attending Seattle Community College.

Leslie Petty's criminal record was already known to me. What I hadn't know was that at eighteen, after the death of the aunt who raised him, Petty had moved from Arkansas to the Northwest with his two older brothers. He'd been an all-state tackle in high school but lacked the grades to take advantage of college scholarships. Both his brothers were dead, one slain at the hands of Tacoma police in a shoot-out in the Hilltop area, the other cut down by hepatitis after an encounter with a dirty needle.

Corliss Dootson grew up in the Puget Sound area and graduated from Ohio State the year before the murders. After a year and a half of postgraduate study at the University of Washington, he joined the Peace Corps. Returning from Africa two years later, Dootson moved to San Jose to work for an architectural firm there, and three years after that was transferred to Seattle. A year later he hired on at Spader and Associates. He had never been married, owned his condominium outright, drove a seven-year-old Audi that was paid for, and owed a combined $180 on the eight credit cards he carried. He had $16,000 in savings and $167,000 in a retirement account at Spader and Associates.

The police probably had hundreds of leads, but, other than his mother and Petty, the only individual I'd linked to Bowers was Dootson, and while he'd cooperated outwardly, I'd had the feeling he was holding something back. It was worth another look.

I left a note on Kathy's desk telling her I probably wouldn't be home for supper, called Bruno Collins, who was "in a meeting" and not available, and decided to launch off alone on foot.

The sidewalks were teeming with pedestrians as I walked to the Rainier Tower on Union. Well aware that there were other exits, I waited in the cold across the street from the east entrance to the tower. Tailing people was usually a waste of time, but when you did it, you never knew what you were going to discover. The downside was that if Dootson got on a bus, I couldn't get on with him, and if he had a car parked downtown somewhere, he'd lose me, for I didn't have a confederate in a car, and the odds of grabbing a random cab off a Seattle street were negligible.

It was after five when Dootson strode out of the building in a long, gray overcoat, a scarf flung around his neck. As big as he was, he walked in an ungainly and slightly disjointed gait, as if he didn't like to walk and did so as infrequently as possible.

Matching him stride for stride, her movements athletic despite rather short legs, was Ione Barocas. She wore a long, plum-colored raincoat.

I kept half a block back, ready to kneel and pretend to tie my shoes if they looked around. At University they went down the hill to Fourth, headed south on Fourth, and a few blocks later walked into McCormick's fish house.

While I waited on a cold street corner, they dined with three men, and an hour and forty minutes later Dootson and the three males left. It was dark, and the fog had dropped her dim skirts onto the city. The four men turned away from me and headed uptown, blurry figures in overcoats.

At the windows in front of McCormick's, Ione Barocas was just slipping into her raincoat when, luxuriating in a blast of warm air laden with the scent of steamed clams, I stepped inside.

"Fancy meeting you here," I said. "Have you eaten?"

"Actually, I have." She looked beyond me at the doorway. "Are you with somebody?"

"No. You?" She shook her head and we looked at each other for a couple of beats. "Hey. Would you like to have a drink?"

"Sure."

We went to the bar and found a small table by the window, fog on one side of the pane, clinking glasses and cheery chitchat on the other. Once, at a critical juncture in our relationship, I'd sat in this same restaurant bar at the same table with Kathy.

I ordered a 7UP, and though I could already smell booze on

her breath, Ione ordered a Scotch on the rocks. This she followed almost immediately with another Scotch. It took me a while to get warm after the long wait outside. We chatted for two hours, during the course of which she continued to sip one hard drink after another. She was catty, which I usually don't mind because I have a proclivity toward cattiness myself. But she so relentlessly berated everyone—coworkers, her sisters, an ex-boyfriend, a man she'd met that evening at dinner—that I was seized with the uneasy feeling that as soon as we parted, she'd be telling tales about me.

I could see that the fact that I was a teetotaler bothered her. Most people weren't impressed one way or the other, but alcoholics were almost always markedly defensive after finding out I was a nondrinker. I was a divining rod for drunks and I knew it.

"Tell me about Corliss Dootson," I said, after she'd imbibed enough that I thought she might answer freely.

"I just had dinner with Corliss and a bunch of his twittering little boyfriends."

"He's gay?" I said, feigning surprise.

"Actually, he's bisexual, but then, when your libido is as suppressed as Corliss's, I don't think it much matters. My experience with bisexuals has always been that they were extraordinarily horny, but not Corliss."

"Gee."

"I came out here years ago to marry him, but when that fell through, we kind of lapsed into this—basically this platonic thing, you know, buddies? I think most people have it figured out by now."

"So Dootson was an item with this guy who got killed, Bowers?"

"I guess that's one way of describing it."

For reasons I'd never been able to figure out, there was a certain type of female who took great delight in hanging out with gay men. Ione Barocas was clearly one of them and assumed no small amount of condescension as she educated me.

"Corliss has always liked younger men. Except when he was young, and then he liked *older* men. When he was in high school, there was a friend of the family, some old Swiss, who took him to Europe. Lately, he's had any number of younger roommates. I don't know why they don't stick around."

"Has he ever fought with any of them?"

"A physical fight? Corliss? Are you kidding? Corliss won't even argue. The worst you could say about him is that he might get bitchy once in a while. Corliss is about the least violent man I've *ever* known. Nat had all the temper tantrums."

"Did you know Nat?"

"I was up at their place a couple of times. He was an ornery kid, always something nasty coming out of his mouth. Not a kind word about anybody. Kind of like me, huh? Say, I've been thinking about this. You didn't meet me here by accident, did you? Somebody in the office told you where we were having dinner. Am I right?"

"I didn't call the office."

"You don't have to be bashful. I know all about bashful. Hell, I was a virgin until I was twenty-four. Corliss and I went together for four years before we did it. Isn't that something? Four years? I thought he was the most incredible gentleman. I sure have made up for lost time." She smirked.

"Did Corliss keep old newspaper clippings?"

"An anal-retentive like him? He didn't keep any newspaper longer than two hours. His place is as neat as a pin."

"So he's never alluded to involvement in a crime?"

"Corliss? You have to be thinking of somebody else."

"Why did he go into the Peace Corps?"

"His mother told him it was the thing to do. It looks great on a résumé."

"What about Bowers? You know anything about *his* past?"

"Bowers?"

"The dead guy."

"Oh, you want to talk about the dead guy? Sure. I'll talk about the dead guy. What was the question? I'm beginning to suspect I've had too much to drink."

"Did Bowers say anything about his past?"

"Just that he had a lot of rough friends. I never met any of them, but that's what he said. Oh, you know what else? He claimed he had some sort of secret from his childhood that was going to make him rich."

"Did he ever hint at what it was?"

"I never paid attention. But he always had some get-rich-quick scheme. He devised a system for picking the numbers on lotto tickets. He had an uncle who sold him a partnership in an abandoned gold mine in Colorado. It was always something."

"Did Corliss get involved in these schemes?"

"Mr. Conservative? Corliss won't even put money into a growth fund."

CHAPTER 29

Friday night Kathy went with a girlfriend to the latest cinematic rendering of a Jane Austen novel while I drove north to Lake Stevens to visit Priscilla Penick at her apartment. It was hard to fathom a connection between her conflict of interest in representing Charlie Groth and our blackmail, but as my grandfather used to say, nobody gets apples without shaking the tree.

It was also hard not to dwell on the $38,000 Penick owed creditors, and at first, given her emaciated physical condition, I wondered if the bills hadn't been run up at some hospital. But Hilda had enumerated Penick's vices for me, and they turned out to be dual weaknesses for clothing and travel. Her clothing was all hand-tailored, and in the past five years she had flown or sailed to Russia, France, Tahiti, the Mediterranean, and only that past summer had spent three months touring Germany.

Lake Stevens, a once rural community northeast of Everett, now dotted with enclaves of new housing, was maybe forty minutes north of Seattle. I got out my Thomas Guide and double-checked the route, taking Highway 2 to East Hewitt, and staying on it when it crossed Highway 9 and became Twentieth Southeast. From a suburban sprawl with housing clusters on either side of the road, it proceeded to become almost a country lane, winding down the hill, woods and brush on either side. In the valley on Machias Road, I stopped to ask directions at a small fire station.

White with blue trim, the complex was perched on a hillside only a mile from the fire station, the driveways steep and sloping. Penick's apartment was halfway up the hill in the second tier, and from her slanted parking area I could see the calm waters of Lake Stevens to the south. I parked next to a silver Lexus.

Her front porch was tucked into a weather-free nook. When I pushed the doorbell, two dogs barked just inside the door, followed shortly by a strained, little-girl voice I recognized as Penick's.

When the door swung wide, a Doberman pinscher stood on either side of her, the animals intent on my every move. Penick wore berry-colored sweats and spotless white aerobic shoes. She looked smaller than she had in her business clothes. She seemed more relaxed and prettier too, more vibrant, her short hair not as compacted against her skull.

"I apologize for barging in on you at home," I said. "On a Friday evening too."

"No, no. That's quite all right. I realize I've been out of town for two days. Come in." She led me into a large room containing a cast-iron fire box with a red enamel door which looked as if it had never been used. The wall-to-wall carpeting was lily-white and so plush I felt guilty dragging my shod feet across it, though I wasn't about to kick my shoes off with those toothy dogs leering at me. The room had white walls, a vaulted ceiling, and two skylights. The furniture consisted of a sofa and an overstuffed chair. There were no tables, no magazines, no television, no stereo, and no personal articles. It might as well have been a demo rental, and she might as well have been a demo renter.

It was a good bet there wasn't any food in the kitchen except celery stalks, dog biscuits, and diet sodas. The rooms were immaculate, and Penick, perhaps just to prove how compulsive she was, walked around in a circle behind me, stooped, picked up a piece of lint, and deposited it into a steel mesh wastebasket next to the sofa. Curling her legs beneath her, she sat in a corner of the couch. At a signal, both dogs lay between us on the carpet. One of them watched me. The other faced a wall.

Still in my bomber jacket, I sat in the chair, peeking into the wastebasket on my way past, my distorted face looking back at me from the shiny steel bottom. It was empty, except for the lint. "I'm following up on this deal where somebody thinks they know the missing witness to Charlie Groth's murder spree," I said.

"First of all, Mr. Black, it wasn't a spree. Second, Charlie probably did not commit those murders. And if you think you know who that missing woman is, you have a duty to step forward."

"I've got more work to do before I hand out names, but I did stumble across an interesting bit of trivia in Melvin Sternoff's notes. Sternoff interviewed a young woman who had at one time lived next door to Tess Hadlock at Hansee Hall on the University of Washington campus. The woman's name was Priscilla Morton. I did some digging and found out she married a man named Penick."

Penick smiled so tightly her cheeks looked like wet knots. "Except for a couple of old dormies who called me at home after the trial, you're the only person to connect that up. How very ingenious of you," she said bitterly.

She sat silently for a few moments before saying, "Why bring it up now?"

"I can't believe nobody caught on. There must have been dozens of people who knew your connection with Hadlock."

"Actually, not that many. I kept a pretty low profile in the dorm. During the trial too."

"Sternoff was at the trial. Didn't he recognize you?"

"I thought he would, but several years had passed. I'd changed my hairstyle and lost some weight. My name was different. Sternoff had spoken to hundreds of people, and besides, for most of the trial I think he was drunk."

Penick leaned forward and calmly petted the head of one of the Doberman pinschers. I had the feeling she was one of those people who kept dogs for protection the way others kept guns. "Why did you represent Groth even though you had known one of his victims?"

Folding her bony hands together, she sat erect and looked at the wall.

"I was obsessed by what happened to Tess. It was five years before anybody had a clue who killed her or why, and for a lot of us, I guess, we were still shocked. I played through every conceivable scenario in my head. And then Groth was caught and began using that horrible public defender from Tacoma, and my husband at the time facetiously said I should go down and volunteer my services so I could make sure Groth got what he deserved. I can't say that's not what I was thinking, but I drove down and made an appointment and talked to Charlie—I just wanted to talk, to see him up close—but while I was there, he hired me. Later on, after he received his sentence, he told me he chose me because he thought I would get him off and then he and I would become an item."

"He thought you were going to become lovers?"

"Yes. Even though he knew I was married at the time."

"You were living up here then?"

"In Lynnwood."

"What sort of description did he give you of the missing woman?"

"Charlie had been drugged up that weekend and was pretty heavy into drugs for almost a year after the murders, so his memory was never that clear. He said she was pretty. That she was small and on the loud side, that she had a foul mouth. Her hair was long and red, but it had been dyed. He said she couldn't get enough of him. All of which he thought was great—until she started killing everybody. He met her on Thursday afternoon, and by Friday night four people were dead. He said there was a second young woman with them before the killings, but his description of her was pretty vague."

"You don't actually think this first woman killed them?"

"I already told you in my office what Charlie said happened. The girl had a gun and did the whole thing herself. I got to know Charlie pretty well, and I just could never visualize him killing anybody."

"Groth's bloody prints were found on the knife that killed Brittan."

"Because Charlie tried to pull it out. But he didn't kill him."

"One victim had been untied. Tess Hadlock. What was Groth's story on that?"

"He said she must have untied herself."

"And the note that somebody sent Hadlock's parents?"

"Bogus. Some creep sent it. Charlie didn't know anything about it."

Her faith in Groth clearly had to do more with empathy than logic. On the other hand, maybe she was bullshitting me and had sabotaged Groth's defense from the beginning. It was obvious that if he'd had another lawyer, he might not be dead now. Her defense, from what little I knew of it, sounded as lame as a runaway turkey. When Groth had been running through his appeals, the simple confession that Penick had known Tess Hadlock would have won him a second trial. If Penick was so convinced of his innocence, why hadn't she stepped forward and confessed? Because she was convinced Groth was actually guilty and had sabotaged his defense? Because self-interest always defeats a noble cause? By not stepping forward, she'd ensured his death.

"We had two different investigators look for the missing woman," Penick said, "but neither of them made any headway. After a few weeks, it became clear it was hopeless."

"If Charlie told you that the girl had a gun, why did he claim in his statements in court that she had a knife?"

"He thought a felony committed with a firearm that resulted in a death was a mandatory death sentence. So he said it was a knife when he made his statement to the police, and then he wouldn't let me bring up the gun in court. He said he'd deny it."

We chatted about the apartment, about Lake Stevens, and about the execution, which Penick had witnessed and which had made her enormously resentful. I'd witnessed a state execution once, and we were on common ground in our dislike for them.

When we ran out of talk, the Dobermans followed lackadaisically as Penick walked me to the door. "Do me a favor," she said. "If it's going to get out, about my conflict of interest, would you warn me?"

"What would you do if you lost your law practice?"

"I guess I'd have to get a real job."

"You don't sound very enthusiastic."

"Who wants to work? If I had my way, all I'd ever do is grow herbs, make pots, and hypnotize people."

"You do those things?" I asked, more to keep her talking than to hear the answer.

"There's no place for a garden here, but I throw pots in the garage. And I have a license to hypnotize. If you smoke, drink, gamble, or snore, I can fix it. Any bad habit. Cussing. Impotence. Overeating. Would you like a session?"

"Not tonight, thanks."

As I backed out and headed down the drive, a red Firebird came up the hill and pulled in front of Penick's apartment. The driver was the same Hispanic man I'd seen walk past her office the day I interviewed her there. He went in without ringing the bell.

CHAPTER 30

Saturday morning, Elizabeth Faulconer met me at the International House of Pancakes across Madison Street from Seattle University. She was forty-five minutes late, which I attributed to rudeness.

Driving an older Chevrolet Suburban, perhaps the largest passenger truck made in America, she bounced around the lot twice before parking crookedly across two stalls catercorner from the window I sat in. The rump end of her Suburban was covered in bumper stickers: MY OTHER CAR IS A SNOWMOBILE; GIRLS KICK ASS; IF YOU DON'T LIKE MY DRIVING CALL 1-800-JERKOFF; NICE GIRLS GO TO HEAVEN, BAD GIRLS GO EVERYWHERE ELSE.

Careening through the restaurant, she bulled past my table and disappeared into the rest room. When she came out, she hurtled past my table again, even though I'd been in the process of getting up to greet her. Finally, from the far end of the aisle, she turned and saw me. She wore no coat, even though the temperature outside was in the mid-forties, and she carried only car keys.

Once again I was impressed with how large and masculine she looked, how reptilian her eyes were behind those huge lenses, how anemic and unwrinkled her skin was.

When she got to the table, she bumped me out of the way,

pushing my empty cocoa cup away with a distasteful wince, as if it had been left by some former diner. It was hard to tell whether she was half blind or just calculatingly ill-mannered.

"Those damn bridges. They make me late for everything."

The radio had said both floating bridges were clear. "Trouble with your teeth?" I said.

She gave me a withering look. "Before that I got tangled up talking to my son in California. It's tough when you have only one child. They expect everything from you. Now what is it you want to discuss?"

I said, "I understand you went out with Melvin Sternoff. Was that before the trial or after?"

"We went out?"

"That's what he said."

"That's what he called it? Going out?"

"That's what he said."

Faulconer paused often when she spoke, as if her listener were hanging on her every word, which, in this instance, I was. She had a way of making whatever she said sound as if it were more important than anything anybody had ever said before.

"I suppose . . . if that's what he wanted to imagine was happening . . . so be it. *I* was gathering information. *He* was dating. Fine. You realize, Mr. Black . . . I know more about Deception Pass than any other living person?"

Again she fixed me with her reptilian stare.

"I know." The waitress came and we ordered. After she left, I said, "Priscilla Penick believes her client was innocent."

"Priscilla was such a little wimp."

"You thought Groth was innocent too, didn't you?"

"In a sense he was. Circumstances killed those people. If Ray Brittan hadn't come back when he did, the crime most certainly would have remained a simple robbery."

"What do you know about a note?"

"A note? You know something about a note? What? What do you know? How do you know there was a note?"

"I'm just asking."

"Oh. I thought you knew something."

"Not much. What about the missing woman?"

"The police found a hundred and eighty-nine different uniden-tified fingerprints in that house, Black. I've talked to witnesses who lived nearby who now claim there were as many as four killers that night."

"Sternoff said the authorities found sixty-six unidentified prints."

"If you want to know the truth, you'll have to buy my book like everybody else."

"I know you were close to Groth, but—"

"You bet your patooties I was close to Charlie. There wasn't anybody closer, not his mother, not his best friend, and certainly not his lawyer. I was *the* closest. But I gathered information from all different sources. I'm *still* gathering information. Did you know about the man who allegedly gave a ride to a young woman on the night of the murders, dropped her off out by the bridge? He fought in World War Two with Jack Kennedy. He knew Jackie."

"Did he identify the girl?"

"I can't tell you any more about that. Like I said before, you'll just have to buy my book. But yesterday I called Mel Ster-noff. He told me you'd been out to see him. Twice."

"That's right."

"You've been busy, Black. You know why I got involved with Charlie in the first place?"

"No."

"I'd lived up there in Skagit County with my first husband, who used to start drinking first thing Monday morning and wouldn't stop until Sunday night. Living with him did things to my ego. I won't even tell you how traumatic it was. But we'd lived up there, and I actually knew where the vacation house was. I was even in it once." She let the import of her words sink in. "We knew the neighbors there, and they knew the Schupp family, the original owners of the cabin. In fact, I ran into the missing woman once, but I can't say any more about that."

"You met the missing woman?"

"I can't say any more. I will tell you I did the story down here in Bellevue about a woman who was murdered in the same apartment complex where Charlie had been living. That case was never solved. I've said too much already."

"Did you tell the police you know who the missing woman is?"

"I didn't realize it until just recently when I was putting this book together. It's too late to do anybody any good. You realize they killed Charlie on June third."

"Do you know where she is now?"

"I'm afraid my lips are sealed."

"And you've linked Groth to an unsolved murder in Bellevue?"

"Did I say that?" She stared like a huge grouper looking out of a tank. "Did you know my editors didn't want to do any feature stories on Charlie? Of course, after I began winning prizes, after we got the governor's award for the series, after all that they sang a different tune."

It occurred to me there were five avenues through which a blackmailer could have gotten information: from Groth himself, from Penick, from Faulconer, from somebody else Groth had blabbed to, or from an unknown person hiding in the attic during the murders. Faulconer, if you could believe her wild boasting, had been closest to Groth.

As our food was served, a young man wearing jeans and a ski jacket approached the table, glowered at Faulconer, and said in a whining voice, "Where's the money?"

"In this family we work for our money," she said coldly.

"How am I going to get a job without a decent car?"

"We're not doing this here," Faulconer said. "We've been through this, and we're not doing it in front of John Q. Public."

"Mom . . ."

"You heard me."

Sulking, he sat next to her in the booth. She moved over just far enough so they weren't touching. I wondered how he'd gotten from California to Seattle in twenty minutes. I wondered why Faulconer felt it necessary to tell so many lies.

Her son had the same waxy-eyed stare as Faulconer. He resembled her too, except that his hair was dark, his brows thick, in stark contrast to her silver-white hair and plucked eyebrows. If he hadn't been so petulant and had so much stubble on his cheeks, he would have been a handsome man. He was in his early twenties, recently released from prison after serving time for a double murder, according to the man at the *Journal American* offices.

As the waitress bustled past, Faulconer caught her attention with a snap of her fingers and said, "He'll have what I'm having."

It wasn't a whole lot of money, but you had to admire her technique. I wondered how many other relatives would stumble in and end up on my tab.

Preoccupied with her own thoughts, Faulconer didn't bother to introduce us, and when I introduced myself, her son rejected eye contact and pretended not to see my outstretched hand. When his meal arrived, he ate the sausages with his fingers and picked over the rest with a fork that he had bent while waiting.

"Jared knew Nat Bowers," Faulconer announced. "They went to middle school together."

"Really? That's a pretty incredible coincidence."

"Life is full of coincidence, Black."

It was full of liars too. Nat Bowers had been blackmailing Lainie Smith with details of the Deception Pass killings. I wondered if Jared and his mother shared knowledge of those details. If they were the blackmailers, Elizabeth Faulconer must have figured out who I was working for and had probably invited her son here to size me up, which was going to be a little difficult since he hadn't yet looked at me.

"You realize the major suspect in the Bowers killing has been released, don't you?" Faulconer said. "Leslie Petty? They let him go."

"How well did you know Bowers?" I asked, addressing Jared, who didn't look up.

When it became clear Jared would continue to ignore my questions, Faulconer said, "When they were younger, every month or so, one or the other would spend the night."

"Did you ever see the house where those people were killed near Deception Pass?" I asked, but it was like talking to a deaf man, his only reply a belch. This time his mother neglected to respond for him.

I paid the cashier and left before they'd finished, and as I passed through the parking lot, I could see them in the window, she wielding knife and fork, he picking at his meal. I drove out the far end of the lot.

CHAPTER 31

I was alone in the office when Lainie Smith phoned half an hour later.

"He wants the money now. He said he would sweep the package for tracking devices and if he finds anything, he's going to leave it where it is and go straight to the papers. Thomas?"

"Where does he want you to put it?"

"In the garbage behind the Promenade Market at Twenty-third and Jackson."

I knew where the market was. I'd been there Tuesday, asking people if they knew Petty. "I hope you stalled for time."

"I said I was all alone, that I'd just gotten up, and I couldn't even carry that much money by myself. He gave me two hours. It's supposed to be in the Dumpster at one o'clock. No tracking devices. No surveillance."

"Is that what you want?"

"I guess."

"Well, unless we're skunked outright, it might get us closer to whoever's doing this."

"I want to go ahead and do it."

"I'll be there in twenty-five minutes to hear the tape and pick up the money."

I arranged for Bruno and some others to meet me in the

parking lot at Washington Middle School about a block from the market. It was Saturday, and the school lot would be empty. I thought about calling in more muscle, maybe a couple of off-duty police officers I'd worked with in the past, but time was short, and I had the feeling this was someone Bruno and I could handle.

Clutching a microcassette tape in her hand, Lainie met me in the lobby of her building and escorted me into the elevator. As soon as the elevator doors closed behind us, she threw her arms around me. It was so sudden and unexpected that at first I thought it was a joke. I patted her back soothingly. She felt like a beach ball that had gone soft in the sun.

"I'm so glad you're here," she said into my chest. "I'm such a mess. I can't believe I'm going to give all this money to a black-mailer."

"It's not too late to change your mind."

Still holding me, she stepped back. "What choice do I have? If I don't pay, my life is over."

We got off on Smith's floor, which appeared to be deserted, and walked to her office, where she put the tape into the machine. It was the same muffled voice we'd heard on the other tapes. When Lainie speculated to her blackmailer that she wasn't sure she should hand over the money, the man spoke quickly and without a trace of panic: "The Parcheesi board? Hadlock wrote her farewell on it. Afterward she wrote *love* eighteen times down one side, twenty down the other."

"That chilled me," Lainie said, pushing the stop button on the machine. "He's seen that board."

"The police have seen it. But I don't think this person is with the police. Originally, nobody knew about it except Groth and you, right?"

"Right."

"It was in Nat Bowers's room. Maybe he saw it there."

"I'm scared."

Carrying a million and a half dollars in three large, military-style duffel bags was like lugging around a couple of weeks' worth of newspapers.

Accompanied by Lainie and one of the building's security

guards, I walked to my car and, one by one, swung the bags into the trunk. It occurred to me that Lainie was putting an extraordinary amount of trust in me, both by handing the money over and by the way she looked at me with her brown eyes and did not look away. When she gave me another hug, the security guard turned away discreetly.

CHAPTER 32

I'd been running around trying to pinpoint Lainie's tormentor, working from past to present and from present to past, confusing myself and everyone around me, when the smart money simply would have engaged a fat surveillance team and waited for the drop.

As it was, I had Hazel, Thelma, and Bruno—not a bad little bunch, but more a squad than a battalion. I'd been lulled by the ease of our original surveillance on Nat Bowers, forgetting Bowers was dead and our new target might be the one who made him dead.

The shopping complex at Twenty-third and Jackson was anchored by a large grocery store called Promenade Market. There was a parking lot on the north side of the market and a narrow ramp that led between two buildings at the southwest corner of the lot to a lower parking lot where the Dumpsters and a bank were located.

I parked a block south on Twenty-fourth so that, through my binoculars, I had a narrow but unobstructed view of the Dumpster enclosure. Thelma was in the lot, a harmless, elderly woman in a Jaguar coupé. Hazel would draw no attention waiting in her car in the upper lot, while Bruno was a block east on

Twenty-fifth South. We were all in radio contact. The odds of a sophisticated operator getting away clean were on his side, but there wasn't much to do about it now.

The sky was darkened by a high cloud cover that the AM radio disc jockeys predicted would produce rain by evening. With the motor off, the inside of the car quickly grew chilly. Though the four of us had been in radio contact, our stint, like all surveillance, quickly became tiresome.

Half an hour late, he walked out of the open corridor through which the bank's main door was accessed, apparently having come down the interior stairs from the upper parking lot where he'd somehow escaped Hazel's keen eye.

As calmly as a man looking for empty soda cans, he strode to the enclosure that hid the Dumpsters and opened the gate. After a few moments I could see him above the wooden enclosure as he walked around on top of the garbage inside the smelliest Dumpster, where, out of spite, I'd thrown the bags.

He lifted the bags one at a time, dropping them onto the cement. Even a block away I could hear the muffled thumps as they landed.

Managing to tie two of the bags at the mouth, he threw them over his good shoulder, one bag suspended in front and one in back, while he lugged the third in the crook of his good arm. With one arm in a sling, it was a tricky balancing act. I had to wonder how far Leslie Petty was planning to walk.

As if it had just that moment occurred to him that somebody might be watching, he glanced around the parking lot until his eyes alighted on Thelma, where they remained for ten seconds. Then he hiked up the ramp that led to the upper parking lot. The pedestrian corridor in front of the bank where he'd come out and the ramp he was now going up were the only paths to the upper lot.

A trill infected Thelma's voice as she gave a textbook description of Petty over the walkie-talkie. She switched on her car motor and tried to follow him up the narrow ramp to the upper lot, but as she neared the ramp's peak, an old white van pulled across the mouth of the ramp in front of her.

Petty had disappeared on foot into the upper lot, and Hazel breathlessly informed us she saw nothing. She hadn't seen him approach the lower lot earlier, and she didn't see him now. It occurred to me that maybe I shouldn't be hiring operatives who were seventy-two years old.

"Bruno, go around the block from the east," I said. "I'll go from the west."

As we drove, Hazel and Thelma continued to communicate between themselves. The van's driver, a large black woman, had climbed out and appeared to be in the process of looking for help. Petty had, I surmised, jumped into a waiting car.

"Hazel," I said. "Write down the license number of every vehicle that leaves the lot."

"I'm doing that right now."

When I found myself trapped behind traffic at a red light at the corner of Twenty-third and Jackson, the future flashed before me. Like D. B. Cooper, Petty would disappear into the mist. We would never recover the loot. Lainie would continue in a state of constant apprehension and would revile me for my incompetence. In six months, a year, five years, Petty would run out of cash and return to blackmail her again.

"He's there!" It was Bruno's voice on the radio.

"Where?"

"Right there."

The light on Jackson turned green, traffic began moving, and as I turned behind a succession of cars, I spotted Petty on foot crossing Jackson toward the new Walgreen's Pharmacy on the north side of the road. I could tell the bags were getting heavy because he was tipping to one side and taking tiny, mincing steps.

In our respective cars, Bruno and I pulled into the drugstore parking lot behind him.

Continuing north, he walked alongside the brick wall of the drugstore toward the Masonic Temple half a block away. Pulling a hat down over my head as a makeshift disguise, I drove quickly past him and swung into the empty temple parking lot, where I parked behind a clump of shrubs as tall as a house trailer. The

Masonic Temple itself was across the parking area. On the west side of the street stood an empty lot infested with brush and blackberry brambles. There weren't any cars parked nearby, so if Petty had confederates, they were well hidden.

I got out of my car just as he came trudging past. "Hey, Leslie."

"You sonofabitch. What are you doing here?"

"Where're you taking those bags?"

Petty thought about it for a moment, then dropped the single bag to the ground and dipped his now-free hand straight down into the waistband of his trousers. As he did this, Bruno pulled up behind him in his Chevy, a distraction that allowed me to lunge forward and grab the gun in Petty's fist before he got it clear of his trousers.

We wrestled wordlessly, his one arm almost equal to my two, until I said, "Go ahead. Pull the trigger. You can wear a dress next time you're in stir."

Handicapped by his bad arm and the fact that he still had two duffel bags full of money slung over his good shoulder, Petty sagged to his knees. I heard his kneecaps hit the sidewalk heavily. Just to make sure he stayed down, Bruno came over and tapped his bad shoulder with the heel of his palm. Petty's gun clattered to the pavement. Petty said, "You shit fuckers."

I hurled the nickel-plated revolver across the street into the vacant lot while Bruno pulled a semiautomatic from his shoulder holster.

"Where you goin' with all that money?" Bruno said.

"What the fuck are you talking about?"

"All that money," said Bruno.

"You want a cut? You two? Is that it?"

"You gonna cut us in?" Bruno said, winking at me. Petty didn't see it; his head was down. The street remained empty.

"I'll cut you in. Sure. You two bastards leave me alone, I'll cut you in."

"How much?" Bruno asked.

"Three hundred each."

"Each?"

"You can't have it all. Three hundred each leaves fourteen hundred for me."

"Your math is funny," said Bruno. "Three hundred thousand for me. Three hundred thousand for Thomas. That leaves nine hundred thousand for you. Not fourteen."

Bewilderment dulling his dark brown eyes, Petty looked up.

"What do you think is in those bags?" I said.

"How should I know? I only just found 'em. I was taking 'em home to look."

"Put the gun down, Bruno," I said. Realizing Bruno had no intention of putting it away, I turned back to Petty. "You and Bowers were doing the extortion together, weren't you? You had a falling out, so you killed him and decided to go big-time."

"Extortion? What the fuck are you talking about?"

If he was feigning surprise, he was an award-winner. I could see Bruno thinking the same thing.

"You weren't working a blackmail with Nat Bowers?"

"I told you. Nat was scared of someone. I went along to protect him."

"What were you doing today?"

"I pick up these bags and I deliver them. I don't know what's in them. I don't want to know what's in them."

"Who are you picking them up for?"

He didn't reply. Bruno had hurt him badly, yet he climbed to his feet and put his chest against Bruno's gun without flinching. After he'd faced the gun barrel long enough and audaciously enough to satisfy himself about his own courage, he turned and stared at me as if everything that had ever gone wrong in his life was my fault.

"What did they tell you was in those bags?" I asked.

"Business papers. They're paying me two thousand bucks to pick up some business papers somebody stole from them. Five hundred down. Another fifteen when I deliver."

"I bet you'd be pissed if you found out you were carrying over a million dollars," Bruno said.

Petty dropped the bags off his shoulder, but he couldn't get them open with his one good hand. Reaching into his trousers pocket, he came out with a switchblade which he flicked open and jammed into the canvas. After a few seconds of sawing, he exposed three heavy plastic sacks of cash inside the first bag.

He looked at us. "What the fuck?"

"My sentiments exactly," Bruno said.

"Somebody paid you two thousand dollars to pick up a million five," I said. "All you had to do was throw these puppies into a cab and head for Tijuana."

Watching Petty's hard brown face, it was easy to believe he hadn't known about the money. It wasn't so easy to believe whoever hired him would have let him get this far on his own.

While I was looking around and thinking about this, Petty took a sudden swipe at Bruno with the knife, nicking Bruno's gun hand. He took a swipe at me too, but I leaped backward out of the way. Then, in one swift motion, he picked up the loose duffel bag and sprinted down the sidewalk past the Masonic Temple.

Bruno, who'd already wrapped a handkerchief around his bleeding hand, was holding the automatic in both mitts now, aiming it at Petty's back.

"Put that gun down," I said.

"Stop! Hey, clown! Stop!"

I hit Bruno's arm from below, sending the bullet into the sky. I held his arm in the air while he emptied his gun, a tiny little smile on his rosebud mouth. The shooting temporarily deafened us both.

"What are you doing, Bruno? We can't shoot people."

"Sure we can."

"We certainly can't shoot anybody in the back."

"I was going to maybe knock the heel off his boot. You know, like Robert Mitchum in *Blood on the Moon*. Make him trip."

"Bruno, are you nuts? You're not that good a shot."

"I could try."

"Try it on a tin can. We're going to have the police down on us any second."

"Ah, nobody pays attention to gunshots around here."

As if to make Bruno into a liar, a police car zoomed down Jackson and slowed in front of Walgreen's, blue lights flashing. I loaded the two remaining duffel bags into the trunk of my car.

Thelma and Hazel helped us canvass the neighborhood, but Petty had either ducked into somebody's yard, sneaked into an apartment house, or had a car waiting around the corner on the other side of the Masonic Temple.

After twenty minutes I dismissed Thelma and Hazel.

The sick feeling in the pit of my stomach didn't get any better five minutes later, when Petty's grandmother, expecting somebody else, hollered for us to come in after we knocked at her front door. We said hello as if we were welcome, and charged through the house looking for Petty. Gramma was eating lunch off a tray in front of the television, and by the time we raced through her small abode, she was too outraged to answer our questions. Who could blame her?

After quizzing three neighbors without result, we stood for some minutes in front of Petty's house like a couple of crows on a wire. It was hard to say what we were doing.

Bruno said, "Fiddlesticks."

"I did this all wrong," I said.

"Circumstances were just running against you. Besides, it could have been worse."

"I don't see how."

"He coulda got *all* the money."

"That's true."

"He coulda cut *you* too." Bruno nursed the wrapping on his hand.

I started laughing. "You're right. I *should* be grateful. I hate knives."

Bruno laughed. "Man, you jumped like a cat. You should have let me shoot him."

"I don't think so."

"I would have nicked him, lightened him up a tad."

I laughed. "Do me a favor. Go back and get that gun I took off Petty. We don't want some kid to find it and shoot his little sister. I'll take the rest of the money back to the client and give her the news. When you get your hand patched up, send me the bill."

"Hey, Thomas. It's not that bad."

"I know. At least I didn't get cut."

We both laughed.

CHAPTER 33

It occurred to me that anybody who was home half an hour after Petty picked up the money most likely was not involved, so I made a few phone calls.

For a while nobody answered Elizabeth Faulconer's phone, but then an elderly woman who sounded austere and rather unpleasant told me her daughter, Betty, had gone to have breakfast with some man, a cop she said, who Betty was going to sell a book to. It was interesting that Faulconer thought of me more as a customer than anything else. Faulconer's son, who, according to the old woman, lived there with his mother and grandmother, had left shortly after his mother and had not returned. As I was about to hang up she blurted that her daughter had just that moment come in.

"Black?" Faulconer said breathlessly. "What do you want now?"

"I wanted to make sure your day was going as well as mine. Is your son with you?"

"Jared went somewhere. And I don't understand why you would give a rat's ass about my day."

There was no polite answer for that.

Nobody answered at Priscilla Penick's apartment or office.

When I phoned Grays Harbor County, Melody Sternoff told

me in a whisper that Sternoff was napping and couldn't be disturbed, not that I thought Sternoff could get out of bed and chase a million dollars around Seattle's Central District.

Corliss Dootson's phone rang unanswered.

The calls didn't tell me diddly. Sternoff was sawing z's. Dootson wasn't home. Penick wasn't answering. Faulconer had just arrived home but lived in Bothell, not twenty minutes from the Promenade Market. Her son was still out.

On a whim, I dialed the pay phone in Nat Bowers's rooming house and asked the young woman who answered if Shanarra Rosenblatt was in. "This is Shanarra. What can I do for you?"

"Shanarra? This is Thomas Black. The man who found Nat's body the other morning?"

"The private investigator?"

"Yeah. When did Nat move in? Do you remember?"

"He lived here last year, but then he was gone all spring. He came back June fourth. I remember because my boyfriend's birthday is the next day."

"Thanks." June fourth, the day after Groth's execution.

If Petty and Bowers had been working together, then none of these other people were involved. If that were the case, Petty had done a royal con job on us, because Bruno and I both believed his surprise upon seeing the cash. But then again, maybe he'd been surprised not because he wasn't expecting it, but because it was the first time he'd seen a million and a half dollars in cash, because he was in awe.

Narrowing the search for Robbie Pedersen by geography was futile because he might be anywhere. If he was listed in the compact disc phone directories for the state of Washington, he wasn't one of the sixty-two entries I reached. Or he was and he lied to me.

As I spoke to these men, it occurred to me that even though Lainie might have found the love of her life, Pedersen might not have given those faraway nights a second thought. She wouldn't have been the first teenager to fall in love with a man who was using her. Perhaps I *had* spoken to him, and he'd guilelessly told me he didn't know what I was talking about because he truly didn't remember it.

Late that afternoon, a fax containing approximately eighteen hundred names arrived from Lainie Smith's office. The cover letter said these were the visitors to her condo and offices during a two-and-a-half-month stretch ballooned around the time she estimated the snapshot on her desk had been stolen. Using the office scanner, I put the names into the computer, then added the names from my own notes, as well as from Melvin Sternoff's notes.

According to Smith's records, neither Bowers nor Petty had visited her condo.

The E. Falconder on Lainie Smith's guest list was buried down around the sixteen hundreds, which might have made it hard to spot once you got name drunk the way I was getting, but it happened to be at the end of a page, where it stood out. There was a J. Falconder too, who might have been Elizabeth's son, Jared. The misspellings, if they were misspellings, could be attributed to someone else writing the names on a guest list.

That evening Kathy and I watched *Persuasion* on the tube— she was on a Jane Austen kick, which I suffered with what I considered to be good humor—and then we went to bed intending to fool around, or so I thought.

Kathy turned to me in bed, propped her head up with one arm, and said, "Don't you feel lousy losing all that money?"

"Geez. Thanks for bringing that up. I thought we were going straight to the monkey business."

"Wasn't Lainie upset when you brought back just the tiniest fraction of the loot?"

"It was a million dollars, not the tiniest—"

"The point is—"

"She was upset, but I don't think it was over the money. She wants to believe that with Bowers dead, Petty is doing this on his own. Her theory makes Petty the probable murderer and consequently somewhat less of a threat, since he'll be running from the law, and if they ever nab him, he'll have almost no credibility. I didn't tell her Bowers grew up in Skagit County and might have been around that house or known somebody who had been. I didn't mention Petty was incarcerated in the same penitentiary as Groth. Those could be coincidence, but they're also long shots. A lot of people grew up in Skagit County. A lot of people donated some of their years to Walla Walla. I didn't even tell her Faulconer had been to her condo. Hey! It just occurred to me. Are these billable minutes?"

"In theory, if we're discussing the case, they are. Wasn't that a pretty dumb way to pick up all that money? To just walk over and carry it away on foot?"

"Petty's no rocket scientist."

"Maybe not, but he got away with five hundred grand and came within a gnat's whisker of getting a lot more."

"A gnat's whisker, huh? Maybe I'm the one who's no rocket scientist."

"I didn't mean it that way. What about this Faulconer/ Falconder deal? You think she visited Smith's office in April? Plus, she claims to know more about the Deception Pass killings than any other living person. Taken together, those facts make her a prime suspect. From what you've told me, she's just the sort who might go snooping around another person's office."

"Yes, she is. She's probably under our bed right now."

"You think we can make it worth her while?"

"If we stop talking and you slip out of those silk pajamas, we can."

"It's a shame Petty got away."

"I can't help thinking Bowers's death is related to some scenario we put into motion. Maybe that first confrontation with Bridget and Petty alerted them. Maybe they got into a dispute over how to proceed. Maybe Petty came along Sunday night, got into a beef with Bowers, sprayed the room with bullets, panicked, and fled without realizing there were no witnesses to call the police. He would have had all night to think about the money. Monday he goes back to see if the cops are there, sees they aren't, goes in, and scarfs up the bills. While he's at it, he lifts the newspaper clippings."

"And forgets the Parcheesi board?"

"Right."

"We should really tell the police about the blackmail. We're walking an ethical tightrope here."

"I'm not even walking it. I'm hanging by my fingertips. I'd

feel worse if the dick handling the case wasn't Arnold Haldeman. Besides, I don't know what you're so bothered about.
You're not the bigmouth who told Lainie her blackmailer's name."

"Now you think Lainie killed Bowers?"

"It wouldn't have been that hard. Walk over. Knock on the
door. Bang bang bang. Lainie had the motive."

"But Lainie isn't blackmailing herself."

"I've been thinking about something else, Kathy. Suppose
there were five people at the cabin that weekend instead of four.
The married couple sleep in one bedroom. The single woman
in the other bedroom. One of the single men on the couch in the
living room. The other person—"

"In the attic," Kathy said. "He could have been up there making up a cot or something when Groth and Lainie came in with
the gun. He would have heard the shouting and seen everything
through the cracks in that plank ceiling."

"And, if he saw Groth with the gun, he might have stayed
put."

"Or if he saw Lainie with the gun."

"If Lainie had the gun, you and I are working for a killer."

"But that was just supposition on my part. Lainie's too nice."

"Or kids were in the attic," I said, "and years later they some-
how figured out who Lainie was. Or *nobody* was in the attic, and
Faulconer—or Penick or whoever—got enough information from
Groth to figure out who Cherokee was."

"Between Faulconer and Penick, which do you think is more
likely?"

"Penick is anorexic and has erased as much of her body and
her personality as she can. She didn't have a personal article in
sight in her office or her apartment, but she's spent big money
on her car, her clothes, and travel. Faulconer, on the other hand,
has all the charm of a bull goring, writes the crime beat, and has
raised a kid who's a killer. Both times I spoke to her, I had the
feeling she would just as soon shoot me as break wind."

"Plus her son knew Bowers."

"She *says* he knew Bowers. She was also, I think, a visitor at
Lainie's condo last spring. But so was the governor. The mayor.

Every Northwest writer and artist I've ever heard of. And about a gazillion other newspaper reporters."

"We need a statistician," Kathy said, "to tell us the odds of one woman having been in the Schupp house at Deception Pass before the murders, having a son who knew Nat Bowers, writing a series of prize-winning articles on Charles Groth, *and* visiting Lainie Smith's condo during the time period Lainie thinks the snapshot was stolen. Somebody should give us the odds of all those things happening without that person being the blackmailer. Let's write this all down. Let's make a list of names and—"

"Tonight?"

"Why not?"

Using one hand, I began unbuttoning Kathy's pajama top. "*This* is why not."

"We can do this anytime."

Reaching into her pajamas, I said, "This? We can do this anytime?"

"No, silly. Make a list of suspects. *This* we have to do right now."

And so we did.

After some time had passed, Kathy said, "I hope whoever's under the bed enjoyed that as much as I did."

"Were those billable minutes?"

"They were, but I won't charge you this time."

CHAPTER 34

Monday morning, after phoning from the office to make sure Dootson was in, I picked an umbrella out of the rack by the door and walked uptown to the Rainier Tower. By the time I arrived at the office of Spader and Associates, my pant cuffs were damp where the umbrella's shadow had failed me.

Corliss Dootson wore dark green slacks, a striped shirt with a rep tie, and a black tweed jacket. He stood in the corner of his cubicle with his arms and legs crossed in a defensive posture. Rain peppered the window behind him. Feathers ruffled by the wind, a gull floated over the street.

"You were gone on the weekend," I said. "I was wondering where you were."

"I had to be out of town suddenly."

"Something happen?"

"Ione and I took the ferry to Port Townsend."

"Friday night?"

"Actually, Saturday afternoon. It was kind of a spur-of-the-moment deal."

Saturday afternoon would have been right after the botched money pickup.

In the building across the street, a man was tilted back in a dentist's chair as three people in masks congregated around his open mouth with mirrors and lights and steel tools. The man kept crossing and uncrossing his ankles.

"Monday a week ago I don't think you were over at Nat's place by accident," I said, speaking a little too loudly. "You went over because you were doing business with Nat."

"Business?" Dootson's voice sank until it was a mere whisper.

"Don't tell me you didn't know about it. Bowers was blackmailing someone."

"He what?"

"If you're going to try to sound surprised, my advice is to practice beforehand. He *what*? He whaaaat? Work on it."

"Nat was a good kid. He was no criminal."

"Why did he move out of your place on June fourth?"

"The fourth? Yeah. I guess it was the first part of June. I told you. I had some emotional problems. He couldn't handle it."

"A guy named Charles Groth was executed on the third of June."

"So?"

"What did Nat know about the Deception Pass murders seventeen years ago?"

"How on earth did that get into the discussion?"

"The extortion Nat was involved in had to do with the Deception Pass murders."

"How on earth . . . ?"

"You really are a piss-poor actor. If you're trying to con me, Petty did a much better job on Saturday. Aren't you curious as to why he never showed up at your rendezvous? Don't you want to know where all that money went?"

"Black, I think you're out of control here. I don't have any idea what you're talking about."

"Nat was blackmailing my client. After he was killed, somebody took over for him. I think that someone was you."

Making quieting motions with both hands, Dootson peered out his cubicle opening at the corridor and looked over the tops of the dividers. He pulled up a stool beside me.

"If you'll please be quiet," he said. "You're going to get me in trouble."

"You know Petty, don't you? Leslie Petty?"

"I know who he is. He was a friend of Nat's."

As uncomfortable as I was with this stabbing-in-the-dark approach, I was willing to plug along until he threw me out, and so far he'd shown no inclination to throw me out. In fact, he was hanging on my every word, which made me more confident than ever about the approach, as well as more suspicious of his involvement. The pictures in his cubicle had interested me when I'd first seen them, and I studied them now. In the baseball team photo Dootson was wearing shin guards. Catchers wore shin guards.

"There are two ways it might have happened," I said. "The first way, your friend, Nat, knew something about the Deception Pass killings. He would have been eight at the time, but he lived in the vicinity, not real close, but up north there, and he might have known kids who'd played in the house. Maybe even kids who'd been in the house the night it happened." I was watching Dootson's face, and he seemed to relax as I went in this direction, so I said, "But now that I've got you in front of me, kids playing in the house doesn't seem nearly as likely as *you* being in the house."

"What are you getting at?" Like a man eating hot peppers, he was starting to sweat.

"Deception Pass. The night of the killings."

"That's ridiculous."

"Ever play baseball, Corliss? There was a man killed up there who played some ball. Jack Leroy Schupp. In fact, he was on the U.W. team. You ever meet him? This wouldn't be you and him on a high school baseball team, would it?" I asked, stepping over to the pictures on his corkboard wall. "Is that you with the knee pads?"

"I played some ball. So what?"

"You took Tess Hadlock's note out of the cabin because it identified you. She said goodbye to Jack's favorite catcher—said she forgave him. If I'm not mistaken, you're on this baseball team here and so is he; you're wearing shin guards. This person over here looks a lot like Jack Leroy Schupp."

"I don't know what the hell you are talking about, Black.

Those four killings? That's ridiculous. I was up at Paradise camping that night."

"Almost twenty years later, and you've got an alibi prepared like a dinner in the freezer. You realize there isn't one person in a thousand who could tell me where he was that weekend? Even the gentleman over there in the dental chair, even on sodium Pentothal, even he wouldn't be able to tell me where he was that weekend. But it was on the tip of your tongue."

Dootson blinked and touched his glasses. He dabbed at his lower lip with his tongue, something he'd been doing a lot of this visit. "I have a very good memory. Besides, at the time it was a big deal on the news. Like the moon walk. You tend to remember those things."

"Do you remember your alibi for the moon walk?"

"I don't know why you're coming to me with this crap."

"Because you knew Bowers, and because you were there the morning after the murder, and because you played baseball long ago. Because in the note one of the victims wrote there was a line that said, 'Tell Jack's favorite catcher all is forgiven.' None of these facts, taken alone, means beans, but poured into one pot, they're enough for me to stand in your office and try to make you nervous." And nervous he was.

"I really don't know what you're talking about."

"Who were you camping with all those years ago?"

"I don't know. Ione perhaps."

"And you've never been to Deception Pass?"

"Of course I've been to Deception Pass. Everybody's been there. Only not that weekend."

"You weren't at that house the night those people were killed?"

Although he shook his head, his face had turned red, as had the scalp under his thin hair. Beads of sweat were standing out on his upper lip. It was hard to believe he hadn't ousted me from the office.

"Let me tell you what I think happened at Deception Pass," I said.

"I don't know anything about—"

"Let me tell you, and then you can deny your involvement in the moon walk and anything else you care to."

He exhaled heavily through his mouth and said, "I don't even know why you're here. This is preposterous."

"Five people went up there to spend the weekend. A married couple, Amy and Raymond Brittan. Jack Schupp, whose family owned the cabin. Tess Hadlock, a friend of Amy Brittan's. And somebody else. An unknown party. A friend of Jack's."

"The papers said there were four people." When I gave him a look, he added, "I told you; I have a good memory."

"Your memory won't tell you who was camping with you?"

"I was camping alone. I remember now."

"When Charles Groth knocked on the door, the fifth person was up in the attic situating his belongings, maybe preparing a cot. Hearing trouble downstairs, that person remained where he was. Maybe he pulled up the fold-up stairs. Maybe the stairs were already up. They've redone it now, but you could see through the cracks in the boards in that old ceiling, through the knotholes down into the main part of the house. Anybody up there would have seen everything."

"I don't know what you're trying to say here. The police investigated. If there'd been somebody else, they would have called the police themselves."

"What I'm really interested in is how you became the worst coward in recent history."

"Black," Dootson whispered, "could you please be quiet?"

"Whoever was up there in that attic must have had a dozen chances to become the spoiler, to go downstairs and put a stop to it, only he hid and he stayed hidden. Which has to be about the most despicable, disgustingly putrid exhibition of cowardice I've ever heard of."

I stared at him for a long time, my cop stare, the one I practiced in the mirror after each run-in with Arnold Haldeman, and after twenty seconds Dootson said, "I didn't do anything to be ashamed of."

"Like hell you didn't."

"I didn't do anything millions of other people wouldn't have done."

"You dirty, stinking coward."

"I didn't *ask* to be there. I didn't *volunteer* to be murdered by some drugged-out cretin."

"You didn't *do* anything to stop it."

Squinting at me, Dootson sat upright on the stool and closed his mouth with a dry, smacking sound. "I'm not going to admit this and end up in jail. Screw you."

For a moment I thought he'd seen the light and was going to stop talking. "They've had the trial," I said. "Hell, they've had the execution. I'm not even trying to solve Nat Bowers's murder. I'm only trying to get my client out of a jam."

"Who is your client?"

"If you were in that attic, you know who my client is."

"I don't know anything about it."

"You had a pretty good memory a few minutes ago. Now you don't remember who was in the cabin?"

"Why don't you leave now?" he said indecisively.

"Listen, Corliss. The police have all sorts of unidentified finger-prints from the house. It won't be hard, once I get them to re-open the case, to match your prints to prints in the house. And they have Hadlock's note, although I don't think they know what it is, because it was found in Bowers's room. At this late date, they'll think you were an accomplice."

"I'm going to talk to a lawyer before I say another word."

"Up until now I haven't told the police about you, but when I do, they'll be on you like a paper hat in the rain."

"I was no coward. Look, supposing that Friday morning somebody ran into an old friend from high school, and when he said he was going camping alone that weekend, this old friend invited him to the cabin instead. Supposing somebody *was* up in the attic and heard yelling and pulled the stairs up. Supposing somebody saw what happened. You could never prove it." He looked at me, his gray eyes as blank as he could make them, though he hadn't erased the raw fear. "What I don't like is you calling me a coward."

"You were in the attic and you didn't come down. You didn't call the police afterward. At least one person was probably still alive. What do you want me to call you?"

"When Groth went up for trial, I might have told the police, but they had a case. They didn't need me."

"Plus, you would have had to admit you were a coward."

"I'm telling you I wasn't," he whispered. "You don't know what it was like. How could you know if you weren't there? I had no options. I got caught somewhere I wish to God I'd never been. I've been trying to live with it ever since. I'm not blackmailing anyone. I'm not a criminal, for God's sake. Or a coward."

"You know who my client is. Otherwise Nat wouldn't have known who to call."

"I never told Nat who the girl was. I didn't know. I still don't."

"Didn't you have a picture of her?"

"You think I was up there taking snapshots? All I know is it was a girl, a young woman, dressed in jeans and a tank top. She was real quiet once things got moving. Hardly said a word."

"How did Nat find out you were at Deception Pass?"

"It was last spring, right around the time of the execution, when all the newspapers and the television people were raking it up again. I got upset, like I always do when it hits the news. Couldn't sleep. Couldn't eat. Had the shits. Nat picked up on it. He went poking around in my apartment and found my files. Since he'd already put two and two together, I told him the rest. That's why we broke up, really. Nat wasn't a natural hand-holder, and he couldn't take my self-pity. My self-loathing, really. When he left, he stole the files. I certainly don't know anything about blackmail, which is illegal. And I have no idea who killed Nat. Heaven forbid."

"You don't know who Nat was blackmailing, who the young woman with Groth was?"

"I said I didn't. I don't know what sort of view you imagine I had from the attic, but it wasn't much. I saw a man with a gun. I wouldn't have been able to identify him or the girl if they'd put them in a lineup, which was part of the reason I never went to the police."

"How could Nat know who this person was and you don't?"

"I don't know."

"What did you see when you climbed down?"

"What do you think?"

Pulling another stool close to Dootson's, I sat, and eye-to-eye, we thought about the situation for a while. Dootson remained jumpy. I could understand how Groth's execution would upset Dootson enough so that somebody living with him would notice. He was a nervous-breakdown type of guy, the kind of man, as I had observed the first time I met him, who borrowed most of his opinions from others more sure of themselves.

"What else happened that night?"

Dootson's thick eyeglasses and tufted eyebrows no longer looked menacing. He was inches taller than me, and as if to advertise the fact, he stood now, but his posture only made him oddly childlike. "What night? What house? I don't know what you're talking about."

"You're going to deny it now?"

"Deny what?"

"Corliss, you're a coward *and* a liar."

"If somebody is being blackmailed, they must have been part of it. If they were part of it, they deserve what they get. And if somebody is blackmailing them, it seems to me there isn't a damn thing you or anybody else can do about it."

"You're beginning to sound involved."

"I made a mistake long ago, Black. I made another one talking to you about it. But I'm not a criminal. I wouldn't even know how to go about it. Now, please leave."

When I stepped into the corridor, Dootson followed and spoke even more softly than ever. "Black?"

"Yeah?"

"You mention a word of this to a soul, I'll deny it. Then I'll sue."

"Ditto."

It was a depressing walk back to the office. I'd caught Dootson in a fortuitous—for me—window of anxiety and had extracted more information than I had any reason or right to expect, something that happened from time to time with reluctant witnesses; but he'd turned resolute, determined not to talk any further, and it wasn't likely I'd catch him off guard twice.

Now that I thought about it, he seemed a little too squeamish to commit a deliberate felony such as blackmail, too high-strung for any crime except the one he'd committed at Deception Pass, the crime of omission.

It was easy enough to imagine him caught up in the tragedy, unwilling to shout downstairs, unable to move or even think, but it was harder to envision him raking it all up in a blackmail plot that could very well draw attention to the original crime and his part in it.

Watching the scene under him as the three victims were gagged and lashed to chairs, Dootson must have been close to heart failure. Then it only got worse when Brittan returned from the store and the fight erupted, when Groth (or Lainie) sank the knife into Brittan's chest, when the others were murdered. How long had Dootson huddled in the attic after the house had gone quiet? How many minutes, or hours, passed before he mustered the sand to go down and see if there were survivors?

Once he regained his wits, he must have cleaned up his belongings, stepped over the pooled blood, climbed into his own car, and put the nightmare as far behind him as he could, which in his case meant joining the Peace Corps a few months later.

Had Tess Hadlock been alive when Dootson came downstairs? Had they spoken? Had she begged for help? It was hard to guess at the catalogue of Dootson's transgressions.

He had to be the one who removed the Parcheesi board with Hadlock's letter on it. He stole it because the obscure sentence about Jack's favorite catcher referred to him.

I found myself detesting Dootson and his cowardice with a passion that made my uneasiness around Lainie Smith pale by comparison.

So intent was I on despising him that I walked bare-headed for a block in the rain, mushrooming my umbrella up only after a woman on the street smiled at me and said, "If you don't want that, I'll take it."

It was curious that she'd smiled and spoken to me, because I must have looked like a madman walking along muttering to myself, my hair matted in the rain, my eyes darkened by hatred.

CHAPTER 35

Back at the office I filled Kathy in, and after fencing with
Kent Wadsworth on the phone, I reached Lainie, who agreed to
meet Kathy and me at the office in an hour.

I got Bruno's pager, and he called back two minutes later.
"Black, my man. We won't be nabbing rough-tough Leslie just
yet, but I found out where he went. He has an old girlfriend
right around the corner on Washington from where you wouldn't
let me wing him. This old gal must be at least sixty-five. She said
they been seeing each other off and on since he was a kid. I told
you he wasn't gay."

"I'm pretty sure he is, Bruno."

"I got proof. I seen her. Petty went in there and hid out until
we were gone. And he's already spending that money, because
when the old gal wasn't in the room, her grandkid told me
rough-tough Leslie gave them a thousand dollars just to borrow
the family car. I'm on my way over there now to tie up some
loose ends."

Arnold Haldeman, the homicide detective, called back ten
minutes after I left a message. "Black? What do *you* want?"

"I was curious if anything had sprung loose on the Bowers
murder."

"Now, why would you want to know something like that?"

"Like I said, curious."

"Black, I shouldn't be telling you this shit, but Bowers had a woman visitor Sunday night. You got any idea who that might have been?"

"A woman?"

"That's what I said. She might have been the last person to see the kid alive."

"You might ask around and see if it was Elizabeth Faulconer, your reporter friend from the *Journal American*."

"The behemoth who's writing about this?"

"I thought she was your friend."

"I hardly know the woman. But she wouldn't have been there Sunday night, Black. The body wasn't found until Monday. What? You think she's involved?"

"Did she tell you she knew him? Did she tell you her son, a double murderer out on parole, also knew him?"

"Black, if this is a line of bullshit, you'll be sorrier than a tax man at the pearly gates. Where did you get this?"

"I had breakfast with Faulconer Saturday morning."

"Okay. But this better not be bogus."

A half-hour later I was calling R. Pedersens and waiting for return calls from people who might work in the next pickup team when Kathy buzzed and said Lainie had arrived.

Lainie was standing by the window in Kathy's office looking somewhat less somber than she was on Saturday, when I'd told her we'd lost half a million dollars of her money. Her eyes were puffy, her black bangs as even and precise as if she'd painted them on.

Kathy was leaning against the corner of her desk. I walked over beside her, and we remained in those positions throughout the discussion, all of us more or less on our feet.

Without naming him, I told Lainie I'd found the individual who'd been in the attic at Deception Pass seventeen years earlier. The news made her legs wobbly, and one hand, when she brought it up to her face, quivered. I got ready to lunge forward and catch her before she could pass out and crack the window with her head, but, as wobbly as she was, she remained on her feet.

"You mean there actually *was* somebody else in the cabin?"

"He admitted it."

Lainie blinked hard several times as if batting away incipient tears. "Somebody else knows everything?"

I nodded.

"He's my blackmailer?"

"Nobody's going to confess to an ongoing extortion. Whoever it is, I think they'll try again, and if you're game, I want to be prepared this time."

"I just . . . Who is it?"

"It isn't anyone you know. There is one remaining problem, but you've faced it all along."

"Which is?"

"In order to stop them, you'll have to come clean with the police and a prosecutor."

"That's to stop them legally. What about if we stop them *illegally*?"

"For the sake of argument, let's say this team is a woman and her son. Let's say we give them a million dollars and we catch them red-handed with the cash. What do you advise at that point? I'm not a killer, and I hope you aren't either. If we take the cops with us, the cops can arrest them for extortion, but then of course, they'll rat you out. If we don't have the cops with us and we catch them red-handed, they'll tell us to get lost, and we won't be able to do a thing about it. You can confront all this head-on, or you can fly to Brazil."

"Or I can keep paying."

"We talked about this in our first meeting. Unfortunately, nothing has changed. I thought it might, but it hasn't."

"You want me to get the police involved? Is that what you want?"

"I would have to advise against that," Kathy said. "There's a high probability you'd do time. Maybe a lot of time."

"Like a life sentence?" Lainie asked.

"There's the possibility of a death penalty."

"But I didn't hurt anybody."

"You were an accessory, which is the same as if you did. That's how the law sees it."

I said, "The man from the attic claims he doesn't know who you are. He claims he didn't get a good enough look at either Groth or Groth's companion to ID them."

"Obviously he does know who I am. I can't decide what to do."

"You don't have to make up your mind now. But you need to think about it. Knowing who they are might be a bargaining chip in itself," I said.

"I thought it was this person you say was in the cabin at Deception Pass."

"I don't know who's doing the blackmail. Not for sure. But now's the time to think it through, what you're going to do. Before the next call."

"Was it a child? Ever since we took that trip, I've been haunted by the possibility a child saw those killings."

"It was not a child."

"Then why didn't they come down and help? Why didn't they do something?"

"Maybe for the same reason you didn't do anything," I said.

Lainie began crying. Kathy gave me a look that said I was a bully.

"It's hard to know what anybody else is thinking," Kathy said gently.

Lainie cried for a while at the window, and then, without saying anything more, she left.

I said, "She didn't take that so badly."

"You really had to let her have it, didn't you?"

"You know what else? She's going to keep paying. She doesn't have the guts to do anything else."

"I'm not sure it's a question of guts," Kathy said. "What else can she do?"

"You know, Bowers mentioned that plastic gun during one of his phone calls, didn't he? Bowers had to have gotten his information from Dootson, so Dootson knew it was a plastic gun. And since he didn't leave with Groth and Lainie and see it break on the street, he knew it while they were in the cabin."

"How could he have known? He said he could barely see anything. That he couldn't identify anybody."

"He was lying. The way that ceiling was constructed, he

would have seen it all. I'm guessing he'd seen that particular model of toy gun before and recognized it."

"Lainie at least thought he had a real gun."

I kissed her brow and walked to the door. "I've got work to do. Besides, with Harold and Curtis and Preston and the rest of the guys, you have enough crosses to bear."

"Don't I ever."

Monday after dinner I put on sweats, snapped a leash on L.C.'s collar, and jogged down to the school dribbling a basketball. We played for two and a half hours: eleven Asians, a five-foot-six-inch high school kid who could dunk the ball, and me. We had more fun than a bunch of dogs in a flower bed.

Two and a half hours later L.C. and I returned home to find Kathy in bed reading. After racing around the living room like an escaped hyena at the zoo, L.C. made a beeline for the bedroom and slobbered all over Kathy's hand before I caught him and dragged him outside, his splayed feet skidding on the floor. Making two or three trips to our one, he'd dashed up and down on the sidelines during our basketball game and would sleep the night as if drugged, snorting and whining in his sleep, both of which were better done on the porch.

When I got out of the shower, Kathy said, "I spoke to Lainie."

"You did?"

"She got another call. She's to take a million in unmarked hundreds to the Bellevue Square mall at six-thirty tomorrow evening. They don't want any middlemen this time."

"What'd she tell them?"

"She said she'd do it."

"How did she sound?"

"For the first time she sounded perfectly calm."

CHAPTER 36

A million dollars in hundred-dollar bills worked out to be a hundred packets of one-hundred-dollar bills, a hundred bills in each packet. Lainie didn't have a whole lot of trouble carrying the package.

She'd been instructed to take the money to the second level of the main mall corridor and sit on a bench just outside the Mrs. Field's Cookies store.

At six-thirty she was on the bench, her plump legs crossed, her brown eyes quiet, almost serene.

Bellevue Square was a busy shopping mall in the heart of downtown Bellevue just across Lake Washington from Seattle. It had three levels with multiple wings and multilevel parking garages on all sides. There were exits in all directions, and because the mall was on the corner of two of Bellevue's busiest thoroughfares, it would be easy for somebody to slip out of our grasp.

Not counting the three uniformed police officers hanging out in the JC Penney store at the south end of the mall, we had seven women operatives and six men inside. Bridget Simes sat on the other end of Lainie's bench sipping from a large cup of Diet Coke, reading a Scientology periodical and wearing a bright fluorescent-green beret that called so much attention to itself her cat wouldn't have recognized her.

As a precaution, I'd obtained, copied, and passed out photos of Petty, Priscilla Penick, Elizabeth Faulconer, Jared Faulconer, and Corliss Dootson; all of them driver's license photos except the younger Faulconer—his a booking photo. Jared, as it happened, had been out of prison for almost a year after serving six and a half years for killing two homeless men by getting them drunk and laying them across the railroad tracks in the train yards in south Seattle.

At 6:37, peering over the railing at pedestrians thirty feet below, our man approached along the upper level. Twenty yards shy of Lainie's bench, he leaned against the railing, and glancing around calmly to see who else might be in the vicinity, he watched Lainie for five minutes. At 6:42 he made his approach.

Stopping in front of Lainie, he gazed down at her and, as she later related, said, "Is it all there?"

"Are you the one who's blackmailing me?" Lainie said.

"Just tell me if it's all there."

"Is all what there?"

"The money."

"How much again?"

"You know how much."

"Not if you don't say it, I don't."

"One million."

"It's all here."

At that point Dootson picked up the duffel bag, pulled on the drawstring and stuck an arm inside. Lainie said, "Why are you blackmailing me?"

Apparently feeling an obligation to answer, an odd trait in one who didn't feel obligated to let her keep either her money or her sanity, Dootson said, "For the money, of course."

Dootson swung the canvas duffel bag over his left shoulder and began walking north on the concourse toward Nordstrom. After he'd gone twenty-five yards, Bridget got up and followed. Standing just inside the entrance of the nearby jewelry store where I'd posted myself, I motioned Lainie over.

"Are you all right?" I asked.

"Yes. Who was that?"

"Corliss Dootson."

"The man in the attic?"

"Yes."

"He just walked away like it was laundry."

"I know."

I followed Bridget Simes, who followed Dootson, and by the time I caught them, Dootson had stopped inside Nordstrom, down one floor, pretending to shop for perfume in front of the cosmetics counter where one of the clerks was applying foundation to a woman's face. It was my guess Dootson was waiting around to make certain he wasn't being tailed, a prospect he undoubtedly deemed unlikely.

Although I could see three of our operatives within shouting distance, and I was only twenty-five feet away myself, Dootson appeared to be satisfied that he was safe. He was only a little nervous, which I found odd for Dootson.

He wore tan slacks, running shoes, and a windbreaker that was still damp from the storm outside. I wasn't familiar enough with the mall to know which parking garages had sheltered entrances and which didn't, but there was one outside Nordstrom that would have given the weather a crack at him.

"Mr. Dootson, my friend," I said a little too loudly. I'd learned the other day that speaking loudly unnerved him.

Up close, he was all nerves. Behind thick glasses, his pupils had shrunk to pinpoints and his fuzzy eyebrows arched like caterpillars crossing a hot road.

"I thought you might be somewhere," he said.

"Everybody's somewhere."

His voice was calm, even if the rest of him wasn't. As we spoke, I stepped close and patted him down for weapons. He smiled halfheartedly. Between his smile, his cologne, and his breath mints, I felt like giving him a big kiss.

"What do you think you're doing?" he said, trying to sound jovial. "Going to arrest me?"

"That's exactly what I'm doing," I said. "You're under arrest for extortion."

Dootson's smile wavered. His gray eyes narrowed. "You can't arrest me. You're not a cop."

"It's done, buddy." I nodded to Bridget, who took a portable radio out of her coat pocket and called the police at the other end of the mall.

Dootson calmly dropped the money on the floor, turned, and began walking away through the narrow aisles of the cosmetics department. As I followed, I cocked my head at Bridget and wondered whether she was carrying her pepper spray.

When Dootson got to the corner of the glass counter, a slender, well-groomed brunette salesclerk of indeterminate age asked if she could help him. As he was sidestepping her, I caught him and grabbed his right hand.

I tried to put a thumb grip on him, but he folded his hand into a fist before I could lock it up, pivoted on his heel, and attempted to walk right through me. I pushed him. He pushed me. The two of us became engaged in a strangely passive-aggressive dance of barely suppressed hostility.

The saleswoman said, "Please. No roughhousing inside the store."

"Out of my way," Dootson said.

I stepped aside, and then, as he tried to walk past, pulled on his shoulder with both hands and put my foot out. He crashed to the floor, landing on a knee and then a hip and a shoulder. On the other side of a display I could see Bridget confiscating the canvas duffel bag.

Dootson rose to his hands and knees and tried to crawl forward, shoving my thighs with his head and shoulders while I tried to push his head down the way you would an overly friendly dog attempting to sniff your crotch. He pinned me up against a cylindrical glass display stand with perfume bottles arranged on four levels, and suddenly it was raining bottles, broken glass and perfume everywhere. We were going to smell like a couple of kindergartners at a vanity table.

Tired of playing at it, he tackled me hard around my thighs. We struggled that way for a few seconds, me standing, him on his knees. Exchanging horrified looks, the cosmetics women abandoned their posts and fled to the perimeter of the store. A good little crowd was beginning to gather in the aisles.

I cupped my hands and slammed them against either side of Dootson's head. If done properly, the move would rupture an eardrum. He sobbed and sat back just far enough away for me to put a knee into his face. It didn't knock him down, but it broke his nose and caused his face to blossom into a splash of red.

When the Bellevue police officers arrived, two cosmetics saleswomen quickly explained that I had assaulted Dootson for no reason. When I attempted to give my version of the story, a loud dialogue ensued.

"This him?" one of the cops asked, looking at Bridget. Dootson was still on the floor, bloodied, puddles of perfume soaking into the knees of his trousers.

"Yes."

"You didn't have to do that," Dootson said, glaring at me, eyes watery, blood dripping off his lips.

Lainie Smith, who had worked her way to the front of the crowd, looked down at the bleeding man with undisguised contempt. She looked at me. "So he's the one?"

"Yep."

When the cops cuffed Corliss Dootson's hands behind his back and hoisted him to his feet, the saleswomen were outraged. "*He's* the one who started it," the brunette said, walking over and stabbing her long-nailed index finger against my chest. "This one here."

Both counterwomen stared malevolently at me. The police patted Dootson down for weapons while Corliss glowered at Lainie and said, "You can't make this stick without getting found out. I know you don't want that."

"Try me," Lainie said.

Dootson inhaled wetly, blood choking his words, and said, "Your life is going to be ruined. You tied up those people. You stood by and watched."

One of the police officers was about to take Dootson by the arm and walk him away, but Bridget, who'd done the liaison work with Bellevue, shook her head and he stopped. Lainie said, "And what did *you* do to stop it? If you were close enough to see it, you were close enough to put a halt to it. You can't have it both ways. If you know about me, you were there. And if you were there, you failed too."

"He had a gun. And I had a bad back," Dootson said.

"And afterward you left without telling anyone. My lawyer tells me that could be construed as accessory after the fact."

"You're the accessory."

"Those poor people must have thought you were going to come down any second and rescue them."

"I don't know what you're talking about."

"You were a . . ." She looked him up and down. "A two-hundred-pound man in his prime. You could have come down out of that attic and saved four lives."

"He had a gun," Dootson said calmly. "There was nothing I could do."

"You could have called the police afterward," Lainie admonished. "You might have saved Hadlock's life. They say Tess Hadlock lived for half an hour."

"She was gone when I got down."

"How do you know? Are you a doctor?"

"He had a gun," Dootson said.

"That's not what your friend Bowers told us." I stepped in front of Dootson and moved forward until I was inches from his face. "Bowers told us the gun was plastic. Now if he'd met Groth somewhere and Groth told him the gun was plastic, that would be one thing. But Bowers never met Groth. *You* told Bowers about the toy gun. Lainie knew he had a gun, but she didn't find out it was a toy until later, so except for the minutes during the struggle in the kitchen, she actually thought she was being held captive by a man with a gun. You believed no such thing. You saw a man and a girl downstairs, and the man was waving what you recognized as a play pistol, and you did nothing."

"I didn't *ask* to be there," Dootson said. "I was set to go camping. I only went with them on the spur of the moment. I didn't even know any of them except Jack."

"You let all that happen, you let those people die, and then you have the brass balls to come after me," Lainie said softly. "I thought I was a gutless wonder, but I could never hold a candle to you."

Dootson looked around, made eye contact with one of the cosmetics ladies and said, "You saw this. You're my witness."

CHAPTER 37

Kathy had come along in the event Lainie needed help, professionally or otherwise, and as she worked her way to the front of the small gathering of shoppers and Nordstrom clerks, she caught my eye and said in a low husky voice, "Did he kill Nat Bowers?"

I looked at Lainie, free of her demons at last, ingenuous, no doubt headed for prison, and happier, more delighted and more content, than I'd ever seen her. Until moments earlier I'd harbored suspicions that Lainie had killed Nat Bowers, but I didn't think so any longer.

"He had enough reason," Kathy said. "He wanted all those materials about Deception Pass back. And Bowers was mucking up his life by blackmailing Lainie. He went to Bowers's apartment and Bowers wouldn't give him back the stuff, so he shot him. Right?"

"I don't think he killed Bowers."

"Why not?"

"Whoever killed Bowers removed all the documentation about Deception Pass. But there was that photo on the floor of Lainie and Robbie Pedersen . . ."

"He probably dropped it when he was leaving."

"Maybe so, but nobody dropped the Parcheesi board. It was on the desk when I went up there the first time, right under the newspaper clippings and the money, and I didn't pay any attention to it. I didn't know what it was. Dootson wouldn't have left it. He would have recognized it in a heartbeat. It would have been the first thing he took."

"So if he didn't kill Bowers, who did? Petty? He took the materials and then came back the next morning for the money?"

"I don't think so. He would have taken everything the night of the killing. Besides, whoever killed Bowers covered him up afterward. That's the sort of thing Petty never would have thought of. It was somebody showing some concern for the victim's nakedness. A former lover, maybe—or a woman."

The police agreed to keep Dootson in the store while I got on the radio and learned that our confederates outside had already identified Dootson's Audi, which was cruising outside the mall with a woman at the wheel.

By the time Bridget and I got out to the narrow lane that ran along the east side of Nordstrom, Bruno's Chevy had boxed in the Audi. A second sedan was snugged up against the rear bumper.

Rain pelted me as I walked in the dark to the driver's side of the car and knuckled the window, my wedding band clicking against the glass.

Lowering the window a notch, Ione Barocas looked up at me through the horizontal opening, her eyes large and dark and lined with black eyeliner and enough mascara that it looked like spackle. Her dark hair was shoulder-length and loose and big against her shoulders. Rain began to trickle off her beige raincoat like drops of mercury.

"What's going on?" she said.

"The jig's up, Ione. We caught Corliss inside. He's under arrest."

"What on earth are you talking about? He told me to wait. We were going to a movie."

"You went over to Nat Bowers's place that Sunday night, didn't you, Ione?"

"What are you talking about?"

"Bowers had a female visitor the night he was killed. You went to retrieve those newspaper clippings. Bowers swiped them from Corliss. Nat was using information supplied by Corliss to blackmail my client. Corliss was too timid to confront him, but you weren't too timid, were you, Ione? You see what you want and you go get it. You wanted to blackmail Smith yourself. After all, Nat was only taking in two grand a week. You would do it right and take millions. You and Nat struggled. He probably didn't know you had a gun until you took it out and popped him."

"This is a waste of time," Barocas said firmly. "I want you to tell those people to move their cars so I can leave."

"You're under arrest, sister."

"Like bloody hell I am."

I reached inside to pull the keys from the ignition, but before I could get them, she put the car into gear and rammed the side panels of Bruno's Chevy. The air bag in the steering column of the Audi deployed, and as it inflated, it smacked Ione in the face with such force that her head bounced back against the headrest. A filigree of blood filled in the outlines of her long, white teeth. A dry, white powder from the air bag adhered to my jacket sleeve after I shut the ignition off. Bridget opened the door and dragged Ione out of the car, put her through the routine, and cuffed her hands behind her back. Ione's complexion took on a sallow look under the fluorescent streetlights. She was furious.

"How dare you! Any of you! Any connection between me and what you think Corliss has done is in your head."

There was no point in making this easy, so we deliberately left her out in the rain in the headlights. Ione Barocas, to my way of thinking, did not sufficiently understand ignominy.

Speaking into the walkie-talkie, I said, "This is Black. Is Dootson still there?"

"Affirmative. Right here," said one of the cops over the walkie-talkie Bridget had left them.

"We've got Barocas out here. She's saying Corliss Dootson killed Nat Bowers. She's willing to testify to that in court."

Dootson's garbled hollering came over the airwaves indistinctly, so it took some seconds to figure out what he'd said. "She knows damn well I didn't kill Nat. *She* did. She told me she did. She's not going to pin that on me. I even know where she hid the gun. It's in her safety deposit box."

"I don't think Corliss is playing on your team," I said to Barocas.

"That was cheap. It won't hold up in court."

"It will when they find the gun where he says it is and start looking at you harder."

On the radio I said, "Ione says she doesn't know anything about blackmail. She says if there was any blackmail, it was Dootson's doing."

More yelling over the airwaves.

Barocas eyed me coldly and said, "You ass."

"Yes, ma'am."

Later that evening as Kathy and I debriefed Lainie, she was all pink cheeks and smiles. It seemed illogical, but her newfound equanimity disturbed me. There had been something natural and deserved about her melancholy, something just and true and right, and now that it had lifted, I was depressed in the same way I would have been depressed if an old enemy had won the lotto.

"I don't know what's going to happen," she said. "But you can't believe how good I feel. Like I'm ready for anything. It's out there now. If they want to charge me, it's out there."

A week earlier, Kathy had heard two college students on the Ave talking about their classes. One of them was taking ethics and the other asked what that was about. "Well, you know. It's when you do something wrong, they teach you how to feel about it." Somehow, that student had missed the point, just as Lainie seemed to have missed the point. Perhaps she wasn't under pressure any longer, and perhaps her worries had been whittled down, but she'd been involved in one of the most vicious crimes ever to depress the Northwest psyche and she had no right to smile.

It was a puerile and unrealistic notion of justice and damnation, but it was my notion and I couldn't shake it.

CHAPTER 38

Two months later the Skagit County prosecutors interviewed Lainie Smith, and then, planning to use Dootson as an eyewitness, charged Lainie with second-degree murder. Following the advice of her new attorneys—Kathy had bowed out—Lainie pleaded not guilty.

Oddly enough, Corliss Dootson was granted immunity, though he admitted failing to report a crime and leaving the scene, and, in all probability, had been responsible for Tess Hadlock's not receiving medical attention in time to save her life. He might have been charged with a lot of crimes, but the prosecutors needed him, so they cut a deal.

Kathy informed me that the extortion, which he had not been granted immunity on, would net him about three years in the cooler. Somehow, it didn't seem enough.

Despite protests that she'd never been there, Ione Barocas's fingerprints were found in Bowers's room, hairs from her head were found on his floor, and fibers from one of her overcoats matched material found under Bowers's fingernails. If that wasn't enough, the police located witnesses who put her in the neighborhood the night of Bowers's death, along with another witness who'd seen her later that same night crying in her car. She was convicted of murder and sentenced to seven-to-ten.

As Barocas was being routed out of the King County court-room the afternoon of her sentencing, a short woman dressed in men's clothing approached her, spit on her, and said she would kill her when she got out of prison: Bowers's mother. The sentencing hadn't seemed to bother Ione, but the threat scared her enough that she was pale and perspiring when I last saw her.

During her pretrial incarceration, Lainie Smith lost thirty pounds. It was widely stated that the judge in the case thought he was three steps closer to God than the rest of us, and perhaps because of this, he made a number of significant and, Kathy said, unfair rulings against the prosecution, tipping the scales decidedly in favor of the defense. I was in the courtroom the day Lainie got on the stand.

She shot me a nervous glance just before she told of going to the house with Charles Groth and seeing three people inside dancing to a Three Dog Night tune. In two hours of testimony it was the only time she looked at anybody in the courtroom except her own lawyers. Predictably, the story she'd told Kathy and me was amended for the courtroom.

"After the car broke down, Groth told me he knew people in the neighborhood who might help us, but then when the door opened and it looked as if the people in the house were not going to help, he pulled a gun and ordered everyone, including me, inside. I was terrified. I didn't even know he had a gun, and I had no idea he was going to commit a robbery."

Her breathing was controlled, her eyes calm as she went on to say she was sure Groth had spared her only because he didn't want to leave her body in the house where it might be linked to him, that it had been obvious he was planning to kill her later, and that she'd spent the remainder of the night, hours and hours, fleeing. Listening to her lies in the courtroom, I couldn't help wondering how deep her complicity actually went.

Despite a long cross-examination from the prosecution, a cross that was quite a bit less than stellar, and a far cry from what anybody would call withering, Lainie stuck to her story and even embroidered it.

The jury was out twelve hours and eventually brought in a verdict of not guilty. While a flood of friends and onlookers congratulated Lainie, I left the courtroom and drove back to King County in what could only be described as a major funk. It wasn't so much that I'd wanted her to be convicted, because I couldn't pretend that I knew that was the right outcome. It was more that I'd wanted her to tell the truth. Of course, telling the truth during a trial for your life was not always a smart move, but that didn't invalidate how I felt about it.

Robbie Pedersen turned up after it all hit the newspapers, a father of six in Spokane, coach to three different Little League teams, happily married for thirteen years, an investment banker. He barely remembered being on the streets in Seattle, but the name Cherokee had rung a bell. He'd had no idea he'd known the killer at Deception Pass.

Later that same year, Lainie sent us a note with an invitation to her wedding, making it clear she would be hurt if we didn't come. Out of curiosity and a lingering faith in Lainie's innate goodness, Kathy went. I couldn't force myself to do it.

"How was it?" I asked, late that summer evening when Kathy came back from the reception.

"He's a stockbroker, quite a bit older than she is. She was radiant and prettier than the last time we saw her."

"Brides are always radiant," I said. "I needed sunglasses to look at you on our wedding day."

"Is that why you wore sunglasses? I thought it was so nobody would see you crying."

"Well, that too."

"I thought so. But at Lainie's wedding, all through the ceremony I couldn't stop thinking about those four dead kids. I couldn't help thinking she beat the rap twice, once by fleeing and getting rich, and once in that courtroom. Maybe I'm nuts, but it ruined the wedding for me."

"That's why I didn't go."

"You know what else I found out? The bride and the groom have been living together off and on for six years. Lainie told us she'd been celibate for ten years. I keep wondering what else she lied about."

"She lied on the witness stand."

"Maybe it *was* the way she told it. Maybe she *was* too scared to do anything but what Groth told her."

"Maybe it was the way she told it which time? She got less and less guilty the more practice she got telling her story. Besides, people always have a choice. Afterward, after something horrible has transpired, they want to pretend they didn't, but they always have a choice."

"She was *so* remorseful. Whatever happened at that cabin, she's still doing a lot of good because of it."

"Maybe."

Because of the last sentence in her note—inserted to notify the police of the identity of their fifth member, who Hadlock must have realized was not going to come down from the attic to help—Dootson removed the Parcheesi board from the cabin and his identity along with it. In the excitement she had probably forgotten his name. "Tell Jack's favorite catcher all is forgiven." It was amazing. Even as she was about to be murdered, Tess Hadlock had forgiven Dootson.

Elizabeth Faulconer, it turned out, was as much of a liar as her coworkers at the *Journal American* had claimed. She had never been to the house where the killings had taken place. Her son had never known Nat Bowers. After interrogations by both the prosecution and the defense prior to Lainie Smith's trial, Faulconer acknowledged that in all their private chats, Charles Groth hadn't told her much of anything.

She never published her book, publishing instead a volume of poetry about her ex-husband, the drunk. The last I heard, her son was in art school.

Priscilla Penick lost her license to practice law and went into real estate, where people didn't get so jacked up over ethics.

That spring Leslie Petty was discovered dead in an apartment in Berkeley, California, the result of a drug overdose. He had a Corvette, $40,000 worth of clothes, enough of a heroin cache for another month, and $290,000 cash.

A few days after Petty's funeral in Seattle, I stopped by his grandfather's house with a bunch of flowers and noticed that the rickety old Maverick in the driveway had been replaced by a late model Mercedes. Other than that, everything looked the same, and the old woman took the flowers and was just as cold to me as she'd been the day we barged in. The death of her grandson had hurt her deeply.

Dootson, we found out much later, had been a visitor to Lainie's condo, but he hadn't been on any guest list. He'd spotted Lainie's feather tattoo on her foot and, recognizing it, decided to snoop around. In her office he found the picture of her with Robbie Pedersen and stole it. After Bowers found out why he was having an emotional breakdown, Bowers decided there was no reason he shouldn't get rich over it.

Later, Ione Barocas conned Dootson into resuming the blackmail. What could go wrong? Lainie Smith wasn't going to let the cat out of the bag.

After I'd had some weeks to think about it, I stopped mentally castigating Dootson for being a coward. Maybe he was, but he'd been placed in a difficult position. I knew from experience that the hardest times to act were those when you thought no action would be required of you. Dootson had gone to an unfamiliar house on an unfamiliar beach with three strangers and an old friend, and through no fault of his own he'd been upstairs when Groth arrived. When the robbery began, he told himself nobody was going to be hurt, that he would simply go down afterward and untie everyone.

A lot of people would have remained hidden. Even if they'd suspected the gun was a toy, a lot of people would have remained hidden. You liked to think you would have taken action, but you never knew. You never knew until it happened to you.

For the rest of that winter when we made love, Kathy called me Curtis or Harold or Preston and then laughed, sometimes so hard she brought the proceedings to a halt. From time to time, when all was said and done, she would playfully push me away and say, "Neeeeext."

About the Author

EARL EMERSON is a lieutenant in the Seattle Fire Department. He is the Shamus Award-winning author of the Thomas Black detective series, which includes *The Rainy City, Poverty Bay, Nervous Laughter, Fat Tuesday, Deviant Behavior, Yellow Dog Party, The Portland Laugher, The Vanishing Smile,* and *The Million-Dollar Tattoo.*

Earl Emerson lives in North Bend, Washington.